REKI KAWAHARA   ABEC   BEE-PEE

SWORD ART ONLINE

EARLY AND LATE

SWORD ART ONLINE

"What is this...? Ramen?"

Asuna § Vice commander of the KoB. A rapier expert nicknamed "the Flash."

"...So, have you come to any conclusions, Commander?"

Kirito § The Black Swordsman, who saved everyone trapped inside *SAO*, the game of death. A solo player with the unique skill Dual Blades.

"Then I will give you an answer worthy of this false ramen's flavor."

Heathcliff § Commander of the powerful Knights of the Blood guild. His unique skill, Holy Sword, gives him tremendous strength. Does not get along with Kirito.

Lisbeth § A girl who upgraded Kirito's swords in *SAO*. In *ALO*, she is a leprechaun blacksmith.

Sinon § A young woman Kirito saved in *GGO*. Plays a cait sith archer in *ALO*.

Silica § A girl Kirito saved in *SAO*. In *ALO*, she plays a beast-taming cait sith character.

"All right! Everyone's weapons are at full capacity!"
"Thank you very much!!"
"Thank you for answering my abrupt summons today, everyone! You have my word that I will pay you back for your assistance—emotionally! And now...let's kick some ass!"
"Yeah!"

Leafa § Kirito's little sister. Real name: Suguha. She plays a magic fighter sylph in *ALO*.

Asuna § Kirito's girlfriend. In *ALO*, she plays an undine magician.

Klein § A good friend of Kirito's. Plays a katana-wielding salamander in *ALO*.

Yui § An A.I. in the form of a little girl. She met Kirito in *SAO*, and now serves the *ALO* party as a navigation pixie.

"Let's go. I'll grab the fruit one's attention while you take out the flowering one as quick as you can."

Kopel § A player Kirito meets during a quest, shortly after the start of the game.

"...All right."

Kirito § A boy trapped in *SAO*, the game of death. Was previously a beta tester.

ANTI-CRIMINAL CODE ZONE

Often called a "safe haven." In *Sword Art Online*, the game is divided into the "field," where monsters and danger lurk, and "settlements," where players can rest, relax, and prepare for their adventures. Settlements are safe-haven zones where players cannot harm one another through any means. Any weapon attack will produce its regular visuals but no HP damage, and poisonous items have no effect. As the name of the system code suggests, within the safe haven, there is no way to commit a direct crime against another player.

However, there are several loopholes in this code. For one, a sleeping player can be challenged to a "full-finish" duel, after which their hand can be moved to touch the OK button, thus opening them up to a lethal end. For another, opponents can be taken outside the safe haven against their will, where attacks are legal. Therefore, even under the special circumstances that nullify damage, murder can occur within the Anti-Criminal Code Zone.

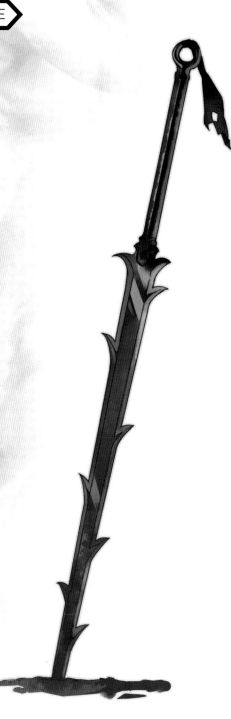

SWORD ART ONLINE
EARLY AND LATE

VOLUME 8

Reki Kawahara

abec

bee-pee

YEN ON

NEW YORK

SWORD ART ONLINE, Volume 8: Early and Late
REKI KAWAHARA

Translation by Stephen Paul
Cover art by abec

SWORD ART ONLINE
©REKI KAWAHARA 2011
All rights reserved.
Edited by ASCII MEDIA WORKS
First published in Japan in 2011 by KADOKAWA CORPORATION, Tokyo.
English translation rights arranged with KADOKAWA CORPORATION, Tokyo, through Tuttle-Mori Agency, Inc., Tokyo.

English translation © 2016 by Yen Press, LLC

Yen On
1290 Avenue of the Americas
New York, NY 10104

Visit us at yenpress.com
facebook.com/yenpress
twitter.com/yenpress
yenpress.tumblr.com

First Yen On Edition: August 2016

Yen On is an imprint of Yen Press, LLC.
The Yen On name and logo are trademarks of Yen Press, LLC.

Library of Congress Cataloging-in-Publication Data

Names: Kawahara, Reki, author. | Abec, 1985- illustrator. | Paul, Stephen (Translator) translator.
Title: Sword art online. Volume 8, Early and late / Reki Kawahara ; illustration by abec ; translation, Stephen Paul.
Other titles: Early and late
Description: First Yen On edition. | New York, NY : Yen On, 2016. | Series: Sword art online ; 8 | Summary: "The game of death took its toll on every player in a different way—when one turns up dead on the fifty-seventh floor, the game is afoot, and it is up to Asuna and Kirito to crack the case—also the story of how Kirito got his Excalibur sword in Alfheim"— Provided by publisher.
Identifiers: LCCN 2016022706 | ISBN 9780316390415 (paperback)
Subjects: | CYAC: Fantasy games—Fiction. | Virtual reality—Fiction. | Internet games—Fiction. | Science fiction. | BISAC: FICTION / Science Fiction / Adventure.
Classification: LCC PZ7.K1755 Swk 2016 | DDC [Fic]—dc23 LC record available at https://lccn.loc.gov/2016022706

10 9 8 7 6 5 4 3 2 1

RRD-C

Printed in the United States of America

"THIS MIGHT BE A GAME, BUT IT'S NOT SOMETHING YOU PLAY."

—Akihiko Kayaba, *Sword Art Online* programmer

SWORD ART ONLINE
EARLY AND LATE

Reki Kawahara

abec

bee-pee

008-001

The Safe Haven Incident

§ 57th Floor of Aincrad
April 2024

1

What's up with this chick?

Yeah, I know it was me who said the weather was nice and worth taking a nap under, and me who was lying down in the grass, and me who actually nodded off for a while.

But I certainly didn't expect to doze for less than half an hour, only to wake up and find her completely passed out next to me. Either she was extremely bold, exceedingly stubborn—or dangerously short on sleep.

I shook my head back and forth with great exasperation as I gazed down at the peacefully sleeping face of Asuna the Flash, vice commander of the Knights of the Blood.

This story began on a day so pleasant that I didn't feel like diving into a dank, smelly labyrinth. Lying on the low hill surrounding the town's teleport square so I could count butterflies seemed like a better use of my time.

The weather was truly incredible. The floating, virtual-reality castle Aincrad had seasons synchronized with the real world, but they were a bit too dedicated to the re-creation, which meant that every summer day was blazing, and the winter was truly freezing. In addition to temperature, there were countless other climate parameters like wind and rain, humidity, pollen, even swarms of bugs. If some aspect were nice on any given day, something else would be just as unpleasant to balance it out.

But today was different. The climate was sunny and warm; the air was full of gentle sunlight; the cool breeze was pleasant, not buffeting, and lacked swarms of bugs to boot. Even in the spring, you didn't get all the parameters lined up this perfectly more than five days a year.

Interpreting this as a sign that the god of digital realms intended for me to take a break from playing and enjoy a nap, I faithfully indulged in His suggestion.

Yet as I lay my head down on the gentle grassy slope and felt myself drifting off to sleep, white leather boots rudely interrupted me by treading right near my head. Meanwhile, a familiar, harsh voice hit my ears, snapping, "Who said that you ought to indulge in napping, when the rest of the game's conquerors are so valiantly vanquishing the labyrinth?"

Without opening my eyes, I replied, "I daresay this be the finest weather we are likely to see this year, and it doth demand savoring."

The even-more-irritated voice noted, "'Tis the same weather as upon any other day."

To which I stated, "Lie down at my side and thou shalt know of which I speak."

Okay, so the conversation was a lot more informal than that, but for whatever reason, the chick actually lay down next to me and just conked right out on the grass.

Anyway.

It was before noon, and the players milling around the teleport gate in the square openly stared at the Flash and me as we lay on the grass. Some were shocked, others giggled, and some shamelessly set off their recording crystals, flashing as they photographed us.

They couldn't be blamed. As the vice commander of the KoB, Asuna was a figure who struck fear into the hearts of children everywhere, the turbo engine who powered the extreme pace of our game conquest, while Kirito the solo player was—against his will—known as the bad boy of the class, the one who got together with miscreants to cause mischief when he ought to know better.

Even I had to admit that I'd find the combination worthy of interest if I'd witnessed it. But I didn't want to wake her up and get yelled at, so my best move would be to get up and leave her behind.

If only I could actually do that.

For as the Flash lay sleeping, she was opening herself to not just several kinds of harassment, but the more-than-zero possibility that she could be PKed as she slept.

Yes, we were in the safe haven of the town square of the fifty-ninth floor's main city.

Yes, we were within the Anti-Criminal Code Zone.

This place made it impossible for a player to harm another player. A weapon strike would produce nothing but purple sparks, a visual effect that did no HP damage, and no poisons would have any effect, either. On top of that, stealing was absolutely impossible.

So within the safe haven, as the Anti-Criminal Code suggested, it was impossible to commit any direct crimes against other players. This was as ironclad a rule within *SAO* as the one that said you would die if your HP dropped to zero.

But unfortunately, there were a number of loopholes.

One of them involved sleeping players. When a player was in an exhausted near-blackout sleep after hours of battling, they might remain sleeping through moderate stimuli. Under this situation, a player could be challenged to a "full-finish" duel, and his hand could be moved by another to touch the OK button on his window. As such, he could be literally murdered in his sleep.

Bolder than that was the plan to physically transport a player out of the safe zone. A player standing tall on his own two feet was protected by the code, but someone placed on a stretcher item was freely transportable.

Both of these cases had been tested and pulled off before.

The horrid, depraved dedication of the "red" players knew no bounds. As a result of those tragedies, every player now made sure to fall asleep in a home or inn room with a locking door. Before I napped on the grass, I made sure to set my Search skill to warn me of incoming targets—and I did not go into a deep sleep, either.

And yet it was clear to see that the Flash was emitting some hardcore delta waves next to me. I could scribble on her face with makeup items and she wouldn't wake. Either she was extremely bold, exceedingly stubborn, or—

"Totally exhausted, I bet," I muttered to myself.

Depending on your build in *SAO*, solo play was the most efficient way of leveling up. And yet she took care of leveling her guild members *and* was managing to upgrade her own numbers at a pace approaching mine. She had to be cutting back on sleep to farm mobs late at night.

I knew how tough that could be. Four or five months ago, I'd been on the same hard EXP pace—and once I fell asleep, I was guaranteed out for several hours afterward.

I swallowed a sigh, taking a beverage out of my inventory, and sat back down in the grass, preparing for a long haul.

It was my suggestion that she sleep. So it was my responsibility to wait there until she awoke.

Asuna the Flash finally arose with a tiny sneeze when the light filtering through the outer aperture of Aincrad was orange with the sunset.

She'd achieved a full eight hours of sleep; this was far more than just a simple nap. My stomach grumbling with the lack of lunch, I stared at her, eagerly anticipating the face she would make when the callous, unforgiving vice commander realized what had happened.

"...*Unyu*..." she mumbled, blinked, and looked up at me.

Her shapely eyebrows contracted only slightly. She unsteadily pushed herself up to a sitting position, her chestnut brown hair waving as she looked right, then left, then right again. Lastly, she looked at me, sitting cross-legged next to her.

Her pale white skin instantly went red (probably shame), then slightly blue (probably panic), then red again (probably rage).

"Wha…Why…How…" the Flash stammered.

I gave her my brightest smile and said, "Morning. Sleep well?"

A hand clad in white leather twitched. But in keeping with her lofty position as the subleader of the most powerful guild in the game, Asuna won the saving roll to maintain clear judgment and did not draw her rapier or sprint away on the spot.

Through gritted white teeth, she grunted, "…One meal."

"Huh?"

"I'll buy you one meal, anything you want. Then we're even. Deal?"

I rather liked that direct nature of hers. Even fresh out of sleep, she instantly recognized that I had stayed with her the entire time—and not just that I had been protecting her from PKers within the safe haven, but ensuring that she got all the sleep she clearly needed to recharge.

I smirked with one cheek, honestly this time, and agreed to the deal. I could have saucily proposed a homemade meal in her personal kitchen, but I too maintained my composure. I rolled back and hopped up onto my feet, then held out a hand.

"There's a place on the fifty-seventh floor that's pretty damn good for an NPC restaurant. Let's go there."

"…Fine," she said bluntly, grabbing my hand and looking away from me. She stretched luxuriously, trying to suck the sunset into her lungs.

A year and five months had passed since the start of *Sword Art Online*, the game of death.

At the start, the path to the hundredth floor of the floating castle Aincrad seemed impossibly long, but we were nearly 60 percent done now, with the current player frontier being the fifty-ninth floor. That meant that we'd been tackling the floors at a pace of one every ten days. As I was right in the middle of it, I couldn't say if that was a fast or slow pace, but given that it was at least a steady one, here in the middle floors, there was now something of a confidence to actually enjoy one's time.

This attitude was found in abundance in Marten, the main city of the fifty-seventh floor. Just two floors below the current front line, this large settlement was both a base camp for the frontier players and a popular tourist destination. In the evening, the conquerors from above would return, and the players from below would come visit for their dinner.

Asuna and I teleported from the fifty-ninth floor and found ourselves squashed shoulder to shoulder among the mass of humanity on the main street. It was enjoyable to see the shocked looks of many who passed us. It was only natural, given that the pristine, valuable flower with her own fan club was walking side by side with a cocky, unsavory solo player. Asuna probably wanted to use every last point of agility to race into the restaurant, but unfortunately for her—and fortunately for me—I was the only one who knew where we were going.

After five minutes of walking and savoring a feeling that I knew I would never experience again through the very last day of *SAO*, a large restaurant came into view on the right.

"This is it?" Asuna asked, equal parts hope and suspicion. I nodded.

"Yup. I'd recommend the fish over the meat."

I pushed the swinging door open and held it in place so the fencer could duck through confidently. Even as the NPC waitress guided us through the somewhat crowded restaurant, I felt eyes on my skin. The pleasure was giving way to exhaustion by now. It couldn't be easy to attract that much attention every day.

But Asuna boldly strode across the floor toward a window table in the back. I awkwardly pulled out the chair for her, which she took smoothly.

Dinner was on her, but I began to feel like I was the one escorting her around instead. I sat down across from her and decided to make the most of my free meal by ordering an aperitif, appetizer, main dish, and dessert all at once, sighing with relief when it was over.

Asuna took the delicate glass that appeared instantly and tasted the drink, then let out her own long sigh. Her light brown eyes were slightly less sharp than before, and in a voice just barely audible, she murmured, "Well...I guess I owe you...Thanks."

"*Wheh?!*"

I stared at her in shock.

"I said, thank you. For guarding me."

"Er...well, um, I, y-you're welcome."

I was so used to her usual cutting remarks and strategic orders in the boss planning meetings about where the boss's weak points were and who should fight at front or rear that I couldn't put together a proper sentence. Asuna chuckled and leaned against the chair's backrest. She looked up into the air with much gentler eyes than usual and murmured, "I think...that might have been the best sleep I've had since I came here..."

"I-I'm sure that's just an exaggeration."

"No, it's true. Usually I wake up within about three hours of falling asleep."

I wet my tongue with the sour liquid in my glass. "Not because you have an alarm set, I take it?"

"No. It's not quite insomnia...but I usually bolt up in my sleep from nightmares."

"...Yeah."

I felt a sharp pain in my chest. I saw the face of someone who had once said the same words to me.

The Flash was a human being like the rest of us. The fact that it took me this long to properly process that made it difficult to string words together.

"Uhh...well...I guess if you want another nap outside, just hit me up."

It was a pretty stupid line, but Asuna favored me with another smile.

"Good idea. Maybe I'll take you up on that if the game gives us a perfect weather day again."

That smile made me painfully aware of just how beautiful she was, and it stopped the language center of my brain altogether. Fortunately, that potentially awkward pause was broken by the NPC waitress and the plates of salad. I shook some mystery spices onto the mystery vegetables and shoved a forkful into my mouth.

After chewing it down, I tried to break the mood by noting, "Isn't it weird how we still eat these raw vegetables when they have no nutritional content?"

"Well, they're tasty, aren't they?" Asuna rebutted, chewing on a leafy green.

"I mean, they're not *bad*...but they could sure use some mayonnaise."

"Oh, totally. One hundred percent agree."

"And some dressing...Some ketchup...and—"

"Soy sauce!" we said at the same time, and burst into laughter.

At that very moment, there was a distant but unmistakable scream of terror.

"*...Eeyaaaaa!!*"

—?!

I took a sharp breath and rose to my feet, hand over my back to my sword hilt.

Asuna had her own hand on her rapier in similar fashion, her voice suddenly sharp.

"That was from outside!"

She leaped out of her chair and raced for the exit of the building. I hurried after the white knight's uniform. When we reached the main street, there was another hideous, ear-splitting scream.

It was probably from the square a block away from us. Asuna glanced back at me and began a proper full-speed sprint. I raced as fast as I could to keep up with the bolt of white lightning, sparks flying from the soles of our boots as we turned east around a corner and leaped into the circular plaza.

I was greeted with a sight I could not believe.

At the north end of the plaza was a stone building that looked like a church. There was a rope hanging from the decorative window in the center of its second floor, and a man hung from the noose at its end.

It wasn't an NPC. He was dressed in full plate armor and a large helmet, probably on his way back from a hunt. The rope bit deep into the neck of his armor, but that was not the source of terror for the packed crowd below. It wasn't possible to die of asphyxiation from a rope in this world.

The root of their horror was a black short spear plunged deep into his chest.

The man had both hands on the hilt of the spear, his mouth working soundlessly. As the seconds passed, red lighting effects spilled from the wound in spurts, just like blood.

In other words, he was taking steady, continuous damage. It was a piercing DOT (damage over time) effect, something that only occurred with certain piercing weapons.

That particular short spear had to be a weapon designed to inflict that effect. I could see countless barbs along the body of the spear.

I snapped out of my momentary shock and shouted up, "Pull it out!!"

The man looked at me. His hands slowly attempted to remove the spear, but the weapon was in too deep. The fear of death was paralyzing him, sapping his strength.

His avatar was stuck to the wall of the building at least thirty feet off the ground. It was too far for me to be able to jump, given my agility stat. Could I cut the rope with a throwing pick? What if I missed and hit him instead? What if that knocked his HP to zero?

Of course, this was the safe haven, so that wasn't possible. But it wasn't possible for that spear to be damaging him, either.

While I hesitated, Asuna was giving orders.

"You go under and catch him!"

She took off for the entrance to the church with astonishing speed. She was going to go inside to the second floor and cut the rope.

"Got it!" I shouted back, dashing for the spot beneath the helpless man.

But just barely halfway to that spot, I noticed that the man's eyes were trained on a single spot in the air. Instinctually, I knew what he was looking at.

His own HP bar—specifically, the moment it went empty.

Amid the screams and shouts of the square, I thought I heard him yell something.

And with a sound like infinite glasses shattering, the night was lit with blue. I could do nothing but watch, dumbstruck, at the flying polygonal shards.

Without its weight, the rope dangled limp against the church wall. A second later, the black spear—the murder weapon—struck the cobblestones with a heavy thud, sticking in place.

The screams of the crowd drowned out the pleasant, peaceful BGM that played over the town. Even in my shock, I had enough presence of mind to look carefully over the entire crowd of the plaza centered around the church. I was looking for something—a feature that had to be present.

The message announcing the winner of the duel.

We were right in the middle of town, within the realm of the Anti-Criminal Code Zone. There was only one way that a player could suffer HP damage, especially all the way to death: to accept a "full-finish" duel, and lose.

There was no other way.

So the moment that he died, there had to be a large system window appearing, announcing the winner's name and time of duel. If I could spot that, I would instantly know who had killed the plate-armored man with that short spear.

And yet…

"…Where is it?" I mumbled to myself.

There was no system window. Not anywhere in the plaza. And it would only be displayed for thirty seconds.

"Everybody, look for a duel winner notice!" I shouted, loud enough to be heard over the crowd. The other players caught my meaning instantly and began to peer in every direction.

But no one called out with an answer. Fifteen seconds had passed.

Could it be inside a building? Perhaps inside a room on the second floor of the church, where the man had been hung? If so, Asuna might see it.

At just that moment, the white uniform of Asuna the Flash appeared through the very window in question.

"Asuna! Did you see a winner notice?!" I demanded, an abnormally rude way to question her, given our relative unfamiliarity, but time was of the essence. Her face, as pale as her garb, only shook from side to side.

"No! There's no system windows in here, and no people!!"

"...How...?" I mumbled, looking around helplessly.

A few seconds later, someone else muttered, "It's no good... That's at least thirty seconds..."

I passed the NPC nun parked permanently at the entrance of the church and raced up the staircase.

The second floor contained four small rooms that looked like bedrooms, but unlike an inn's, these did not lock. The first three rooms did not have any signs of players, either visually or through my Search skill, as I passed. I bit my lip and entered the doorway of the fourth.

Asuna turned away from the window toward me, putting on a brave face, but I could tell that she was as shocked as I was. I couldn't hide the consternation in my brows, either.

"No one else is inside the church," I reported.

The KoB vice commander promptly asked, "Is it possible they were hidden with a cloaking cape?"

"Even on the front line, there have been no drops powerful enough to override my Search skill. Just in case, I have people standing in a line outside the entrance to the church. Even if invisible, they'd be automatically revealed if they tried to go outside among that much attention. There's no rear exit to this building, and the only window is this one."

"Hmm...all right. Look at this," Asuna said, pointing to a corner of the room with her white glove. It was a simple wooden table, a "fixed-location object" that could not physically be moved.

A thin but sturdy-looking rope was tied around one of the table legs. By "tied," I don't mean it was done by hand. Tapping the rope for a pop-up menu, hitting the TIE button, then clicking the target object would automatically tie the rope. Once tied, that rope could not be undone unless it held a weight over its durability rating or was sliced by a sharp blade.

The dark, gleaming rope stretched about six feet through the room before dropping out of the south-facing window. Though I couldn't see it from here, it eventually ended in a noose that immobilized the man in the plate armor.

"Hmm..." I muttered, shaking my head. "What does this mean?"

"Well, using common sense," Asuna said, mimicking my action, "it seems likely that the victim's dueling opponent tied the rope, stuck the spear in his chest, then looped the rope around his neck and pushed him out of the window..."

"As a warning to others? Wait, more importantly..." I took a deep breath. "There was no winner announcement. There are dozens of people in the plaza down there, and no one saw it. If it were a duel, it would have to be displayed nearby."

"But...that's impossible!" she shot back. "The only way to damage someone's HP in a safe haven is for both sides to agree to a duel. You know that as well as I do!"

"Yeah...that's correct."

We fell into silence, staring at each other.

Asuna was right: The impossible had just happened. And all we knew was that a player had died in a highly public place, with no answers or clues as to whom, why, or how.

A stream of crowd noise washed constantly through the open

window. They, too, recognized the abnormal nature of this incident.

Asuna stared into my eyes and said, "We can't just let this go. If someone's found a new way to PK others in a safe haven, we have to figure out how and announce a way to stop it—or this will lead to disaster."

"...It's rare for me to say this, but I am in complete and total agreement with you," I said with a pained grin. The Flash thrust out her right hand.

"Then I guess you'll be working with me until we solve this. And no time for naps, just so you know."

"I think that would be more your concern than mine," I mumbled under my breath, and held out my own hand.

And so a partnership of makeshift detective and assistant—though which was which remained a mystery—was formed with a handshake of black and white gloves.

2

Asuna and I retrieved the rope as evidence in the case and left the room, returning to the entrance of the church. I'd already placed the black short spear in my inventory before going into the building.

I thanked two familiar players who'd stood guard at the door, and they confirmed that no people had emerged since I went inside. I walked into the plaza and raised a hand to the crowd of onlookers, calling out, "Pardon me, but whoever first spotted what happened, please come and speak to us!"

A few seconds later, a female player reluctantly emerged from the crowd. I didn't recognize her. She had a normal NPC-made longsword—probably a tourist from the middle floors.

Unfortunately, she looked a little frightened of me, so Asuna took the lead and gently inquired, "Sorry, I know this has been scary. What's your name?"

"Uh…uh, my name is Yolko."

Something in her frail voice was familiar to me. I interjected, "Were you the one who screamed first?"

"Y-yes."

The woman named Yolko nodded, her wavy, dark blue hair bobbing. Based on the appearance of her avatar, I judged her to be seventeen or eighteen years old.

Her large, innocent eyes, as blue as her hair, suddenly filled with tears.

"I…I am…I *was*…friends with the person who was just killed. We just had dinner together, and then we separated in the square…and…and then…"

She covered her mouth with both hands, unable to continue. Asuna put an arm around her slender shoulders and guided her into the church. They made their way to one of the long pew benches and sat down together.

I kept a bit of distance and waited for the girl to calm down. If she did see her friend PKed in such a cruel manner right before her eyes, the shock would be unbelievable.

Asuna rubbed Yolko's back until she stopped crying, and the girl apologized in a weak, tiny voice.

"No, it's fine," Asuna assured her. "I'll wait as long as it takes. You just tell me more when you're ready, okay?"

"Okay. I…I think I'm fine now."

Yolko moved away from Asuna's hand and nodded, showing herself to be tougher than she appeared.

"His name is…was Kains. We were once in the same guild together…We still party up and eat together sometimes…So today, we came here to have dinner…"

She shut her eyes, then continued, her voice still trembling. "But there were so many people…I lost sight of him in the plaza. I was looking around for him when suddenly, a person—Kains—fell out of the church window, hung on that rope…with the spear in his chest…"

"Did you see anyone else?" Asuna asked. Yolko paused.

Then she slowly but surely nodded. "Yes…For just a moment, I felt like I saw someone standing…behind Kains…"

Unconsciously, I clenched my fists. The killer had been in that room. Which meant that right after pushing the victim out of the window, the killer had just waltzed right into public to escape.

That would have to mean they used some kind of Hiding-enabling gear, but such items were less effective when the user was moving. Perhaps they had an ultra-high personal Hiding skill that would be enough to make up the difference.

The term *assassin* flickered ominously through my mind.

Could there be a category of weapon skills in *SAO* that even Asuna and I didn't know about yet? What if it were capable of nullifying the Anti-Criminal Code...?

Asuna's back trembled for a moment—she had arrived at the same conclusion. But she looked up at once and asked Yolko, "Did you recognize the person?"

"..."

Yolko pursed her lips in deep thought, then shook her head.

This time it was my turn to ask gently, "I'm sorry if this is unpleasant, but...can you think of any reason why Kains might have been targeted...?"

As I was afraid, Yolko instantly tensed up. It was understandable— she had just witnessed the murder of her friend, and I was asking if he'd done something to deserve it. It was a hurtful question, I knew, but it had to be done. If someone out there held a grudge against Kains, that would be our best clue.

But this time, Yolko only shook her head. Disappointed, I said, "I see. Sorry to ask that."

Of course, it was possible that Yolko just wasn't aware of such a thing. But whoever killed Kains was both an actual murderer and a PKer in the traditional MMO sense. Player-killing was an act that some players engaged in for that reason alone. The red players lurking in the darkness of Aincrad at this very moment were tried-and-true examples of that archetype.

That meant the potential suspects were every orange or red player, of which there were hundreds, as well as anyone who might be subconsciously harboring that desire within them. There was no way to know how to narrow down that list.

Once again arriving at the same conclusion simultaneously, Asuna let out a powerless sigh.

*   *   *

Yolko was afraid to return to the lower floors alone, so we sent her to the nearest inn and came back to the teleport square.

Thirty minutes had passed since the incident, and the crowd was thinning out by now. Still, there were a good twenty players, mostly front-line fighters, who were waiting to hear an update from us.

Asuna and I told them that the deceased was named Kains, and that we had no clues yet on how the murder was achieved. And most importantly, that there might be some kind of undiscovered method of safe-haven PKing at work.

"...So can you send a warning far and wide that for the moment, it's not entirely safe even in town?" I finished. The group accepted the task with grim faces.

"All right. I'll ask an info broker to include this in the next newspaper," said a player in one of the major guilds, speaking for the group. They trickled away after that. I checked the time in the corner of my view and was surprised to see that it was still just after seven o'clock.

"So...what now?" I asked Asuna.

She instantly replied. "Let's examine the information we currently have, particularly the rope and spear. If we can tell where they came from, we might be able to track down the killer."

"I see...So if there's no motive, we have to go on evidence. We'll need the Appraisal skill for that. Hey, you...I don't suppose you've been working on that."

"Neither have you. In fact," Asuna added, fixing me with a sudden look, "would you mind not calling me just 'hey, you'?"

"Huh? Uh...oh, right...So, um...My Lady? Vice Commander? ...Our Lady Flash?"

The last one was a special term used by the members of her fan club in their periodical. Sure enough, she blasted me to shreds with her eye lasers before turning away in a huff. "Just 'Asuna' is fine. You called me that earlier."

"G-gotcha," I said, trembling. It was time to change the topic.

"So, the Appraisal skill. Got any friends who are handy with that...?"

"Hmm." She thought briefly, then shook her head. "I have a friend who runs an armory, but this is her busiest period, and I doubt she'll be able to help right away..."

True enough, this was the time of day that the most adventurers would be performing equipment maintenance and purchases—the end of their day's travels.

"Good point. Well, I could ask a general store ax wielder I know, though I don't think his skill with it is the best."

"Are you talking about that...big fellow? Agil, right?" she asked as I opened my window and started to type a message. "But if he runs a shop, he'll be just as busy right now."

"Don't care," I said, mercilessly striking the SEND button.

Asuna and I emerged from the teleport gate into Algade, the city on the fiftieth floor, and the usual hustle and bustle it featured.

It hadn't been long since this city was activated for the benefit of the player population, but the market district was already crammed with countless player-run shops—primarily because the base cost for establishing a shop here was far cheaper than in the cities on lower floors.

Naturally, that also lowered the average space and appearance of the shops, but the cramped, uniquely Asian chaos—or that of a particular electronics district in Tokyo—was a favorite of many players. I happened to like it, too, and was making plans to buy a home here so I could move in.

Amid the exotic BGM, raucous hawking of wares, and scent of cheap stall food wafting through the air, I guided Asuna quickly through the market. Her pristine miniskirt and bared legs were just a bit too notable in this place.

"C'mon, let's hurry," I said, then noticed that the sound of her heels was growing distant, so I turned around and shouted, "Hey, what are you doing buying cart food?!"

The Flash was purchasing a dubious skewer of meat from an equally dubious cart. She took a bite and boldly pronounced, "Well, we only started poking at our salads when we left dinner... Hey, this is pretty good."

As she chewed, she held out her other hand toward me, holding another skewer.

"Huh? For me?"

"That was the agreement, wasn't it?"

"Oh...right..."

I automatically ducked my head as I accepted the meat, then realized that my free full-course meal had just been downgraded to a free skewer of meat. And the cost from that restaurant was automatically deducted from both of our accounts the moment we left the building.

As I chewed on mysterious, exotically spiced meat, I swore to myself that one day, I would get her to cook me a homemade meal.

We had just cleaned off the two skewers when we reached our destination. The skewer itself vanished into thin air as I wiped my perfectly clean hand on my leather coat and called out to draw the shopkeeper's attention.

"Heya. I'm here."

"I don't give the usual welcoming routine to noncustomers," Agil grunted, the sulky voice out of place on the shopkeeper-slash-ax-warrior's massive, brawny figure. He motioned to another customer and said, "Sorry, closed for the day."

He bowed politely and apologized as the customer complained, and once they were alone, he opened the shop-management window to set the business to closed status.

The chaotic, cramped display cases automatically shut themselves, and the front shutter clattered down as well. Agil turned to me at last.

"Listen, Kirito, when it comes to making a living as a merchant, number one is trust. Number two is also trust, and even with nothing at number three and number four, only by the time you get to number five do you reach 'making easy money...'"

This rather baffling admonishment faded out as the bald shop-keeper caught sight of the player standing next to me. His whiskers shook as Asuna gave him a brilliant smile and bowed politely.

"It's been a while, Agil. I'm sorry to bother you out of the blue like this. We need immediate help with this, I'm afraid..."

Agil's grumpy features turned pleasant in an instant. He thumped his chest bracingly, told her he would handle it, and prepared some tea.

There's just no way for a man to overcome his innate parameters, it seems.

Upstairs, once we had explained the incident, Agil's jutting brow knotted and his eyes turned sharp.

"His HP ran out in the safe haven? And you're certain it wasn't a duel?" he rumbled in his deep baritone. I leaned forward in the rocking chair and nodded.

"I can't imagine that no one would see the victory announcement, so it seems to be the natural conclusion now. Plus...even if it were a duel, there's no way he would accept a duel when he was out getting dinner, especially a full-finish duel."

"And if he was walking with that girl Yolko beforehand, it couldn't possibly have been a sleep-PK," Asuna added, swirling her mug over the small round table.

"Plus, the details are too complex for a spontaneous duel. I think we can assume that this was a preplanned PK. So that brings us...to this," I said, opening my menu and manifesting the rope from my inventory, so that I could hand it to Agil.

Naturally, the knot that had been tied around the table leg was undone when I'd retrieved the rope, but the other end was still done into the large noose. Agil dangled the loop in front of his face, snorted with disgust, and tapped it.

He chose the "Appraisal" menu from the pop-up window. If Asuna or I had tried that, we'd just get a failure notice, since we lacked the proper skill level, but Agil the merchant would be able to learn more about it.

The large man looked over the window, which was visible only to him, and described the contents in his deep voice.

"I'm afraid this wasn't player-made, just your garden variety NPC-sold rope. Not a high-ranking item. It's got about half of the durability left."

I replayed the horrible sight in my mind and nodded. "That figures. It was holding a guy in heavy armor; that had to be a considerable load to bear."

But all the killer needed was for the rope to hold out the few dozen seconds necessary for the man to lose his remaining HP and explode into nothing.

"Well, I wasn't expecting much from the rope to begin with. The real kicker is this one," I said, tapping my still-open inventory to materialize another item.

The dark, gleaming spear and its heavy presence cast an eerie mood over the cramped room. As a weapon, it belonged to a rank far, far below those Asuna and I equipped, but that wasn't the point. This spear was a murder weapon, a tool that had cruelly taken a player's life.

I handed the spear to Agil, careful not to let it bump against anything. The entire weapon was made of a single black metal, a rarity for that category. It was about five feet long, with a foot-long grip, a long handle, and a sharp six-inch point at the end.

Its main feature was the rows of short, sharp barbs that ran along the entire length of the handle. They served to make it harder to remove the spear once it had stabbed its target. It therefore required very high strength to pull out.

In this case, strength referred to both the player's numerical strength stat, and also the force of the brain's mental signal being absorbed by the NerveGear. In that moment, Kains had been too gripped by the fear of death to produce a clear, crisp signal to move his body. He could hardly be blamed for not being able to move the spear.

That only strengthened my hunch that this was not a spontaneous PK but something premeditated, planned. There was nothing crueler than death by continuous piercing damage. He wasn't felled by an opponent's skill or superior weaponry—but by his own terror.

Agil brought me out of my thoughts as he finished examining it.

"It's PC-made."

Both Asuna and I suddenly bolted upright. "Really?!" I shouted. If it were PC-made—crafted by a player with the Smithing skill—the name of that player would be listed there. And that spear was likely a one-off special-order weapon. If we could ask the crafter directly, there was a very good chance we'd learn who ordered and paid for it.

"Who made it?" Asuna prodded him. Agil looked down at the system window.

"Grimlock...Never heard of 'im. At any rate, it's not top craftsmanship...Still, it's not like regular players have never thought of boosting Smithing to craft their own weapons..."

If Agil the merchant didn't know this crafter, then Asuna and I certainly wouldn't. Silence fell on the cramped room again.

But it didn't take long for Asuna to note, "We should still be able to track him down. I can't imagine that a solo player would have gotten to the point of being able to craft a weapon of this type. If we ask around in the mid-level floors, we're sure to find someone who's been in a party with a 'Grimlock' before."

"True. There aren't many idiots like this guy," Agil agreed. He and Asuna looked at me—the idiot.

"Wh-what? I join a party every now and then."

"Only for boss fights," she quipped. I had no rebuttal to that.

Asuna snorted and examined the spear in Agil's hands again. "Based on this...I'm not sure if I really want to have a nice chat with Grimlock, even if we do find him..."

I had to agree. It must have been some unknown red player who commissioned and used this spear, not Grimlock the blacksmith. Killing someone in *SAO* with your own handcrafted weapon, where your name was permanently saved on it, would be like writing your own name on a knife you stabbed someone with in real life. On the other hand, any crafter with a certain amount of smarts and experience should recognize what a weapon like this was designed to do.

Piercing damage over time had a very limited effectiveness against monsters. That was because monsters were just a series of algorithms that felt no fear. If stuck with a piercing weapon, they would simply pull it out once they got the chance. And since no monster would thoughtfully hand back the weapon, it usually got tossed far away, irretrievable until the battle was over.

Which meant that this spear could only have been crafted for the purpose of PvP. All of the crafters I knew, at least, would have refused the job when they learned what it was for.

But this Grimlock had not.

It was very unlikely that this was the name of the killer himself—given how easy it was to pin down the name—but it was possible that this crafter was at least a person of loose morals or perhaps secretly affiliated with a red guild.

"...At any rate, we're not likely to get an answer for free. If we're forced to pay for the information..." I murmured. Agil shook his head, and Asuna fixed me with a piercing glare.

"We'll split the cost."

"...Fine. No turning back now," I said, giving in. I turned to the shrewd merchant and asked, "I doubt it'll be much of a clue, but I might as well ask what the name of the weapon is."

The bald man considered the invisible window for a third time.

"It says it's called...Guilty Thorn."

"...Hmm."

I looked at the barbs bristling out of the short spear's handle again. Of course, the name was simply randomly generated by the game. So there couldn't be any personal will behind those particular words.

But...

"Guilty...Thorn..."

Asuna's whisper imbued the words with a chilly edge.

3

Asuna and I, with Agil in tow, stepped through the teleport gate in Algade to visit the very bottom floor: The Town of Beginnings.

We needed to check the Monument of Life found in Blackiron Palace. The first step to contacting Grimlock the blacksmith was ensuring that he was alive to speak to us.

For being springtime, the Town of Beginnings was cloaked in dreariness. This was not just due to the weather parameters—few players strolled the wide streets at night, and it seemed as though the NPC musicians providing BGM were all in a minor-key mood.

I'd heard the rumors: Lately, the Aincrad Liberation Front, largest of the guilds and governing force of the lower floors, had supposedly enacted a night curfew. It sounded like a joke, but based on this, it might be true. The only people we saw were ALF guards, all wearing matching gunmetal armor.

Even worse, the way they raced over when they saw us was nerve-wracking—I felt like a middle-schooler being chastened by police officers. One absolute-zero glare from Asuna was usually enough to send them scurrying.

"No wonder Algade is booming, despite the price of living," Agil murmured, then noted lowly, "I hear the Army intends to start taxing players."

"Huh? Taxes?! How do they intend to collect them?"

"I don't know...Maybe they automatically skim off the top from monster drops."

"Or maybe they'll confiscate a portion of your sales."

Agil and I bickered pointlessly for a while, but once we stepped into the interior of Blackiron Palace, we fell silent.

As the name suggested, the building was a massive structure constructed solely of metal beams and plates, filled with an even colder atmosphere than outside. Even Asuna rubbed her bare arms as she walked ahead of us.

There were no other people inside, probably due to the time. In the middle of the day, the cries were endless, as players came to confirm the deaths of friends and lovers, faced with the cruel horizontal lines striking through the names of the deceased. Tomorrow, the friend and witness of Kains's death, Yolko, would likely pay her own visit. I, too, had done the same thing, not too far in the past. I still wasn't completely over that bitter memory.

We quickly strode through the empty hall, which was lit by lanterns with bluish flames. Once we reached the Monument of Life, which stretched for dozens of feet side to side, we looked for the G section of the alphabetized list.

Agil kept walking to the right, while Asuna and I examined the rows of player names, finally finding the right one at the same time.

Grimlock—no line.

"...So he's still alive."

"Yep."

We breathed sighs of relief. Meanwhile, Agil came back from the K block and said, "Kains is indeed dead. Died in the Month of Cherry Blossoms, April 22nd, 6:27 PM."

"...The date and time match up perfectly. That's just after we left the restaurant tonight," Asuna noted. She looked away, her long lashes downcast. Agil and I held a short vigil. We also knew it was the right man, because Yolko had told us how to spell "Kains."

Once everything was done and we promptly exited Blackiron Palace, the three of us let out held-in breaths. The in-town BGM was now in late-night waltz mode. The NPC shops were all shuttered, and the only light on the streets was from the occasional streetlamp. There were no Army patrols at this hour either, it seemed.

We proceeded silently to the teleport square, at which point Asuna turned around and said, "Let's begin the search for Grimlock tomorrow."

"Good idea," I agreed.

Agil's powerful brows tilted downward. "You two realize that my main occupation isn't 'warrior,' it's 'merchant'…"

"Understood. You are hereby laid off from assistant duty here," I reassured him, patting him on the back. He grunted a relieved thanks.

Thoughtful Agil was not truly prioritizing his business, nor shirking the responsibility to investigate—he just didn't want to come face-to-face with the person who crafted that wicked-looking spear. Not out of fear, but out of the possibility that the rage he normally reserved for monsters might explode out of his control.

Agil wished us luck and disappeared through the portal. Asuna needed to return to her guild HQ for a minute, so we decided to call it a day.

"Let's meet at nine o'clock before the fifty-seventh-floor portal tomorrow. No sleeping in!"

She was like a teacher or an older sister—not that I would know, not having one in real life.

"Fine, fine. And you'd better get a proper night's sleep. If you need it, I could sleep next to—"

"No, thank you!" the vice commander of the KoB snapped, then spun on her heels and leaped into the portal, leaving only a blur of white and red.

All alone now, I stood in front of the wavering blue gateway, reflecting on the day's events. It started off as a day with very nice weather, but once I got roped into standing guard over Asuna the Flash's nap, we ended up having dinner, only to leave early when a sudden murder took place within town, thus thrusting me into the role of detective—or assistant.

Naturally, every day I spent within the floating castle Aincrad was "abnormal," but now that a year and a half had passed since the start of the deadly game on November 6th, 2022, most of the players—at least in the mid-levels or higher—were able to consciously forget their lives from the real world and engage in a "normal" schedule of swords, battle, gold coins, and dungeons.

But today's incident had once again drawn me to a kind of abnormality. Perhaps it was the harbinger of some kind of perpetual change to our status quo...

I took a few steps forward into the blue portal. I called out "Lindarth," the city on the forty-eighth floor where my current lodgings were found, and felt a momentary loss of weight as the portal flashed around me.

When my boots touched ground again on stone of a different color, the surrounding scenery was nothing like the place I'd just been. I'd only set up base in Lindarth about a week earlier, but I liked the canals that ran through the town in every direction, dotted with peaceful waterwheels. Of course, after ten o'clock, the curtain of night had descended here, too, with no blacksmith hammers to be heard.

I was just considering whether I should heed the vice commander's advice, and get to sleep early, or find an NPC pub for a drink first, when, just steps out of the portal, I was rushed by a group of six or seven players.

At first, I nearly drew my sword. The assumption that one was safe in town, even surrounded by dozens of people, had just been shaken to its core in the last few hours.

But I managed to control my instinct, holding it to just the twitch of a finger. I recognized the faces in this group—they were members of the Divine Dragon Alliance, the largest of the front-line guilds. I found the member who seemed to be the leader of the semicircle and said, "Good evening, Schmitt," with a smile.

The tall lancer paused for a moment, then spoke quickly, his voice troubled. "We were waiting here, hoping to ask you something, Kirito."

"Oh yeah? I'm guessing it's not my birthday or blood type..." I joked automatically. Beneath Schmitt's sports-captain buzz cut, his thick eyebrows trembled.

As fellow front-line fighters, we weren't exactly enemies, but the Divine Dragon Alliance and I did not generally see eye to eye. I was probably on better terms with Asuna's Knights of the Blood.

I couldn't help but feel that while the KoB's goal was "beating the game as fast as possible," the DDA's particular aim was to "bask in the glory of being the strongest guild." They didn't form parties with nonmembers, and they never shared their knowledge of game info. They were also unpleasantly fixated on scoring the Last Attack on every boss—the final blow that gave its winner extra item rewards.

In a way, they were enjoying *SAO* more than anyone else, so I'd never raised a fuss about them, but I had turned down two invitations to join their guild. So we weren't particularly close, to say the least.

Even now, as I leaned against the stone wall of the teleport square, surrounded by the seven in a half circle, there was an odd sense of distance between us. It wasn't quite the "boxing in" harassment method of preventing a player from moving; it was more like a "boxed in by manners" state, where the need to make rude physical contact to break out of the circle kept those concerned with etiquette where they were.

I held in a sigh and offered to Schmitt, "I'll answer any questions you have. What's up?"

"It's about the PK that happened on the fifty-seventh floor tonight."

Obviously, that had been coming. I nodded and folded my

arms, still leaning against the wall, then prompted him to continue with a glance.

"Is it true…that it wasn't a duel?" he asked in a hushed tone. I thought it over and shrugged.

"At the very least, no one witnessed a victory display screen. I suppose we can't deny the possibility that somehow everyone present missed it."

"…"

Schmitt's square jaw clenched hard. The armored plate at the base of his neck creaked. The DDA members all wore silver plate armor with blue highlights. His lance jutted upward to six feet tall, the guild flag hanging from its sharp point.

After a long silence, he spoke again, even softer this time. "I heard the victim's name was Kains…Is this correct?"

"That's what the friend who witnessed the incident said. We went to check at Blackiron Palace, and the date and time matched up."

I noticed his throat twitch and, for the first time, realized that something was going on. "Did you know him?"

"…It's none of your business."

"Hey, you asked your questions, you can't just ignore mine—" I started to protest, but Schmitt's bellow cut me off.

"You're not the police! I understand you've been working with the KoB's vice commander, but you don't have the right to monopolize that information!"

His voice must have carried all the way to the edge of the plaza. The other members there looked at one another in concern. Apparently Schmitt had rustled them up without giving a full explanation.

Which meant that any likely connection to this incident came not from the DDA as a whole, but from Schmitt himself. I tucked that fact away for future reference. Suddenly, a gauntleted hand was pointing directly at my face.

"I know that you collected the weapon that was used in the PK. You've had your turn to examine it; now hand it over."

"…Oh, come on."

This was an obvious breach of manners. In *SAO*, weapons that weren't equipped on one's figure reverted to having no ownership rights after three hundred seconds of being left on the ground, or handed to someone else, or left stabbed in a monster, or so on. At that point, it was both system protocol and commonly accepted fact that whomever picked it up next owned it. The black short spear had no listed owner by the time it took Kains's life. So according to the game system, it now belonged to me.

Demanding another player's weapon was beyond rude, but on the other hand, that spear was a piece of evidence in a crime, more than it was just a weapon. A small part of me did agree that, as I was neither a policeman nor a soldier, it wasn't right for me to hog that evidence for myself.

So this time I sighed openly and waved a hand to engage my inventory window. Once the black spear had materialized in my hand, I made a show of jamming it down into the cobblestones between us.

Schmitt faltered back half a step at the tremendous clatter and shower of sparks the metal spear produced.

Looking at it again, I was struck by what a wicked-looking weapon it was—not that it should be a surprise, given that it was designed to kill players. I tore my eyes off the drop counter that only I could see and told the lancer, "I'll save you the trouble of appraising it. The name of this spear is Guilty Thorn. It was crafted by a blacksmith named Grimlock."

This time his reaction was unmistakable: Schmitt's narrow eyes bulged, his mouth fell open, and he let out a rasping moan.

The athlete was undoubtedly connected somehow to the black-smith Grimlock, and possibly to the victim Kains as well. It was clear that he shared some kind of past with them.

If that past was enough to be a motive to murder Kains, then perhaps my fears that the safe-haven killing was the indiscriminate act of a red player were wrong. I wanted to know what had happened in the past, but I knew Schmitt would never freely say.

As I contemplated what to do next, he reached down with his thick gauntlet and awkwardly pulled the spear out of the ground. He practically swung it against his inventory to stash it away, hurling the thing so as not to touch it any longer than necessary. Afterward, he abruptly turned toward me.

Rather predictably, the lanky lancer's parting comment was: "And don't go snooping around about this. Let's go!"

The members of the Divine Dragon Alliance marched through the teleport gate and disappeared.

Very interesting.

4

"The DDA?" Asuna repeated suspiciously, when I told her what had happened.

Those three letters were normally a source of fear and consternation, the kind of threat a parent would conjure to shut up a crying child, but as the vice commander of the KoB, Asuna was completely unaffected by them.

On the twenty-third day of the Month of Cherry Blossoms, the weather parameters were in a foul mood, and the morning was shrouded in thick fog and rain. Given that the only thing overhead in Aincrad was just the bottom of the next floor up, it didn't seem very fair that it could rain on us—but then again, the same thing applied to the ample sunlight we got over the course of a day.

After meeting at nine o'clock on the dot at the fifty-seventh floor's teleport square—where the previous day's incident had occurred—Asuna and I headed for a nearby open café for breakfast so that we could reexamine the information. Naturally, the biggest topic of discussion was Schmitt of the DDA, who had ambushed me last night and all but seized the weapon and details from me.

"Oh, yes, I remember him. The big lancer?"

"That's the one. He looks like the captain of a high school jousting team."

"That's not a real thing," she snapped, ruining my brilliant joke, then picked up her café au lait and considered the information. "I suppose we can rule him out of being the killer?"

"It's dangerous to make assumptions, but I don't think it's him. If he wanted to retrieve the weapon to cover his tracks, he wouldn't have left it in the square to begin with. If anything, I think that spear was a message from the killer."

"I see…Good point. The way the murder happened, plus the name of the weapon…It seems less like an extravagant PK than a public execution," Asuna muttered, looking gloomy. I had to agree.

This was not indiscriminate PKing, but an execution specifically targeting Kains. And something had happened in the past involving Kains, Grimlock, and Schmitt. I delivered my conclusion in hushed tones.

"Meaning the motive was either vengeance or justice. Kains committed some 'crime' in the past, and this was his righteous punishment, the killer would have us believe."

"In which case, Schmitt isn't the culprit behind the murder, but among the targeted. He did that something *with* Kains, and when Kains turned up dead, he panicked…"

"If we figure out what that something is, I think we'll know who the person swearing vengeance is. But it's also possible that this was all an act by the killer. We've got to be careful not to act on assumptions."

"True. Especially when we talk to Yolko," Asuna agreed. I checked the time. At ten o'clock, we were going to meet Yolko at a nearby inn to go over more details about the incident.

Even after our simple breakfast of black bread and vegetable soup, we had plenty of time yet, so I sat back and gazed at the figure of the KoB's vice commander across from me.

Today she wasn't wearing her usual uniform of red on white, probably because it was a personal matter she was on. She wore a shirt with narrow pink and gray stripes and a black leather vest, a black frilly miniskirt, and shining gray tights.

Her shoes were pink enamel, and her beret was pink as well,

which made her whole outfit look very carefully coordinated—but whether this was intentional or just ordinary feminine attention to fashion was something I was sadly unable to determine, what with my own lack of fashion sense. I couldn't even tell if it were an expensive outfit or not. Though it didn't track that she would dress up for a murder investigation...

Suddenly, Asuna looked up and met my gaze, only to quickly turn away. "What are you looking at?"

"Uh...er, well..."

I couldn't just ask her how much her outfit cost, and I could tell that complimenting her on it would just lead to an explosion of anger, so instead I improvised. "Umm...is that thick, drippy stuff good?"

Asuna looked down at the mystery potage she was stirring, looked back at me with a very odd expression on her face, and heaved a deep sigh.

"...It's not very good," she mumbled, pushing her dish to the side. She cleared her throat and assumed a more officious tone.

"I was thinking, late last night. About the penetration DOT on that black spear..."

I nodded, suddenly realizing that it might be the first time I'd ever seen her without her usual rapier equipped. "Yeah?"

"Could he have been hit with the piercing weapon out in the field? Do you know what would happen if you moved into a safe haven while the effect was active?"

"Uh..."

I had to think. I'd never experienced that situation; I'd never even thought about it.

"I don't know. But...DOT from poison or burns disappears the moment you step into the safe-haven zone, right? Wouldn't piercing damage work the same way?"

"But what happens to the weapon piercing you, in that case? Does it automatically come out?"

"That's a creepy thought...All right, we've got some time to kill; let's do an experiment," I suggested. Her eyes bulged.

"E-experiment?!"

"Picture's worth a thousand words," I offered ominously, getting to my feet and checking my town map for the nearest gate.

Right outside of Marten, the main city of the fifty-seventh floor, was a field dotted by the occasional gnarled old oak. I'd passed down this road plenty of times just a few weeks ago when this was the front line of our progress, but my memory of it was already dim. Of course, it did look different now with the greenery blooming in the spring, but in general, front-line players didn't have much use for the wild terrain of floors they'd already beaten.

The moment we walked out of the gate into the drizzling mist, a warning reading OUTSIDE FIELD appeared in my view. It didn't mean that monsters would immediately begin attacking, but it always caused a part of my mind to automatically tense and grow watchful.

Now that Asuna had her familiar rapier equipped again, she brushed aside the drops collecting on her bangs and asked suspiciously, "So how are you going to do this experiment?"

"Like this."

I felt around on my belt for the throwing picks I always kept there, three at a time, and pulled out one. Every weapon in Aincrad corresponded to one of four damage types: slashing, thrusting, blunt, and piercing. The one-handed sword I used all the time was a slashing weapon, while Asuna's rapier was thrusting. Maces and hammers were blunt weapons, while Schmitt's lance and the spear that killed Kains were piercing.

What was a little harder to tell was how the many throwing weapons fit into this system. Even in the same category, boomerangs and chakrams were slashing, throwing daggers were thrusting, and my throwing picks fell under piercing. It might only look like a foot-long needle, but the throwing pick was a perfectly good piercing weapon capable of inflicting a small damage-over-time effect.

I didn't mind sacrificing some HP for the experiment, but it would be foolish to lose armor durability over it, so I took off my left glove and aimed the pick at the back of my hand.

"W-wait, stop!" Asuna shrieked, causing me to flinch. To my surprise, she was opening her inventory to pull out a very expensive healing crystal.

"Oh, don't be dramatic. This pick will only take a percent or two off of my total HP."

"You idiot! You don't know what might happen out in the field! Form a party with me so I can see your HP bar!" she thundered, like a sister scolding her little brother, then hit a few buttons to send me a party request. I meekly accepted, and below my HP gauge, a smaller one representing Asuna's appeared.

I realized it was the first time I'd ever been in a party with her. We'd met many times, owing to our positions among the game's best players, but she was a senior officer of the game's most powerful guild, and I was just an outcast solo player. We had hardly ever even spoken before this.

And yet here we were, forming a party of just two. And it wasn't that long ago that we'd had a one-on-one duel because of an argument about boss tactics. Now she was looking on nervously, a pink crystal clutched in her hand. I couldn't help but stare at her.

"…What?"

"'S nothing, I just…didn't think you'd be so worried for my sake…"

To my surprise, as soon as I said it, her white cheeks went the color of the crystal in her hand. She promptly summoned a bolt of angry lightning.

"Th-that's not true! W-well, it is, but…Just do it already!!"

With a little shiver, I readied the pick again. "A-all right, here goes," I announced, took a deep breath—and made the motion for the starter throwing weapon skill, Single Shot.

The pick began to glow with a faint effect between my two fingers, and it shot straight forward, piercing the back of my left hand. After the initial shock, I felt an unpleasant numbness and a dull pain.

My HP bar lost more than I expected: about 3 percent off its total. I remembered belatedly that I'd equipped a new, rarer set of picks I'd looted recently.

As the pain continued, I watched the spot where the needle was sticking out of the skin. After five seconds, there was another flash of red light, and I lost about half a percent of HP. This was the same piercing DOT effect that stole Kains's life.

"Get in the safe zone already!" Asuna snapped nervously. I nodded, glanced at my HP bar and the pick, then headed for the nearby town gate. When my boots crossed from soggy grass to hard stone, the notice reading SAFE HAVEN appeared.

My HP bar stopped decreasing.

The red effect was still flashing every five seconds, but my hit points weren't decreasing at all. The safe haven ensured that all damage was nullified.

"…It stopped," Asuna stated, and I nodded.

"Weapon's still stuck good, but the damage has stopped."

"Do you feel it?"

"Yeah, the sensation is there. I guess that's probably to ensure that no idiot can wander around the town without realizing that there's still a weapon stuck in them…"

"Meaning you?" she asked drily. I shrugged and yanked out the pick, grimacing at the fresh discomfort. There were no external wounds on the back of my hand, but the cold metal sensation was still there. I blew on it a few times.

"So the damage is gone…" I muttered. "But then, why did Kains die? Was it a special effect of that weapon…or some skill we don't know about ye—Wh-whoa!!"

The shout at the end was because Asuna had grabbed my left hand with both of hers and clenched it tight to her chest.

"What the…What…are you…"

After a few seconds, the vice commander let go and shot me a sideways glance. "That got rid of the sensation, didn't it?"

"...Uh...yes...it did. Thanks."

The only reason my heart was racing was the suddenness of it all.

Yes, it definitely wasn't anything else.

Yolko emerged from her inn at exactly ten o'clock on the dot. She must not have slept much, because she was blinking a lot as she bowed to the two of us.

I bowed back and said, "Sorry to keep dredging this up for you, right when you're dealing with the passing of a friend..."

"It's all right," the slightly older girl mumbled, shaking her blue-black hair. "I just want you to catch whomever did this..."

But the moment she caught sight of Asuna, her eyes widened. "Ooh, wow! Those are all handmade items from Ashley's store, aren't they? I don't think I've ever seen anyone with an entire outfit!"

I didn't recognize that name, so I asked, "Who is that?"

"You don't know?!" Yolko said, stunned, looking at me like I was wasting my life. "Ashley is the first seamstress to completely max out the Sewing skill to one thousand! She won't even take a request unless you can bring the rarest and most deluxe crafting materials to make it!"

"Ohhh," I said, impressed. All I ever did was fight and fight like a simpleminded fool, and it wasn't that long ago that I'd maxed out my One-Handed Sword skill. I gave Asuna another light-speed examination from head to toe. Her cheek twitched.

"It...It's not what you think!"

But I had no idea what she thought I thought.

With the impressed Yolko and dubious me in tow, Asuna guided us through the door of the restaurant we failed to eat at last night.

Due to the time of day, there were no other players present. We headed for the farthest table back, checking the distance to the door. This far away, our conversation wouldn't be audible outside unless we screamed it. I used to think the best place for secrets was an inn room behind a locked door, but I'd recently learned that it only made you more vulnerable to someone with the Eavesdropping skill.

Yolko had already eaten breakfast, so we ordered three teas and got right down to business.

"First, a report...Last night we check the Monument of Life in Blackiron Palace. Sure enough, Kains died at that very moment."

Yolko sucked in a brief breath, shut her eyes, and nodded. "I...I see. Thank you for going to the trouble to check..."

"No, it's fine. There was another name we wanted to check while we were there," Asuna said, shaking her head. She asked the first important question: "Yolko, do you recognize these names? The first is Grimlock, most likely a blacksmith. The other is a spearman named...Schmitt."

Yolko's downcast head twitched. Slowly, hesitantly, she made a gesture of recognition.

"...Yes, I know them. They were both members of a guild with Kains and me, long ago," she murmured. Asuna and I shared a glance.

So it was true. In that case, we had to confirm our other suspicion—that *something* in the past of that guild was the cause of this incident.

I asked the second question: "Yolko, I'm sure this is hard to answer...but in order to solve this incident, I have to ask for the truth. We believe that this murder was either vengeance or judgment. Perhaps because of a past event, Kains may have earned himself someone's hatred and desire for revenge...As I asked yesterday, I want you to think hard. Is there anything that comes to mind, anything that might shed light on this...?"

Her answer was not immediate this time. Yolko stared downward for a long time, silent, then reached for her tea with trembling fingers. She wet her tongue with a sip and nodded at last.

"...Yes...I do. I'm sorry I couldn't tell you about it yesterday...I just want to forget it all. I was hoping that it wasn't related, so I just couldn't bring myself to mention it right away…but now, I will. That…'event' was what caused the breakup of our guild."

The name of our guild was Golden Apple. We weren't trying to help beat the game; it was just a small guild of eight, hoping to do some safe hunting so we could earn enough for beds and meals.

But half a year ago, at the start of fall…

We were adventuring in an unremarkable sub-dungeon on one of the middle floors when we encountered a monster we'd never seen before. It was a little lizard, all in black, but extremely fast and hard to spot…We knew it was a rare monster at a glance. We were beside ourselves with excitement, chasing it all over…and someone's dagger throw got lucky and just so happened to strike true and kill the beast.

The item it dropped was just a simple ring. But we were amazed when we identified it. It raised agility by a whole twenty points. I doubt you can find loot that powerful even on the front line today.

I'm sure you can imagine what happened next.

We were split between using it for the sake of the guild and selling it and splitting the proceeds. The argument got so heated, it nearly resulted in a fight, and we took a vote to determine our plan: five to three in favor of selling. An item that valuable was too much for merchants on the middle floors, so our guild leader went to a big city on the front line to leave it with an auctioneer.

It would take time to research a trustworthy auction house, so our leader was supposed to spend a night there. I remember eagerly awaiting the end of the auction and return of our leader. Even split among eight, we were bound to get a ton of money, so I was thinking about weapons and fancy personal-brand clothes I wanted to buy, poring through catalogs…But I had no idea it was going to turn out like that…

…there was no return.

Over an hour after our scheduled meeting time the following night, there hadn't been a single update message. We tried to track the leader's location and got nothing, and there were no responses to any of our messages.

We couldn't believe that our boss would just take the item and run. This gave us a very bad premonition, so a few of us went to the Monument of Life to check.

And then...

Yolko bit her lip and simply shook her head back and forth. Asuna and I didn't know what to say. To our relief, Yolko gave us a reprieve by wiping her eyes and saying in a trembling but firm voice, "The time of death was one hour after taking the ring to the upper floor. The cause of death...piercing damage."

"...There's no way you'd take a valuable item like that out of the town. So it must have been...a sleep PK," I muttered. Asuna's head bobbed.

"Half a year ago was just before that method started getting around. Back then, there were more than a few people who slept in public spaces, to save the money on an inn room with a locking door."

"And the lodgings at the front line are expensive. But...I have a hard time thinking that's a coincidence. Whoever went after your leader had to know about the ring...meaning..."

Yolko nodded, her eyes shut. "One of the other seven members of Golden Apple...We considered that as well, of course. But... there's no way to go back and look up who was doing what and when...So with everyone suspecting everyone else, it didn't take long for the guild to fall apart."

Another heavy silence settled over the table.

It's a very nasty story. But also very plausible. It all adds up.

It wasn't that hard to find stories about perfectly friendly guilds with no dramatic storm clouds overhead being thrown into sudden turmoil by the lucky advent of a powerful item. The only reason they didn't pop up in rumors more often was because the people involved just wanted to forget it ever happened.

But at this point, I had to ask Yolko something.

As the older girl looked down in pain, I took a practical tack.

"Just tell me one thing. What were the names of the three people who were against selling that ring?"

Several seconds later, Yolko steeled her resolve and looked up, answering clearly, "Kains, Schmitt...and me."

The answer took me by surprise. As I blinked, Yolko noted ironically, "But their reason for opposing it was not the same as mine. Kains and Schmitt were both forwards, and they wanted to use it themselves. And I...had just started being involved with Kains at the time. So I prioritized his opinion over the good of the group as a whole. I was a fool."

She closed her mouth and stared down at the table again. Asuna finally broke her silence to ask softly, "Yolko, are you saying...that you and Kains were still an item from the end of your guild breakup until now...?"

Yolko shook her head almost imperceptibly, without looking up. "When the guild broke up...we did as well. We met from time to time to catch up...but we couldn't stick around for very long before thinking about the incident with the ring. It was like that yesterday, too. We were only getting dinner...but before then, well..."

"I see...It doesn't change the fact that it's a terrible shock. I'm sorry for asking you about these painful things."

Yolko shook her head briefly again. "No, it's all right. Now... about Grimlock..."

That name brought me back to my senses. I sat upright.

"He was the sub-leader of Golden Apple. He was also the husband of the guild leader. Husband in *SAO* only, of course."

"Oh...your leader was a woman?"

"Yes. She was very strong...for a mid-level player, that is...But good with a one-handed sword, pretty, and smart...I admired her so much. So...it's still so hard to accept that she was so cruelly PKed in her sleep..."

"I suppose it must have been a terrible shock to Grimlock, too, losing someone you love enough to marry..." Asuna mumbled.

Yolko shivered. "Yes. Until that point, he had been such a kind and cheerful blacksmith...and after the incident, he was a terrible wreck...Once we fell apart, he fell out of touch with everyone. I have no idea where he is now."

"I see...I hate to ask all these painful questions, but there's just one more. Do you think it's possible...that Grimlock killed Kains yesterday? We took that black spear that was stuck in Kains's chest and appraised it...and it said that Grimlock was the crafter."

It was tantamount to asking if the true culprit of the ring incident half a year ago was Kains. Yolko looked hesitant for a while, then very briefly nodded.

"...Yes...I think it's possible. But neither Kains nor I would have PKed our leader to steal that ring. I have nothing to prove my innocence...but if it were Grimlock who did that yesterday... then maybe he ultimately means to murder all three of us who were against selling the ring: Kains, Schmitt, and me..."

We walked Yolko back to her inn, gave her several days' worth of food items, and told her not to leave under any circumstances. In order to make things more bearable, we paid for a week's worth of time in a three-room suite, the largest the inn had to offer. But in Aincrad, there were no MMORPGs to play to pass the time, so we promised to solve the case as quickly as we could before we left her behind.

"Actually, I would have felt most secure leaving her at KoB headquarters," Asuna noted. I recalled the splendor of their new HQ building in Grandzam, the City of Iron on the fifty-fifth floor.

"Good point...but if she insisted she didn't want to go, there's no forcing her."

In order to have Yolko under the KoB's protection, she'd have to reveal the full details of her situation to the guild—in other words, to make public every sordid detail of the dissolution of Golden Apple six months earlier. She'd probably resisted to protect Kains's honor.

Right as we reached the teleport gate, the town bell rang eleven o'clock. The rain was finally letting up, only to be replaced with thick mist. Through the haze, I looked at Asuna in her black and ashy pink outfit and said, "So now…"

"…?"

Asuna gave me a curious look, waiting for the rest of my sentence.

It seemed awkward to bring it up now, but late was better than never, so I cleared my throat and said, "Ahem! Well, err. I just was…going to say…you look nice."

I did it. I was a *gentleman*.

But no longer had the thought run through my mind than her face crinkled so sharply, it nearly cracked. She thrust her index finger into my chest and growled, "If that was your reaction, then you should have said it the moment you saw me!!"

She spun at light speed and announced that she was going to change outfits. Her red ears had to be from rage.

It made no sense. Truly, I would never understand women.

Asuna emerged from a nearby empty home in her usual knight's outfit, swinging her long hair behind her back. "So what do we do now?"

"Ah, r-right. Our choices are…One, ask around the middle floors for Grimlock to pin down his location. Two, look for the other members of Golden Apple to get confirmation on Yolko's story. Three…a more thorough examination of the clues in Kains's murder."

"Hrrm," Asuna mumbled, crossing her arms and thinking hard. "One is too inefficient with just the two of us. If Grimlock is the culprit as we currently suspect, he'll be hiding out. Two…the other members are the ones involved, so it's impossible to get an accurate picture…"

"Huh? How so?"

"Well, let's assume they give us some information that con-tradicts Yolko's story. How will we determine which story is the truth and which is a lie? It'll just confuse us. We need more objective material to go off of..."

"So...three, then?"

We glanced at each other and nodded in agreement. For one thing, hard as it would be to admit to Yolko, the reason we were so interested in solving the case was not to expose the truth of the Golden Apple killings but to identify the method of the safe-haven PK that had killed Kains.

All we'd been able to certify so far about the murder last night was that it was *not* caused by piercing damage inflicted outside of town and then brought inside. We needed to have a long, thorough discussion about what other ways it could possibly have happened.

"It's just...I think we need the help of someone with a bit more knowledge," I mumbled.

Asuna looked at me curiously. "Yes, but it wouldn't be fair to Yolko to go spilling the details of her story everywhere we go. And there aren't many people who are absolutely trustworthy and know even more about the *SAO* game system than us..."

"...Ah."

A single name popped into my head, and I snapped my fingers. "That's it. I know just the person."

"Who?"

When I told her the name, Asuna's eyes nearly popped out of her head.

5

The fact that the man actually showed up thirty minutes after Asuna sent the message was somewhat of a surprise. I doubted it was because of my insistence that I would buy lunch.

The moment his silent, tall figure strode through the center square of Algade, the passing players in the crowd burst into murmurs. His long blond hair was tied to spill neatly across the back of his dark red robe, and he wore no weapon on his waist or back. His sheer presence alone gave him the image of an imperious mage—a class that didn't actually exist in *SAO*. Heathcliff the Holy Sword, leader of the Knights of the Blood and Aincrad's greatest swordsman, smoothly approached us, his only reaction a raised eyebrow.

Asuna gave him an audibly crisp salute and quickly explained. "Forgive me for the sudden summons, Commander! This id... Er, this man has some questions that he refuses to back down from..."

"Well, I was just planning to eat lunch, myself. It's not often I get the opportunity to receive a treat courtesy of Kirito, the Black Swordsman. I have a meeting with our gear managers this evening, but I have time until then," Heathcliff said in a smooth, steely tenor. I looked up at his looming face and shrugged.

"Well, I haven't thanked you yet for drawing aggro for so long in the last boss fight. In exchange, I'll tell you a very interesting story."

I guided the top two members of the strongest guild in the game to the sleaziest, scummiest NPC-run restaurant I knew of in Algade. It wasn't because I liked the taste there, just that the overall aesthetic of the place somehow struck a chord in me.

For five minutes I walked them through a maze of alleys, turning right, ducking down, spinning left, climbing up, and so on, until we finally reached the dingy-looking restaurant. Asuna looked at it and said, "You'd better guide us on the return trip. I don't think I can find my way back to the square."

"From what I hear, there are dozens of players who got lost and didn't have a teleport crystal, still wandering the alleys to this day," I joked with a macabre leer.

Heathcliff flatly pointed out, "You can pay ten col to an NPC on the side of the road to guide you back. And if you don't have that much…"

He lifted the palms of his hands in a shrug and walked into the building. Asuna made a face and joined me in following him.

As I had hoped, the cramped interior was totally empty. We sat at a cheap four-seat table and ordered three servings of "Algade soba noodles" from the suspect-looking owner, then sipped ice water from cloudy cups. On my right, Asuna grimaced and said, "It feels like we're having a consolation party…"

"Just your imagination. Anyway, let's cut your busy commander a break and get to business," I said, glancing across the table at the cool-faced Heathcliff.

His expression did not change the tiniest bit as Asuna offered an efficient explanation of the events of last night. The only reaction he gave was a twitch of an eyebrow at the scene of Kains's death.

"…So we were hoping, if it's not too much trouble, to make use of your knowledge, sir," Asuna finished. Heathcliff took another sip of ice water and grunted.

"First, I'd like to hear Kirito's conjecture. What do you make of the means of this safe-haven murder?"

I relinquished the hand that was propping up my cheek and lifted three fingers. "Basically...I have three theories. The first is that it was a proper in-town duel. The second is some kind of loophole in the system using a combination of already known methods. And the third...is some kind of unknown skill or item that nullifies the Anti-Criminal Code."

"You can rule out the third," he replied immediately. I couldn't help but stare. Similarly taken aback, Asuna blinked a few times.

"You seem...very certain of that, Commander."

"Just imagine. If you developed this game, would you insert a skill or weapon with that power?"

"Well...I suppose not," I said.

"And why do you think that?"

I looked back into those brassy eyes, their gaze full of a magnetic power, and answered, "Because...it wouldn't be fair. While it pains me to admit it, at its core, the rules of *SAO* are fair. With the one exception being *your* Unique Skill."

I threw in that last comment with a little smirk, which Heathcliff silently returned. That caught me by surprise, but I didn't show it. Even the commander of the KoB couldn't possibly know about the secret skill I'd been hiding recently.

Asuna watched the two of us exchanging enigmatic smiles, then sighed, shook her head, and interjected, "At any rate, it would be a waste of time for us to speculate on the third option, since there's no way to be sure of it. So let's begin with the first possibility: that it was a duel-based PK."

"Very well...By the way, this place certainly seems to take its time serving the food," Heathcliff said peevishly, looking back over to the counter.

I shrugged. "As far as I've seen, the guy here is the least motivated NPC in Aincrad. In a way, that's worth enjoying. And there's all the ice water you can drink," I said, filling the commander's cup to the brim from the cheap pitcher on the table. "If a player dies within a safe haven, then it's common sense that it was from a duel. But—and I assure you of this—when Kains died, there was no victory display. Have you ever heard of a duel like that?"

Next to me, Asuna wondered, "By the way, it never occurred to me before to ask, but what determines the location of the victory screen?"

"Huh? Umm…"

I hadn't given that any thought, either. But Heathcliff answered the question immediately.

"It is the median point between the two duelists. If they are over thirty feet apart at the time of the finish, a window will appear in the near vicinity of both players."

"…I'm surprised you know a rule like that. Which means that, at the very farthest, it would have been within fifteen feet of Kains."

I replayed the atrocity in my brain and shook my head. "There were no windows in the open space around him. There were dozens of witnesses, so that's a certainty. Now, if it appeared in the church behind him, that's a different story, but the killer would have to still be inside, and Asuna would have encountered him when she burst into there before Kains's death."

"And I didn't see any winner's display inside the church, either," Asuna added.

I grunted in acknowledgment. "So…I guess it wasn't a duel…"

It felt as though an even darker shadow had fallen over the gloomy restaurant.

"Are you sure you chose right with this place?" Asuna mumbled, finishing her cup of water and smacking it onto the table. I wasted no time in refilling it. She shot me a look and thanked me, then held up two fingers. "That leaves only the second option: a loophole in the system. I just keep coming back to one thing."

"Which is?"

"Piercing DOT."

Asuna picked up one of the toothpicks from the holder on the table—a useless item, as teeth didn't get dirty here—and jabbed it like a tiny weapon.

"I don't think that spear was just for a show of public execution. I feel like the damage over time was necessary for the PK to work."

"Yeah, I'd agree with that," I said, only to shake my head at another thought. "But remember our experiment? If you're pierced by a piercing weapon out in the field, then go into town, the damage stops."

"When you walk back, yes. But what about a corridor crystal? If you had a crystal set up to teleport into that church room, then traveled through it from outside of town...would the damage stop then?"

"It would," Heathcliff said promptly. "Whether on foot, or through a corridor teleportation, or if thrown by another player, the code works on any player as soon as they enter the town. Without exception."

"Hang on. Does 'the town' only count on the ground and in buildings? What about the air?" I asked, struck by a sudden revelation.

The rope. Could it be possible to hang a rope around Kains's neck so that he hung out of the church window from a corridor crystal, bleeding out from the spear, as he did not touch any surface of the town?

Even Heathcliff showed a moment of doubt at this thought. But two seconds later, his ponytailed hair shook from side to side.

"No...strictly speaking, the safe-haven zone extends vertically from the borders of the town up until it touches the 'lid' of the floor above. As long as a player intersects with that pillar of space, they are under the code's protection. So even if they set the exit of a corridor crystal to the air hundreds of feet above the town and tossed a victim in from outside its borders, they would suffer no fall damage. Not that the resulting nerve shock would be at all pleasant."

"Ohhh," Asuna and I marveled in tandem. Not at learning the shape of the town's safe-haven zone, but the sheer mental and observational skill of Heathcliff that he knew such a thing.

Part of me wondered if that was just the kind of mentality one needed to be a guild leader, but then the scraggly face of a certain katana-warrior floated into my mind, dashing that notion to pieces.

However—that meant that as long as Kains was within the town borders, even that piercing damage-over-time effect would stop. Which meant the source of the damage that eliminated his HP came from outside the Guilty Thorn. Could that be where the loophole was?

I thought hard, and I eventually conjectured, "The Monument of Life included the cause of Kains's death along with the time. It said 'piercing damage.' And the only thing his disappearance left behind was that black spear."

"Right. I have a hard time imagining that another weapon was secretly involved."

"Listen," I said, recalling the stomach-churning feeling of taking a critical hit from a powerful monster, "what happens to your HP bar when you suffer a really nasty critical hit?"

Asuna looked at me as though the answer was obvious and said, "You lose a ton of HP, of course."

"I mean, the way it happens. It doesn't just immediately eliminate a huge chunk of the bar. It slides downward from the right. In other words, there's a small period of lag between suffering the blow and your HP bar reflecting the proper amount."

She finally understood what I was getting at. Meanwhile, Heathcliff's face was an emotionless mask, so there was no way to guess what he was thinking. I looked at each in turn and gestured. "Let's say that Kains's HP is reduced from full to nothing from a single spear blow outside of town. He looked like a tank based on his armor, so he must have had lots of HP. Someone like that, it might take...let's say, five seconds to drain all the way. In that time, Kains was sent through the portal and through the church window..."

"W-wait a minute," Asuna rasped. "He might not have been a front-line fighter, but Kains was an above-average player in the high-volume zone. I don't have a one-hit sword skill that could wipe out all of his HP...and neither do you!"

"That is true," I agreed. "Even a critical hit of my Vorpal Strike wouldn't take down half of his HP. But there are thousands of players in *SAO*. We can't deny the possibility of an extremely high-level player unaffiliated with any of the front-line progress, lurking out there somewhere."

"Meaning, we don't know if it was Grimlock himself who killed Kains with the spear, or if it was another red player hired to do the job, but whoever it was, they were strong enough to kill a full-armored tank with one hit?"

I shrugged in a sign of affirmation, then turned to the man across the table, awaiting the teacher's grade. Heathcliff looked down at the table through half-closed lids, then slowly nodded.

"That methodology is not impossible. If you took down a player outside of town with one hit, then instantly teleported them with an already built corridor, you might be able to give the appearance of a PK inside the safe haven."

For a second, I thought I was actually correct.

"But," he continued, "as I'm sure you know, piercing weapons are prized primarily for their reach, then their armor-puncturing power. In terms of basic strength, they are weaker than blunt and slashing weapons. Especially when you're using not a large, heavy lance but a short spear."

He had hit a sore spot. I pursed my lips like a sulking child. Heathcliff smiled thinly and continued. "Using a non-elite short spear, a one-hit kill of a tank fighter in the volume zone would require...at least level one hundred, in my opinion."

"A hundred?!" Asuna yelped. The fencer's hazelnut-brown eyes looked back and forth between Heathcliff and me, and she shook her head rapidly. "N-nobody's that good. You haven't forgotten how hard we leveled to get where we are now, have you? Level one hundred...You couldn't even get there by now if you spent twenty-four hours a day in the latest labyrinth."

"I agree."

With the two lead members of the strongest guild in the game both in agreement, there was no way for a simple solo player like me to argue. I was near the very top of the players in the frontier group, and even my level was still barely over 80.

But I just couldn't give up. "Th...there could be an issue of skill strength, not just statistical strength. For example, someone might have found the thir...The second Unique Skill in the game."

The commander's red robe swayed as he chuckled. "If such a player truly existed, I would have laid out the red carpet to the KoB already."

Something in the way he was gazing at me with those impenetrable eyes made me uncomfortable, so I gave up on that line of logic and leaned back into the cheap chair.

"Hmm, I thought I was on to something. That leaves..."

Before I could come up with a stupid idea like having a boss monster strike him before teleporting, a shadow leaned over my other side.

"...Eat up," the NPC cook said tonelessly, setting three white bowls down from a square tray. His face was hidden behind the long bangs coming down his grease-stained cook's hat. He returned to his spot behind the counter as Asuna stared at him in shock—she was clearly used to the clean, polite, and punctual NPCs from other floors.

I took a pair of disposable chopsticks from the table and cracked them apart, pulling one of the bowls closer. Asuna followed my lead and murmured, "What is this...? Ramen?"

"Or something like it," I replied, pulling curly noodles out of the light-colored broth.

The only sounds in the dingy restaurant were three lonely sets of slurps. A dry breeze budged the cloth that hung in the entranceway, and some kind of bird squawked outside.

A few minutes later, I pushed my empty bowl to the side of the table and looked at the man across from me.

"...So, have you come to any conclusions, Commander?"

"…"

His bowl totally empty, including the broth, Heathcliff stared at the kanji-like pattern at the bottom and said, "This is not ramen. I am certain of that."

"Yeah, I agree."

"Then I will give you an answer worthy of this false ramen's flavor." He looked up and politely placed the chopsticks on the rim of the bowl. "Based on the information we have now, it cannot be determined what exactly happened. However, I can say this… The only rock-solid information we have about this incident is what you saw and heard firsthand."

"…What do you mean…?"

"I mean…" Heathcliff fixed me, then Asuna, with a stare from his brass-colored eyes. "That everything you see and hear directly in Aincrad is digital data that can be converted to code. There is no room for phantom visions or auditory signals. On the other hand, that means that all information that doesn't originate as digital data can be shrouded in mistakes or deceit. If you're going to track down the truth of this safe-haven murder…then you should only trust the information received directly by your eyes, ears, and brain."

With one last thanks for the meal, Heathcliff got to his feet. I stood as well, pondering the meaning of the mysterious swordsman's words, thanked the cook, and walked through the doorway.

I just barely overheard Heathcliff mutter to himself, "Why does this place exist…?"

As the commander melted away into the maze of streets, I turned to look at Asuna and asked, "Did you understand what that meant?"

"…Yes," she said. I was impressed.

"It was Tokyo-style shoyu ramen, without the soy sauce. No wonder it felt so lonely."

"Wha—?"

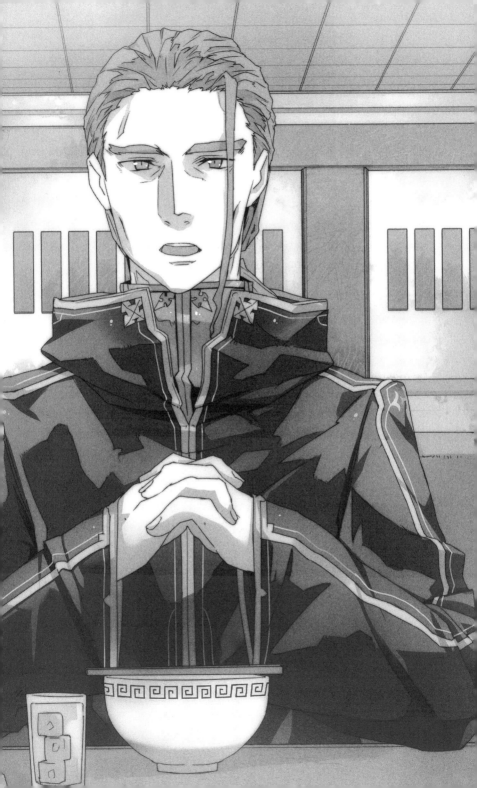

"I've made up my mind. I'm going to find a way to make soy sauce. Otherwise I will never recover from this feeling of dissatisfaction."

·"…Uhm, good luck with that?" I muttered, then abruptly shook my head. "No, not that!"

"Huh? What did you mean?"

"Look, I'm sorry about feeding you some weird food. Just forget about it. What I meant was, what did Heathcliff mean with that weird Zen philosophy?"

"Oh…" Asuna said. She nodded firmly this time. "He just meant, don't take secondhand sources too seriously. In this case, that would be the motive arguments…The whole thing with Golden Apple and the magic ring."

"What?" I groaned. "You want me to suspect Yolko? I mean, sure, there's no evidence of anything…but like you said, Asuna, there's no way to get proof backing up anything anyway, so doubting her is also pointless."

For some reason, she blinked, nonplussed, then looked away and shook her head a few times.

"W-well, you might be right about that. But like the commander said, we still don't have enough material to confirm the PK method yet. So let's go get a story from the other person involved. If we throw the whole ring story in his face, he might just let slip with some answers."

"Huh? Who?"

"The guy who took the spear from you, of course."

6

The numbers in the bottom right corner of my view said that it was exactly 2:00 PM.

Normally, lunchtime would be over, and the afternoon schedule of labyrinth conquest would be in full swing. But there was no time to leave the town today. Once I had passed through the wilderness and reached the unexplored sections of the dungeon, the sun would already be down.

I was willing to ditch my normal duty at the tip of a hat because the weather was nice, so it meant nothing to me, but the same could not be said of the Flash, who was absent from advancing the game for the second day in a row.

And yet, as far as I could tell from side-eyeing Asuna as we walked together, she seemed in a softer, gentler mood than usual. She was browsing the mysterious-looking shops in Algade's back alleys, peering into dark culverts that went God-knows-where, and when she noticed my gaze, she actually gave me a little smile along with her questioning look.

"What is it?"

I shook my head rapidly. "N-nothing, nothing at all."

"You're weird. That's nothing new, though."

She giggled, locked her hands behind her back, and practically skipped forward.

Who was being weird here? Was this really the same possessed warrior of game progress who had dropped a thunderbolt on me in the middle of a nap yesterday? Or did she really like that Algade soba that much? If that was the case, she really needed to try the even more chaotic flavor of the "Algade roast" at that restaurant next time.

Eventually, the bustle of the teleport square came into range ahead. Fortunately, we hadn't needed to pay for the assistance of any NPC guides this time.

I was unusually restlessness, so I cleared my throat to snap out of it and said, "Ahem. So next up is talking to Team Captain Schmitt. Though now that I think about it, I suppose the DDA would be out questing at this time of day."

"Mmm, I wouldn't be so sure," Asuna said with a finger to her delicate chin, the smile gone now. "If we take Yolko at her word, Schmitt was one of the people against selling the ring...meaning he's in the same boat Kains was. Based on how he was acting last night, we can assume he's quite aware of this. If he's under attack from an unknown red player...do you really think he'd venture out of a safe zone?"

"Uh...that's a good point. But there's also a very good chance that red player has a means of killing someone within the safe zone. We can't be absolutely certain that he's not in danger in town, too."

"So he'll need to find the greatest security he possibly can. Which means locking himself in an inn room, or..."

At that point, I understood what Asuna was getting it. I snapped my fingers and continued. "Or hiding out in the DDA's headquarters."

It was just recently that the Divine Dragon Alliance, one of the foremost guilds in Aincrad, had moved their guild home to its stately location on the fifty-sixth floor. It could not have been a coincidence that it was located one floor above the Knights of the Blood's headquarters. Their extremely indulgent and fanciful welcoming party included me, for some reason, and I found that their building was less a "home" than a "castle" or "fortress." As a subtle way to needle them back, I joined Klein and Agil in running a train on their buffet spread, but the excessive intake of flavor signals caused the game to give me an unpleasant stuffed sensation around my gut for three days afterward.

I glared up at the house of overeating horrors situated on a steep hill overlooking the city, and even felt a momentary gag reflex. Asuna showed no visible reaction to the sight as she strode up the red brick road.

As I looked at the white pinnacles flying the guild flag of blue dragons on a silver field, I grumbled, "I'm surprised that even the great and mighty DDA had enough money to buy this place. What do you think about that, KoB Vice Commander?"

"Well, in terms of numbers alone, DDA's got twice our ranks. But even then, it doesn't quite sit right with me. Our accountant, Daizen, says, 'They must got a whole lotta real efficient farmin' spots.'"

"Ahhh."

Farming was an MMO term, referring to a rotation system of high-speed mob-killing. One of the most notable of these spots was the so-called Ant Valley on the forty-sixth floor, where I had engaged in a reckless level-grinding spree last winter. However, once the experience intake in a particular location surpassed a certain rate, the Cardinal System, *SAO*'s digital god that managed every aspect of the game, would automatically enact a penalty that lowered the experience rate.

So it was publicly discussed and agreed among the front-line players that the best farming spots should be announced to all players, so that the spoils could be shared equally until they dried up. But Asuna was referring to a suspicion that the DDA might be secretly harboring a number of spots they had discovered on their own.

It was unfair, of course, but if the DDA got stronger, it ultimately strengthened the entire front-line population as a whole, so it was difficult to openly criticize them for such actions. Doing so would reveal the inherent contradiction of being among the best of the game. It was all of our individual egos that were upholding an extremely unbalanced hierarchy, in which a small minority monopolized a majority of the system resources—under the guise of freeing everyone from this game of death.

In that sense, the competing philosophy of the Aincrad Liberation Front—that all the player-earned resources should be confiscated and then fairly redistributed—couldn't be dismissed as a mere pipe dream. If the Army's goal had been put into practice, this safe-haven murder would not have occurred. The ring at the center of it would have been taken away, sold, and the profits split up among all the players in the game.

"I swear...whoever created this game of death was a real nasty piece of work..."

Why did it have to be an MMO? A real-time strategy game or a first-person shooter would be fairer, quicker, and easier to finish. But *SAO* was testing the egos of its high-level players. It demanded that one balance a meager sensation of superiority against the lives of one's friends—or all the players in the game.

The culprit of the ring murder gave in to ego.

I couldn't claim to be totally immune, either. I myself was hiding a secret in my status window, something so huge it couldn't even be compared to a single magic item.

And having heard my murmur and traced my every thought to that point, Asuna whispered, "Which is why we have to solve this case."

She momentarily squeezed my hand and gave me a little grin that completely eradicated all of my doubts. As I stood there, uncharacteristically panicked, Asuna asked me to wait where I was and headed steadfastly for the gate of the massive complex ahead. I thrust my still-warm hand into my coat pocket and leaned back against a nearby tree trunk.

The grounds of buildings registered as guild headquarters were generally off-limits to nonmembers of the guild, the same way that a player home worked. So there wasn't truly any need for guards, but many of the larger guilds with the personnel to spare would have guards on shift—not for security but to handle visitors.

True to the pattern, the DDA had two heavy spearmen standing imperiously in front of their stately front gate.

They look more like minor bosses in an RPG than guards, I thought, but Asuna maintained her composure and headed straight to speak with the guard on the right.

"Hello. I am Asuna of the Knights of the Blood."

The towering warrior leaned backward momentarily and piped, "Oh, hey! Yo, how's it going? What brings you over here?!"

He wasn't imposing or a minor boss in any sense. Asuna favored the other guard with a radiant smile when he trotted over, and she cut right to the chase.

"I'm here because I have business with one of your members. Do you think you might be able to get in touch with Schmitt for me?"

The men looked at each other, and one of them wondered, "Wouldn't he be in the latest labyrinth?"

The other one answered, "Oh, but I think I remember him complaining about a headache and saying he'd take the day off this morning. He might be in his room inside—I'll go check."

I was surprised they were so accommodating. The DDA and KoB were not on friendly terms by any means, but it seemed that such attitudes didn't extend to individuals. Either that, or Asuna's personal-charm parameters were so high that they couldn't resist. If it were the latter, I'd probably be better off hanging back here.

As I stayed stuck to the tree near the gate earning Hiding skill points, one of the guards typed up a quick message and sent it off.

A response came within thirty seconds, so he opened his window back up. Schmitt was inside the castle after all—he couldn't possibly respond that fast if he was busy adventuring in the latest dungeon.

The guard read the message, looking troubled. "It seems he wants to take a break today…but he wants to find out what you want first."

Asuna thought it over and said, "Just tell him I want to speak about the incident with the ring."

It worked like a charm. The man complaining of a debilitating headache raced out of the castle at phenomenal speed, said, "Let's find somewhere else," and then continued running down the hill. When Asuna passed my tree chasing after him, I joined the chase. Schmitt looked back at us but only picked up his speed and otherwise didn't react. He probably knew that Asuna and I were working as a team on this one.

Just as when he'd snatched the spear from me last night, Schmitt was wearing his expensive-looking plate armor as he powerwalked several paces ahead of us. He even had a lighter chainmail on underneath. He wasn't carrying his massive lance, but the weight of that equipment had to be extraordinary. The way he raced forward as if wearing nothing at all made him less like a tank and more like a burly American football player.

The large man, one of the rare few in Aincrad who actually had an athletic build, only came to a stop once he'd descended the hill into the town. He turned around, armor clanking, and lit into me, rather than Asuna.

"Who did you talk to?"

"Huh?" I responded, then realized that he had omitted the phrase *about the ring*, and I chose my words carefully. "From a former member of the guild Golden Apple."

Beneath his short, spiky hair, his heavy eyebrows twitched.

"Who?"

I hesitated here but realized that if Schmitt had actually done the killing yesterday, he would also know that Yolko was with Kains at the time. There was no point in hiding it.

"Yolko," I answered, and the large man looked up briefly, releasing a long breath. I kept my face passive as my mind raced. If I was correct in taking that reaction as relief, that would be because he knew that Yolko was on his side in opposing the sale of the ring.

Schmitt, too, had come to the conclusion that the killing yesterday was very likely revenge from one of the "sell the ring" voters, which included Grimlock. That's why he'd faked an illness to stay within the safety of the guild building.

It was looking increasingly unlikely that Schmitt was responsible for the murder of Kains, but that didn't mean he had no motive. If both Kains and Schmitt had carried out the killing over the ring, one might still kill the other to silence him. With this in mind, I decided to be direct.

"Schmitt, do you know where we might find Grimlock, the creator of the spear you took yesterday?"

"I...I don't know!!" Schmitt shouted, shaking his head violently. "I haven't talked to him since the guild fell apart. I don't even know if he's alive!" he babbled, his eyes dancing over the various buildings of the town. He seemed to be afraid another spear might come flying at him any second now.

At this point, Asuna broke her silence and gently said, "Listen, Schmitt, we're not searching for whoever killed the leader of Golden Apple. We're looking for who caused the incident last night...Specifically, any clues to it. It's the only way to ensure that the safe haven stays safe for everyone."

She paused, then continued in a tone more serious than before. "I'm afraid that currently, the most suspicious character is the creator of that spear and husband to your guild leader: Grimlock. Of course, it's possible that someone is trying to frame him, but in order to judge that possibility, we need to speak to Grimlock directly. If you have any idea of where he is now or how he can be reached, will you tell us?"

With those large hazel-brown eyes trained on him, Schmitt leaned back slightly. So he was not particularly comfortable with talking to female players. A kindred spirit.

He looked away and clenched his lips. If Asuna's head-on attack wasn't going to do the trick, he was a worthy foe indeed.

I resigned myself to a tougher time than I'd hoped for, but then Schmitt began to mumble.

"...I don't know where he is. Truly. At the time, Grimlock really loved a particular NPC restaurant. He went there practically every day, so maybe he's still a regular..."

"R-really?" I asked, leaning forward.

In Aincrad, eating was essentially the only pleasure to be found in the game. But it was also very rare to find a satisfactory flavor among the cheaper NPC restaurants. If he'd found a place he liked enough to visit every day, that was a tough habit to break. Even I took my daily meals on a rotation of just three particular establishments—and that mysterious eatery from earlier was not one of them.

"Can you tell us the name of the—"

"On one condition," Schmitt said, interrupting me. "I can tell you, but you need to do something for me in return. Help me... see Yolko again."

Asuna and I had Schmitt wait at a nearby general store and huddled together to discuss the deal.

"There's...no danger in this, right? Or is there?"

"Hmmm..." I grunted, unable to make a judgment on that question in the moment.

If Schmitt—or even more unlikely, Yolko—was really the culprit in yesterday's safe-haven murder, then it was highly probable that they would make the other person their next target. It wasn't out of the question that as soon as they met in person, that safe-haven PK trick would come into play again, leading to a new fatality.

But if that were the case, they would have to equip a weapon and utilize a sword skill. And that required at least four or five seconds to open the window, switch weapons on the equipment mannequin, and hit the OK button.

"As long as we don't take our eyes off of them, there shouldn't be any opportunity for a PK. But if that's not the point of this meeting, why is Schmitt asking us to bring him together with Yolko?" I asked, spreading my hands. Asuna inclined her head, thinking hard.

"Let's see...I'm guessing it's not so he can finally express his love for her."

"Huh? Really?"

I started to spin around to look at Schmitt, who looked like he *could* possibly be that innocent, but Asuna grabbed the collar of my coat to stop me. "I just said it *wasn't* that! Anyway, if there's no danger in it, then it just depends on Yolko. I'll shoot her a message to see."

"Y-yes, ma'am. Please do."

She opened her window and typed away on her holo-keyboard with blazing speed. Friend messages were a convenient function that allowed you to speak immediately with someone in a remote location, but they had strict requirements: You had to be registered either as friends, guildmates, or spouses. So just because we knew Grimlock's name didn't mean we could just send him a message. Technically, there were "instant messages" that could be sent if you knew a player's name, but they only worked if on the same level, and there was no confirmation for the sender that the message was seen.

Yolko must have replied immediately, as Asuna didn't even need to close her window before she muttered, "She says okay. I can't say I'm not nervous...but let's take him. We can go to Yolko's inn, right?"

"Yeah. It's still too dangerous for her to be out and about," I agreed, then fully turned to Schmitt this time, who was still waiting at the store behind us. I flashed him the okay sign, and the heavily armored man made an expression of obvious relief.

By the time the three of us teleported from the fifty-ninth floor to Marten on the fifty-seventh, the city was already blanketed in evening sun.

The square was full of the raucous cries of NPCs and merchant players hawking wares. Adventurers walked among them, easing the fatigue of the day's fighting, but there was one spot in the plaza that was desolate.

It was the facade of a small church, the place where the man named Kains had died under mysterious and shocking circumstances just twenty-four hours earlier. I had to keep my gaze fixed straight ahead to avoid staring at it.

After a few minutes of walking the same path we'd taken yesterday, we reached the inn and headed upstairs. The room at the very end of the hallway was the place where Yolko was staying—or hiding for protection.

I knocked on the door and said my name.

She responded in a tiny voice, and I turned the knob. The door lock was set to only open for friends, and it clicked lightly as I pushed it open.

Yolko was sitting on one of the two sofas facing each other in the center of the room, directly through the door. She got to her feet and bowed, dark blue hair swaying.

Without taking a step, I looked from Yolko's tense expression to Schmitt's equally nervous face behind me and said, "Well… just to confirm that it's safe, we're going to ask that neither of you have any weapons equipped or open your windows. I'm sorry to force that upon you, but I hope you understand."

"…Yes."

"I understand."

Yolko's hesitant whisper and Schmitt's disgruntled mutter came at the same time. I stepped inside and motioned to Schmitt and Asuna.

The two former Golden Apple members, who were meeting again for the first time in months, stared at each other in silence for a long time. Yolko and Schmitt had once been guildmates, but now there had to be at least twenty levels between them, given that Schmitt was a busy member of a major front-line guild. But to my eyes, it was the sturdy lancer who was more nervous about the meeting.

In the end, it was Yolko who spoke first.

"...It's been a while, Schmitt."

She smiled thinly. Schmitt pursed his lips, then rasped, "Yes... and I thought I'd never see you again. May I sit?"

Yolko nodded, and he clanked in his plate armor over to the sofas, sitting on the other one. It looked uncomfortable to me, but he did not remove his armor.

I made sure that the door had locked itself again, then took position on the east side of the parallel couches. Asuna stood on the other end.

We'd gotten the most expensive room for Yolko while she had no choice but to stay in hiding, so even with the four of us inside, it felt spacious. The main door was on the north wall, the doorway to the bedroom was to the west, and there were large windows to the east and south.

The south window was open, the pleasant spring breeze rustling the curtains. Of course, the window was protected by the game system, so no one could get inside, even when it stood wide open. It was a taller building than those around it, so there was a good view of the darkening town past the white curtains, as the light deepened into purple.

The bustle of the city outside was interrupted by Yolko's voice. "You're in the Divine Dragon Alliance now, Schmitt. That's very good—they're the best, even among the front-line players."

It sounded like an honest compliment, but Schmitt's brow furrowed unhappily. He rumbled, "What do you mean? You find that unnatural?"

His suspicious, barbed response took me by surprise, but Yolko was not affected.

"Hardly. I just think that you must have worked really hard after the end of our guild. It's very admirable of you, when Kains and I gave up on leveling further."

She brushed back the dark hair resting on her shoulders and smiled. While it wasn't to the same level as Schmitt in his plate armor, Yolko, too, was more dressed up than usual. She wore a thick one-piece dress with a leather vest, then a purple velvet tunic, and even a shawl on her shoulders. Even without any metal, this much clothing would provide a significant armor boost. While she was acting calm and collected, she had to be nervous on the inside.

Meanwhile, Schmitt made no attempt to hide his discomfort. He leaned forward, armor clattering. "Enough about me! The only reason I'm here…is to ask about Kains." His tone of voice dropped lower. "Why would he be murdered, after all this time?! Did…did he steal the ring? Was he the one who killed our leader in GA?"

I realized at once that "GA" stood for Golden Apple. His question essentially announced that he had nothing to do with the ring incident or the safe-haven murder. If it was an act, it was a good one.

For the first time, Yolko's expression shifted. Her faint smile vanished, and she glared at Schmitt. "Of course not. Both Kains and I fully revered the leader. We opposed selling the ring because we wanted to use it to strengthen the guild, rather than have us split the money and waste it. I'm sure that she felt the same way about it."

"Yeah…I felt that way, too. Don't forget, I also opposed selling it. Besides, it's not just the anti-sellers who had a motive to steal the ring. One of the pro-sellers might have wanted to seize it so they could get all of the money themselves!"

He slammed his gauntleted hand against his knee, then held his head in his hands.

"So…why would Grimlock go after Kains now…? Is he going to kill all three of us for voting against selling? Is he coming after you and me?!"

It couldn't possibly be an act. When I looked at Schmitt's profile, with the way he clenched his teeth, I saw clear, undeniable fear.

Meanwhile, Yolko had regained her calm composure. She said, "We don't know for certain that it was Grimlock who killed

Kains. It could have been one of the other members who asked him to make that spear. In fact..." She looked down at the low table between the two sofas and mumbled, "Couldn't it have been the leader's revenge? There's no way for any ordinary player to kill someone like that in a safe zone."

"Wha..."

Schmitt's mouth gaped wordlessly. I couldn't deny that I felt a tiny chill run up my back, too. He looked back at the grinning Yolko and said, "But you just said that Kains couldn't have stolen the ring..."

Yolko stood without responding and took a step to the right. With both hands clasped behind her back and her face toward us, she stepped backward toward the open window to the south. As her slippers softly snickered against the ground, she murmured, "I stayed up all night thinking. Someone among the guild killed the leader, but in the end, it was also all of us. We shouldn't have taken a vote when the ring dropped. She should have just made an order for us to follow. In fact, she should have used it herself. She was the best swordfighter of all of us, and she would have made the best use of the ring. Yet none of us suggested it, because we were all too blinded by greed in our own ways. We all claimed we wanted to make GA a front-line guild, but we just wanted to strengthen ourselves as individuals."

When her long speech ended, Yolko's back was resting against the windowsill. As she leaned back, she added, "Only Grimlock said he would leave it up to her discretion. Only he abandoned his greed and thought of the guild as a whole. So he has the right to seek vengeance against all of us for not giving up our desires for the sake of the leader..."

Amid the silence that fell, the only sound was the chilly whispering of the evening breeze. Eventually, the sound of clattering metal broke the silence: Schmitt's plate armor as he trembled. The veteran player, his face pale and downcast, mumbled, "...You must be kidding. You must be kidding. Now...? All these months later, *now* he wants revenge...?"

He sprang upward, shouting. "And you think that's fine, Yolko?! After all the efforts we've made to survive, you think it's fine for us to be killed in some bizarre, inexplicable way?!"

Schmitt, Asuna, and I all looked at Yolko. The fragile-looking woman was gazing here and there into empty space, as though looking for the right words.

Finally her lips moved, preparing to say something.

At that very moment, a dry sound echoed off the walls. Her eyes and mouth shot wide open. Next, her frail body swayed. She took a heavy step to steady herself, then wobbled around, placing a hand on the open windowsill.

A sudden gust of wind sent Yolko's hair swaying off of her back. There, I saw something I could not believe.

From the center of her shining purple tunic jutted something like a small black stick. It was so insignificant and cheap-looking that for an instant, I didn't recognize it. But when I saw the blinking red light surrounding the stick, I felt a chill of terror.

It was the hilt of a throwing dagger. The entire blade was buried in her body. In other words, the knife had flown from outside of the window and pierced Yolko's back.

Her body wobbled backward and forward, until she tilted perilously over the sill.

"Ah—!" Asuna gasped. I leaped forward, reaching out to grab Yolko and pull her back.

But my fingers only grazed the end of her shawl, and she fell silently out of the building.

"Yolko!!" I screamed, leaning out of the window.

Down below, her body bounced off of the cobblestones, surrounded by a blue glow.

There was the tiniest, most insignificant shattering sound. The mass of polygons expanded, pushed by the burst of blue light...

And a second later, only the black dagger was left behind, clattering against the stone.

7

That's impossible!! the voice in my head screamed, a sentiment that came for multiple reasons.

The inn room was protected by the game code. Even with the window open, there was absolutely no way to get inside, let alone throw a weapon through.

And it was hard to imagine such a small throwing dagger having enough piercing damage, even over time, to wipe out the entirety of a mid-level player's HP. It hadn't taken more than five seconds at the longest for Yolko to disappear after being hit by the dagger.

It was impossible. This was more than just a safe-haven PK; it was an instant kill.

I forced myself to look down at the cobblestones where Yolko had fallen, fighting off the breath caught in my throat and the terrible chill racing up and down my back. Then I looked up, eyes wide, tracking the outline of the town like a camera.

And then I saw it.

The roof of another building the same height as this one, about two blocks away from the inn. And standing atop it, a black figure against the deep purple gloom.

I couldn't see the face due to the hooded black robe he was wearing. I shoved aside the word *Death* as I bellowed, "You bastard!!"

I planted my right foot on the sill and, without looking back, yelled, "Take care of the rest, Asuna!!"

Then I jumped, leaping straight to the roof of the building across the street.

However, even with an excellent agility stat to boost my jump, it was a bit naive of me to think I could clear fifteen feet without a running start, so rather than landing on my feet, I just barely managed to snag the lip of the roof with an outstretched hand. Now it was my strength stat that helped me flip myself upward and over the roof, back onto my feet.

From behind me, I heard Asuna's panicked voice cry, "You can't, Kirito!"

The reason for her command was obvious: If I took a hit from that same throwing dagger attack, I might die just as quickly as Yolko had.

But I wasn't going to let fear of my own mortality keep me from getting a glimpse of the killer in the flesh. I was the one who had guaranteed Yolko's safety. I had shortsightedly assumed that the game system would keep her safe, and I failed to think of other possibilities. If I was going to rely on the system's protection, it would have worked anywhere in town. Why hadn't I considered that a player who would pull off a safe-haven PK could also break through the protection of an inn room?

Over the distant roofs, I saw the black robe flapping in the wind, mocking my regret.

"Just you wait!" I shouted, and began to sprint, drawing the sword on my back. I wouldn't be able to damage him with the blade in town, but I might be able to use it to deflect any thrown objects.

I leaped from roof to roof, careful not to slow my sprint. The people in the streets below must have thought it was an incredibly lame stunt to show off my agility stat, but that wasn't my concern now. I kept jumping through the darkness, the hem of my coat flapping behind me.

The hooded assassin did not run nor even prepare to attack; he simply watched as I raced closer and closer. Once there were only two buildings between us, the assassin's right hand plunged into the depths of his robe. I held my breath and took a forward stance.

But when the hand emerged, it was not holding a throwing dagger. It was glowing a familiar sapphire blue in the gloom. A teleport crystal.

"Shit!" I swore, pulling three picks from my belt as I ran. Holding them aloft, I flung them all together. It wasn't to damage him but to inspire an instinctive dodge and delay the process.

But the assassin was infuriatingly calm. The three needles and their silver bands of light did not faze him in the least as he raised the crystal.

Just before the hooded robe, the picks ran into a purple system wall and fell onto the roof. I listened hard, trying to at least catch the sound of the voice command. If I heard the destination, I might be able to follow with a crystal of my own.

But once again, my plan was foiled. At that very moment, the entirety of Marten was enveloped in the massive tolling of a bell.

My ears—technically, the sound-processing center of my brain—were drowned in the bells signaling five o'clock, preventing me from hearing the assassin give the command for his destination. The blue teleport light flashed, and from a street away, I saw the black silhouette vanish without a trace.

"...!!"

I heaved a wordless bellow and swung my sword at the spot he had stood just three seconds before. More purple light flashed, along with a system tag, impassively warning me that it was an Immortal Object.

I returned to the inn dejected. I took the street this time, stopping at the place where Yolko had vanished so I could stare at the black throwing dagger.

It was impossible to believe that a woman had died there just minutes ago. In my experience, a player's death came only when all effort, attempts to avoid the impossible, or personal strength had finally given way. There was no way someone could be killed in such an instantaneous, inescapable way. It just wasn't fair.

I crouched and picked up the dagger. It was small but heavy, cast of a single piece of metal. On the sides of the razor-thin blade were carved barbs that looked like a shark bite. It was clearly crafted by the same designer of the short spear that felled Kains.

If I stabbed it into my own body, would I take huge, sudden damage as well? I was possessed by an urge to try it out, only maintaining control of myself by shutting my eyes tight and shaking my head.

Inside the inn, I knocked on the room door and turned the knob. The lock clicked open again, allowing the door to swing open.

Asuna had her rapier drawn. When she saw me, she gave me a look of equal parts fury and relief, and then said in a barely controlled growl, "You idiot! How could you be so reckless?"

But then she sighed and, more quietly this time, added, "So… what happened?"

I shook my head. "No good. He teleported away. In fact, I couldn't even tell if it was a man or a woman. Of course…if that were Grimlock, then it's a man…"

SAO had no same-sex marriage rule. If Golden Apple's former leader was a woman, then her spouse, Grimlock, automatically had to be a man. Not that this information would be very useful as a filter—a good 80 percent of the game's population was male.

It was just a throwaway comment. But to my surprise, it got a reaction: from Schmitt, whose large body was scrunched into a ball, the plate armor rattling as he trembled.

"…No."

"What do you mean, 'no'?" Asuna demanded.

He ducked his head in even farther and mumbled, "That's not him. Whoever it was in that robe on the rooftop wasn't Grimlock. Grim was taller. Besides…besides…"

What he said next took our breaths away.

"That hooded robe belonged to the leader of GA. She always wore that plain old thing when she went out. In fact…Yeah! She was wearing it when she went to sell the ring! That…that was her. She's come back for revenge against us all. That was her ghost."

He began to laugh maniacally. He was unhinged. "Ghosts can

do anything. PKing in town? No problem! I wish she'd go and beat the last boss of *SAO* for us. You can't die if you have no HP to begin with…"

As Schmitt continued to laugh hysterically, I tossed the dagger onto the table between the sofas. It landed with a dull thud, a switch that abruptly cut through Schmitt's mood. He stared silently at the jagged blade that gleamed evilly in the light.

"Gah—!"

The large man bolted upright, leaning away from the weapon. I kept my cool and explained, "It's not a ghost. That dagger is a physical object—a few lines of program code that exists somewhere in the *SAO* server. Just like the short spear that's still sitting in your inventory. If you don't believe me, you can take this one, too, and examine it to your heart's content."

"N-no way! You can have the spear back, too!!" Schmitt shrieked, opening his menu window and, after several input mistakes, materializing the black spear. The weapon appeared in midair and fell, clanking down next to the dagger.

The large man put his head in his hands again. Gently, Asuna offered, "Schmitt, I don't think it's a ghost, either. If ghosts in Aincrad were real, there would be many more than just the Golden Apple leader. Nearly three and a half thousand people have died, and they've all got the same grudges to settle. Right?"

She was completely right. If I died in this game, I would sure be mad enough about it to come back as a ghost. Though, if there was anyone I knew serene enough to just accept fate and move on, it had to be the man who led the KoB.

But Schmitt just shook his head, still downcast. "You just… don't know her. Griselda was so strong and so noble…and so incredibly strict when it came to corruption and doing wrong. Even more than you, Asuna. So if someone walked her into a trap…Griselda would never forgive them. She'd come back as a ghost to punish them, if she had to…"

A heavy silence filled the room.

Outside the window, which Asuna had shut and locked, the

sun was down and orange lanterns lit the streets. It would be full of lively players looking to relax, but oddly, the sound seemed to be avoiding this individual room.

I took a deep breath and broke the silence.

"…If that's what you think, then do as you wish. But I won't believe it. There has to be a logic to these two safe-haven murders that fits within the rules of the system. I'm going to find it…and you're going to help me, like you promised."

"H-help…?"

"You said you'd tell us where Grimlock likes to eat. That's our only clue now. I'll stake the place out for days on end, if I have to."

To be honest, while I could find Grimlock, the blacksmith who created the black spear and probably the dagger next to it, I had no plan for what to do after that. I wasn't in the Army, so I couldn't just lock him up and try to interrogate him.

But if what Yolko said before she died was right—"he has the right to seek vengeance against all of us, for the sake of the leader"—and Grimlock was motivated by revenge against the three who voted against selling the ring, or against all the guild members equally…If he was motivated by something as strong as the love for a deceased wife…

If I could sit with him face-to-face and speak to him, maybe something might get through to him. That possibility was the only thing I could bet on at this point.

Schmitt hung his head again but heavily, reluctantly lifted himself from his seat. He stumbled over to a writing desk along the walls, took the pre-supplied parchment and feather quill, then wrote down the name of the restaurant.

As I watched, a thought occurred to me, and over his back I said, "By the way, can you write the names of the other former Golden Apple members? I'll go back to the Monument of Life and check for survivors."

The man nodded and picked up the quill again to continue writing. He brought back the parchment eventually and handed it to me, saying, "It's pathetic to admit this, as a front-line player…but

I don't feel like going out into the open anytime soon. When the time comes for the next boss raid party, leave me out. Also..."

With a gaunt expression devoid of his former boldness, the DDA's lancer and team leader asked, "Can you escort me back to headquarters?"

Neither Asuna nor I could mock Schmitt for the cowardice.

As we walked the terrified giant from the inn on the fifty-seventh floor back to the DDA fortress on the fifty-sixth, the two of us never stopped scanning the darkness. If anyone had coincidentally been unlucky enough to cross our path wearing a hooded black robe, they might have been jumped.

Even through the massive gates of his headquarters, Schmitt's face did not lose its fear. As I watched him trot hastily into the building, I sighed and turned to Asuna.

She was biting her lip. "...It's...very frustrating...what happened to Yolko..." Asuna mumbled. I rasped an acknowledgment.

To be honest, Yolko's death was at least twice as shocking to me as Kains's. I couldn't get the mental image of her falling through the window out of my mind.

"Until now, I'd kind of felt like I was along for a ride...but now I can't see it that way anymore. We have to solve this mystery—for her sake. I'm going to scope out this restaurant. What about you?" I asked.

Asuna looked up at me with a start and replied firmly, "I'm going, of course. We'll get to the bottom of this together."

"...All right. Let's do this."

In truth, I was a bit hesitant about involving Asuna further. If we kept going with this case, we could easily turn ourselves into Grimlock's next targets.

But Asuna turned on her heel, crisply silencing my concerns, and strode toward the teleport gate square. I sucked in a deep breath of cold night air, let it out in a burst, then chased after that long chestnut-brown hair.

8

The place on Schmitt's parchment was a small pub in a cramped section of the twentieth floor's main city. Based on the look of the place, squashed into the twisting alley with a forlorn little sign, it did not look like the kind of restaurant that served meals that could be eaten every day without tiring.

But it was also true that the best spots to eat were found in out-of-the-way places like this, and it was difficult for me to stifle the urge to rush in and start trying everything on the menu. If Grimlock were the hooded assassin, he had already seen my face, and he would never show up here again if he saw me here.

After a survey of the surroundings, Asuna and I hid in the shadows nearby, then noticed that there was an inn within view of the restaurant. When the foot traffic dried up, we darted over to the inn and rented an upstairs room that overlooked the alley.

As we hoped, the window had a clear view of the pub entrance. We extinguished the lights and took seats beside the window, hunkering down to observe.

It wasn't long before Asuna turned to me and asked dubiously, "Hey…we've got a good position now, but how are we going to recognize Grimlock if he goes in there?"

"Good question. That's why I originally thought of bring-ing Schmitt with us, but that didn't seem likely, the way he was acting…Anyway, despite the robe, I got a pretty up-close look at this possible Grimlock. If someone with the right build comes along, I can force myself into a duel challenge to check out his name."

"Whaaat?" Asuna yelped, her eyes wide.

In *SAO*, visually focusing on another player brought up a green or orange "color cursor" with information about them. But the only information it would display for a stranger was an HP bar and a guild tag, but not a name or level.

This was a common-sense measure to minimize criminal activity. If a player's name could be identified at a glance, they could be harassed with malicious instant messages, and if their level were publicized, it would make it easier to pick out a weak target to hunt down or extort in the open when they were vulnerable.

However, not having access to strangers' names also made it rather difficult to search for an individual player, as we were currently doing.

The only surefire method I knew to confirm a player's name was to challenge them to a one-on-one duel. By hitting the duel button in the menu and pointing out the target's cursor, a system message would appear, notifying me that I'd just challenged so-and-so to a duel. This method would show me the official player name as recognized by the system, spelled in the Western alphabet.

However, the same message would also appear with my name in front of the target. So it was impossible to use such a method while also staying secretive about it, and naturally, it was extremely rude behavior. On top of that, there was no stopping the other player from accepting and drawing his weapon.

Asuna opened her mouth, about to say something about my idea—probably that it was dangerous. But she closed it just as quickly and nodded, looking stern. She understood that it was the only way, but she advised, "If you do talk with Grimlock, I'm going to be there, too."

When she put it that flatly, there was no way I could force her to stay here in the room. Now it was my turn to reluctantly accept the plan. I checked the time: 6:40 PM, just around the time that adventurers would be returning from their travels to eat at their favorite restaurants. For having such an unassuming appearance, the little pub's swinging door was in a state of nonstop flux. Yet so far, I hadn't seen a single player who matched the height and build of that robed figure.

We had no clue to rely upon other than this restaurant, but in fact, there was one other worrisome element on my mind. In that inn on the fifty-seventh floor, Schmitt had moaned that the robed figure on the roof wasn't Grimlock, that "Grim was taller than that." It seemed unlikely that the rattled Schmitt would be calm enough to make that snap judgment, but if it were true, this whole stakeout was a waste of time that would get us nowhere. We would be staring at the door of a hidden legend of a restaurant, never to sample its wares…

Suddenly, I clutched my stomach, overtaken by a wave of hunger.

At that moment, something passed in front of my eyes. It was wrapped in white paper and smelled very good. I stared closely at the object Asuna was holding in front of me, keeping her eyes on the pub door. She said, "Here." I had to be sure.

"Y-you're…giving it to me?"

"What else would I be doing? Waving it under your nose to make you jealous?"

"A-ah. Of course not. Sorry—and thank you."

I took the wrapper, ducking my head in apology. Asuna was deftly producing another object of the same likeness, never taking her eyes off of the door.

I quickly unwrapped the package to see a large baguette sandwich. Between the crispy toasted bread was a pile of vegetables and roasted meat. I gazed at it in amazement, only for Asuna to coldly note, "It's going to run out of durability and vanish if you don't hurry up and eat it."

"Oh! Er…right! Here goes!"

There was no time to stare. The durability of food items was, with the exception of certain special ingredients, generally quite low. On a number of occasions, I'd had a packed lunch disappear in my hands as I was about to eat. There was a special item that could be crafted only by master crafters, a little box called a "Permanent Storage Trinket" that could keep food ingredients fresh permanently, even if left out in the open field. Sadly, the box was so small that you couldn't fit anything larger than two peanuts in it.

So I took big, quick bites, savoring the volume of the sandwich as best I could. The flavoring was simple but tastefully vivid, encouraging more bites. Durability of food had no effect on its flavor, so as long as it existed, it tasted freshly made.

I chowed down on the large baguette, keeping my eyes on the pub at all times, and heaved a sigh of satisfaction when I was done. Next to me, Asuna was still chewing politely.

"Thanks for the food. Anyway, when did you have time to arrange a meal? They don't sell proper food like this at the street carts, do they?"

"I told you, it was about to run out of durability. I had a feeling it might come to this, so I put them together this morning."

"Ohh…No wonder you're the manager in charge of the KoB's daily activities. I never even thought about our meal plan. By the way, where's it from?"

The taste of the baguette, with its crispy bread, veggies, and roast meat, was good enough to rank highly on my personal list of best restaurants, so I was eager to insert it into my regular rotation. But Asuna's shrugged response was not what I expected.

"You can't buy it."

"Huh?"

"It's not from a store."

She clammed up and didn't seem likely to share any further detail. It took me a while to figure out what she meant: If it wasn't sold at an NPC shop, it must therefore be player-made.

I sat in dumbfounded silence for a good ten seconds, then panicked and realized I needed to say something, anything. I couldn't afford a repeat of my abysmal mistake in ignoring Asuna's fashion statement from the morning.

"Uh…well, gosh, how should I say this…I w-wish I hadn't just gobbled it down like that. I mean, I could have sold it at auction in Algade and made a killing, ha-ha-ha."

Wham! Asuna kicked the leg of my chair with a white boot, and I sat up straight, trembling.

After several extremely tense minutes, in which Asuna quietly finished her meal, she muttered, "…He's not coming."

"Er, y-yeah. Well, Schmitt made it sound like he doesn't visit every day. Plus, I kind of doubt that Grimlock's going to show up in his black robe to chow on some grub, right after committing a PK…We might need to stake out this place for two or three days," I said quickly, checking the time. It had only been thirty minutes since we started. I was ready to wait until I saw Grimlock, no matter how many hours or days it took, but Her Excellency the Vice Commander might have different plans.

I glanced over at her again, but Asuna was sunk deep into her chair, and not about to get up anytime soon.

Belatedly, I realized that my statement could be interpreted as "two or three nights staying here," and my palms flooded with sweat. But then, Asuna broke the silence.

"Hey, Kirito."

"Y-yes?!"

What she said was fortunately—or unfortunately—totally unrelated to my statement.

"What would you have done? If you were in Golden Apple and they got a super-rare item like that, what would you have said?"

"…"

After several seconds of shocked silence, then several seconds of hard thought, I said, "Good question…But trouble like that is why I fly solo in the first place…In the games I played before *SAO*, a number of guilds I was in fell apart due to members pilfering the best items and selling them for profit…"

It was an unavoidable fact that one of the big motivating factors for a majority of MMO gamers was the feeling of superiority over the rest of the populace. And the easiest measurement of superiority was strength—defeating powerful monsters or other players with upgraded stats and powerful gear. That pleasure could not be found anywhere outside of online games. The reason that I was spending countless hours grinding for levels was none other than to enjoy the feeling of superiority inherent in being a front-line player.

If I was in a guild now, and a phenomenal piece of gear dropped for the party, and it was perfectly suited for another member of the guild—would I be able to say, "You ought to use this"?

"...No, I couldn't," I muttered, shaking my head. "I might not be able to say that I wanted to use it, but I'm not enough of a saint to happily hand it over to someone else. If I were a member of Golden Apple, I would have joined the pro-selling side. What about you?"

Her answer was instantaneous: "It belongs to the person who got the drop."

"Eh?"

"That's the rule in our guild. Any random drop when in a party is the property of whomever got it. And there's no combat log in *SAO*, so there's no public record of who got what. It'd have to be announced on the honor system. So the only way to avoid people keeping secrets and causing trouble is to make it policy. Plus..."

She paused, her gaze on the pub door softening somewhat.

"That system actually makes the concept of marriage here more meaningful. You know that people who get married share a common inventory, right? The moment you get married, you can't hide things from your spouse. It also means that any player who tries to steal items from the guild can never get married to a fellow member. A shared inventory is a very pragmatic system, but I also find it quite romantic."

I blinked in surprise at the note of longing I detected in her voice. A tension that made no sense rose within me, and I thoughtlessly stammered, "Y-yeah, that's a good point. W-well, if I'm ever in a party with you, I'll be sure not to hog all the drops."

Asuna's chair slammed backward. Without the lights on, I couldn't make out her face very well, but in the pale moonlight, I saw the Flash go through a rotation of varying expressions. She raised her right hand as if to strike and shouted, "A-are you nuts?! You can wait decades, and that day will never come! Ah, w-well, that's in regards to being in a party with you, of course. I mean, look…Just keep watching the pub! What'll we do if you miss him?!"

Once she had the bellowing out of her system, Asuna turned away in a huff. As I was making sure not to take my eyes off the door for more than a second while we talked, her accusation stung. I mumbled a pathetic rebuttal that I *was* watching, and stopped to think.

When the ring that caused the downfall of Golden Apple dropped, who was it who scored the item?

Perhaps it was a pointless question now. But if it was desirable enough to kill their leader over it, surely just concealing it from the start would've been easier. That would mean whoever announced they had won the drop couldn't be the killer.

I grimaced, thinking I should have asked Schmitt when I had the chance. Neither Asuna nor I were registered friends of his, so we couldn't send him a message to check. There were instant messages that could be sent to any player whose name you knew, but it required being on the same floor, and had a very short cap on length.

It could easily happen the next time I saw Schmitt. We weren't chasing the culprit of the ring killing of half a year ago, but the one responsible for the ongoing safe-haven murders. Still, I couldn't get over it. I took out the list Schmitt had made for me.

Asuna was still looking away with a weird expression on her face, so I asked her not to take her eyes off the pub, and I examined the list of Golden Apple members handwritten on the parchment.

Griselda. Grimlock. Schmitt, Yolko, Kains…The scrawled list of names was eight long. And at least three of them were no longer present in the floating castle.

We couldn't allow for any more victims. We had to stop Grimlock's revenge and find the logic behind the safe-haven murders.

I was about to put the memo back into my item storage, but right at the moment the small sheaf of parchment was about to be converted back into a digital storage, one particular point drew my notice.

"…Huh…?"

I took a closer look. The detail-focusing system kicked in, refining the texture of the letters on the parchment to bring them into sharper detail.

"Um…what does this mean…?" I mumbled.

Without taking her eyes off the pub door, Asuna asked, "What is it?"

But I didn't have the presence of mind to answer. My brain was working feverishly, trying to decipher the meaning, the reason, the intention of what I was seeing.

Several seconds later, I shouted, "Aaa…aaaah!!" and leaped up from my chair. The sheet of parchment trembled, reflecting the weight of the shock that overwhelmed me.

"I see…So that's what it means!!" I moaned.

In a voice made of equal parts hesitation and frustration, Asuna hissed, "What? What did you figure out?!"

"I've been…We've been…"

I struggled to squeeze the words out of my dry throat; I clenched my eyes.

"We've been missing the entire picture all along. We thought we understood, but we were looking at the wrong thing. There's no weapon, skill, or loophole behind this whole safe-haven-PK thing…There was never any way to begin with!!"

9

Later, I got this background to the story.

Schmitt, defensive team leader for the Divine Dragon Alliance and notable front-line figure, didn't go to bed after returning to his chambers in the safety of the guild headquarters. He didn't even remove his armor.

His room was deep within the stone castle—fortress, really—and without a window. Not only that, the building was impossible to enter for nonmembers, so he was perfectly safe as long as he was in his room. But no matter how much he told himself that, he couldn't help but stare at the doorknob.

The moment he took his eyes off it, would it turn without a sound? Would the silent, shadowy, hooded figure of the grim reaper sneak in and stand behind him without him realizing it?

Others thought of him as a stalwart, fearless tank, but as a matter of fact, the motivation that kept him among the ranks of the top players of the game was none other than the fear of death itself.

On the day we were all trapped in this game, a year and a half ago, he stayed in the center square of the Town of Beginnings and thought. No, agonized. What could he do to avoid dying? The most surefire means was not to take a step out of the city. There was absolute protection within the purview of the Anti-Criminal Code, so there was no fear of losing a single pixel of his HP—the numerical representation of his life.

But as an athlete in real life, Schmitt understood that the rules could change at any time. Who could state for a certainty that *SAO*'s rule about the towns being absolutely safe would remain constant, to the very moment the game was beaten? What if one day, the code simply stopped working, and all manner of monsters poured into town? Those players who never stepped out of the Town of Beginnings and never earned a single experience point would be completely helpless.

If he were going to survive, he needed to be stronger. And in a safe way, without any risk. After a full day of pondering his position, Schmitt chose to be "tough."

First, he went to an armory and bought the toughest-looking armor and shield that his purse would allow, then used the remainder to purchase a long polearm. Out of the many impromptu parties soliciting members at the north gate, he applied to join the one that promised the safest activity. Their first hunt involved ten people surrounding and killing the weakest monsters in *SAO*: small boars.

Since then, Schmitt chose to make up for the low pay of such activity with sheer time. His leveling pace couldn't match the beaters, who played in small parties or solo, risking powerful foes for great reward, but his never-ending fixation on "toughness" eventually took him to the rank of team leader in the prestigious DDA guild.

His hard work was worth it: Schmitt's maximum HP, armor strength, and various defensive skills were almost certainly the greatest to be found in all of Aincrad.

With his massive guard lance in one hand and a tower shield in the other, he knew he could handle front-facing attacks from three or four mobs of his level for a good thirty minutes. To Schmitt, those who wore paper-thin leather armor or focused on damage-dealing with non-defensive weapons—even certain solo players dressed all in black, whom he'd met just minutes before—might as well have been insane. In truth, the build with the lowest possibility of death was a tank covered in thick armor. And because they sacrificed power to do that, it was vital that they join a large party to make use of their talents.

In any case, Schmitt had finally achieved the ultimate toughness, the only thing that could nullify his fear of death. Or so he had thought.

But vast sums of HP, high-level armor, defensive skills, and all other manner of systematic defenses meant nothing to a killer who could bypass them. And after all this time and effort, such a person was coming after *him*.

He didn't really believe it was a ghost. But even that wasn't a certainty anymore. The grim reaper had slipped through the absolute rule of the Anti-Criminal Code like black mist and callously, easily taken two lives with wimpy little spears and daggers. Was that not the work of a digital ghost, the aftermath of all of her rage and resentment, imprinted into the NerveGear?

In that case, solid fortress walls, that heavy lock on the door, and the protection of the guild building meant nothing.

She was coming. She would come for him tonight, after he had fallen asleep. And with a third barbed weapon, she would stab him and steal his life.

Schmitt sat on his bed, head held in his silver gauntlets, and thought desperately.

There was only one way to escape her revenge. He would beg forgiveness—get on his knees, press his forehead to the ground, groveling and apologizing, until her anger abated. He would admit to his one crime—a means to find greater strength and toughness, and use it as a launching pad to a better guild—and repent with all of his heart. If he did this, even a real ghost would surely forgive him. He had been manipulated. He had been taken for a ride, tempted into a tiny little crime—in fact, it wasn't even a crime, just a bit of poor manners. He couldn't have realized what a tragedy it would lead to.

Schmitt unsteadily got to his feet, opened his inventory, and materialized one of the tons of teleport crystals he kept for emergencies. He clutched it with weak fingers, took a deep breath, and in a hoarse voice, mumbled, "Teleport: Labergh."

His sight filled with blue light. When it subsided, he was standing amid the night.

It was after ten o'clock, and on a floor far removed from most player activity, so the nineteenth-floor teleport square was completely empty. The stores around were all shuttered, and there were no NPCs walking about, so it almost felt like he was out in the open wilderness, despite being in town.

Just half a year ago, Golden Apple had a small guild home on the outskirts of this town. It should have been a familiar sight, but Schmitt felt alienated, like the town was shunning him.

His body trembled in fear underneath his thick armor. He walked on unsteady legs for the edge of town. After twenty minutes out of the town, he came to a small hill. It was in the open, of course, not protected by the Anti-Criminal Code. But Schmitt had a very firm reason for being there. It was his only means to escape the wrath of the robed harbinger of death.

He dragged his resisting legs up to the top of the hill and found what he was looking for beneath a single twisted tree at the top. Schmitt kept his distance, quaking all the while.

It was a weathered, mossy gravestone. The grave of Griselda, lady swordsman and leader of Golden Apple. The pale moonlight, which emanated from nowhere in particular, drew a shadow of the cross on the dry ground. Barren branches overhead creaked in the occasional breeze.

The tree and grave were just environmental details, objects placed by a designer to create an aesthetic effect, and nothing deeper. But on the day Golden Apple disbanded, a few days after Griselda's death, the remaining seven players had decided to make that her grave, and they stuck the longsword that was their memento of her into the earth. Technically, they just laid it at the foot of the grave and allowed the durability to slowly run out until it vanished.

So there was no name on the grave. But there was no other place to go to apologize to Griselda.

Schmitt fell to his knees and crawled miserably over to the grave. He pressed his forehead to the sandy ground, his teeth chattering, as he used all of his willpower to open his mouth, emitting a voice that was quite clear, all things considered.

"I'm sorry...I apologize...Forgive me, Griselda! I...I didn't think that would happen...I never imagined that it would lead to you getting murdered!!"

"Really...?"

It was a voice. A woman's voice, oddly echoing, bouncing off the ground from above.

Trying desperately to retain his quickly vanishing consciousness, Schmitt looked upward.

From the shadows of the gnarled branches came a silent figure dressed in black. Specifically, a hooded black robe. With dangling sleeves. The contents of the hood were invisible in the darkness of night.

But Schmitt felt the cold gaze emanating from that depth. He held his hands over his mouth to trap in a bloodcurdling scream, then repeated, "I-it's true. I didn't hear any details. I just...I just did what I was told...It was just a little...Just a little..."

"What did you do...? What did you do to me, Schmitt...?"

With bulging eyes, Schmitt caught sight of a dark, slender curve, sliding out of the sleeve of the robe.

It was a sword. But an incredibly thin one—an estoc, a one-handed close-range piercing weapon that hardly anyone bothered to use. The conical blade, which looked like a very large, long needle, was growing a spiral of delicate thorns.

It was the third barbed weapon.

A tiny shriek escaped from Schmitt's throat. He slammed his head against the ground, over and over and over.

"I…I just—! On the day…that it was voted we'd sell the ring, a piece of paper and crystal just showed up in my belt pouch…and there were directions on it…"

"From whom, Schmitt?"

This time it was a man's voice.

"Whose orders were they…?"

Schmitt froze in place, his neck suddenly tense. His head felt as heavy as iron, but somehow, he lifted his head for just an instant. A second grim reaper had just appeared from the shadows of the branches. It was wearing an identical black robe. This one was slightly taller than the other.

"…Grimlock…?" Schmitt just barely whispered, his face downward once more. "Did…did you die, too…?"

The new reaper ignored this question and took a silent step forward. From the hood came a voice dripping and twisted.

"Who…? Who was manipulating you…?"

"I…I don't know! I swear!!" Schmitt shrieked. "The…the memo just said…follow the leader. Wh-when she checked in to an inn and left to eat dinner, I'd sneak into her room and save the location with the corridor crystal, th-then place it in the guild's shared storage…Th-that's all I did! I didn't lay a finger on Griselda! I-I never…I never thought she'd be k-k-killed, just lose the ring…I never thought that would happen!"

The two grim reapers did not move a muscle as he pleaded his case. The night breeze stirred the dried branches of the tree as it passed, along with the hems of their robes.

Even in the grips of his terror, Schmitt was reviewing a memory burned into the recesses of his brain.

On that day half a year ago, when he first pulled the parchment out of his pouch, he thought it was ridiculous—but was also surprised at how effective a move it was.

Inn room doors were automatically locked by the system, but by default, they would unlock for friends and guildmates, except when the room guest was asleep. By placing a corridor crystal marker there while she was gone, they could sneak into her room even when she was asleep. After that, it was as simple as making a trade request, moving her arm to press the accept button, then selecting the ring and hitting "trade."

There was the danger of being detected, but Schmitt innately sensed that this was the only way to steal an item within the safe zone. The reward listed at the end of the memo was half of the selling value of the ring. If he succeeded, he would instantly get four times the money, and if he failed and the leader actually woke up in the middle of the trade, she'd only see the person who gave him the memo, the actual thief. He could just ignore any accusations from the thief and pretend he didn't know anything. Sneaking into a bedroom and setting portal coordinates left no traces.

Schmitt wrestled with temptation, but that temptation alone was essentially a betrayal of the guild and their leader. He was doing it to get into a better guild. Schmitt justified it to himself by saying that it would ultimately help the guild leader by making the end of the game come sooner. He followed the memo's instructions.

The next night, Schmitt learned that the leader had been killed. The day after that, he found a leather sack on his bed filled with the gold coins he'd been promised.

"I was…I was scared! I thought that if I told the guild about that note, I'd be targeted next…S-so it's true that I have no idea who wrote it! F-forgive me, Griselda, Grimlock! I r-really had no intention of aiding a murder. You must believe me, please!" he whined, scraping his forehead against the ground repeatedly.

Another dark breeze rustled the branches. When it left, the woman's voice took its place. But her eerie echo was completely gone, as though it had never been there.

"We recorded all of that, Schmitt."

It was a familiar voice—one he'd just heard recently. Schmitt looked up and gaped in total disbelief.

The black hood was pulled back now to reveal the very face of the person this grim reaper had supposedly killed just hours earlier. The wavy, dark blue hair swayed in the breeze.

"…Yolko…?" he whispered.

When the other robed figure did the same, Schmitt sounded as though he was going to faint.

"…Kains."

10

"Th-they're alive…?!" Asuna gasped.

I nodded slowly. "Yes, alive. Both Yolko and Kains."

"B-but…but…" she panted, then clutched her hands atop her lap and rasped, "But…we saw it last night. We saw Kains stuck with a black spear, hanging out of a window…We saw him *die*."

"No," I replied, shaking my head, "what we saw was Kains's avatar spray a bunch of polygons, give off a blue light, then *vanish*."

"B-but isn't that how death happens here?"

"Do you remember how Kains was staring off at a specific point in space when he was hanging out of that church window last night?" I asked, holding an index finger out in front of my face. Asuna nodded.

"He was looking at his HP bar, right? At the effects of the piercing damage as it ticked down bit by bit…"

"That's what I thought, too. But that wasn't it. He wasn't actually looking at his HP bar but the durability level of the plate armor he was wearing."

"D-durability?"

"Yes. Remember how I removed my glove when we did the test with the piercing damage outside of town this morning? Nothing you can do to a player in the safe haven will damage HP. But an object's durability will drop…just like the sandwich earlier.

Of course, armor durability doesn't cause it to just vanish in the middle of town like food does, but that's only if it's not damaged. Remember, there was a spear piercing Kains's armor. What the spear was damaging was not Kains's HP but his armor durability."

At this point, Asuna went from a look of bafflement to sudden surprise.

"Th-then...what we saw disintegrating and flying off wasn't Kains's body..."

"Right. It was just the armor he was wearing. I always thought that was weird; why would you wear a huge set of armor if you're just going out to eat dinner? It must have been to ensure the visual effect of the explosion was as attention grabbing as possible. And so Kains waited for the exact moment the armor would shatter, then..."

"Used a teleport crystal," Asuna muttered, closing her eyes to replay the scene in her mind. "And the result of that was the blue light, a shattering spray of polygons, and the disappearance of the player...Something extremely close to the death effect but totally different."

"Yes. I'm guessing that what Kains actually did was stab himself through the chest with the spear, armor and all, outside of town. Then he used a corridor crystal to teleport to that upstairs room in the church, placed a rope around his neck, then jumped out of the window right before his armor broke. At the exact moment it was about to break, he used a teleport crystal to zip away...Thus completing the effect."

"...I see..."

Asuna nodded, eyes still closed. She let out a long breath. "In that case...Yolko's disappearance tonight must have worked the same way. So...she's still alive..."

I could see her silently mouth the words, *Thank goodness*, then clamp her lips shut. "B-but, while she did seem to be wearing a lot, when did she hit herself with the throwing dagger? The Code would have stopped her. She shouldn't be able to even touch it to her body."

"It was in there from the very start," I said flatly. "Think back. From the moment that you, Schmitt, and I walked into the room, she was very careful not to show us her back. When she got the message that we were on our way, she must have run out of town, stuck in the dagger, put on a cloak or robe, then returned to her room. With how thick her hair is, it would be easy to hide the hilt of that tiny dagger as long as she sat tight to the sofa. She kept us talking while her clothes ran low on durability, then she timed it to walk backward to the window, then kicked the wall behind or something to make the right sound before turning around. To us, it just looked like the dagger hit her through the window at that very moment."

"And then she fell out of the window...to make sure we didn't hear her giving the teleport command. Which means...the person in the black robe you were chasing..."

"I'm almost positive it wasn't Grimlock. It was Kains," I stated.

Asuna looked out into space and sighed. "So he wasn't the culprit but the victim. Oh...but wait." She sat up, looking puzzled. "Remember how we went down to Blackiron Palace last night to check the Monument of Life? Kains's name was crossed out. It was right at the correct time, and even caused by piercing damage."

"Do you remember how the name was spelled?"

"I think it was...K-a-i-n-s."

"That's right. That was what Yolko told us, so we believed it, of course. But look at this."

I showed Asuna the piece of parchment that had started me on the path toward this understanding. It was the list of Golden Apple members that Schmitt had written down for us a few hours earlier.

Asuna reached out and took it, examined the names, then exclaimed in disbelief.

"Caynz?! Is that the real spelling for Kains's name?!"

"One letter off could just be a typo or misremembering, but Schmitt wouldn't get three letters wrong on accident. In other words, Yolko intentionally fed us the wrong spelling of his name. She wanted us to see the K-Kains's death report and believe that it was for the C-Kains."

"Th...then..." Asuna said, lowering her voice and looking tense. "At the very moment when we were witnessing Caynz's faked death at the church, the other Kains was dying of piercing damage somewhere in Aincrad? That can't be...a coincidence, can it? No way..."

"No, no, no." I grinned, waving a hand. "Yolko and her conspirators didn't time it out to kill Kains at the same time. Remember how the death listings on the Monument of Life went? It said '22nd of the Month of Cherry Blossoms, 6:27 PM.' That's April in the Aincrad calendar—and yesterday was the second April 22nd we've had in the game."

"Ah..."

Asuna gasped, paused for a moment, then returned that exhausted, powerless grin.

"...Oh my God. I never even considered that. It was last year. On the same day, at the same time, Kains died in a way that was totally unrelated to any of this..."

"Yes. I think that was the starting point for their entire plan."

I took a deep breath and put all of the pieces together once more in my mind.

"At a very early stage, Yolko and Caynz must have noticed that someone named Kains, pronounced the exact same way as Caynz, had died last April. Maybe it just started off as a note of interest between them. But at some point, one of them came up with the idea to take advantage of that to fake Caynz's death. And not just through normal monster-related death...but with the menace of a faked safe-haven PK."

"...Well, they certainly fooled me and you at first. The death of an unrelated player with the same name, destruction of equipment through piercing damage over time, and a simultaneous teleport crystal...These three elements combined to make what looked to all the world like a PK within the safe haven of town...

And it was meant…" Asuna lowered her voice to a whisper. "To draw out the culprit of the ring incident. Yolko and Caynz used the fact that they would be suspected of the act to their advantage, faking their own murders and creating an illusory killer meting out vengeance. A horrific god of death that could pull off a PK in the safe haven of town, regardless of the Anti-Criminal Code…And the one who gave in to fear and took action was…"

"Schmitt," I said, rubbing my chin with a finger. "He probably must have been the first one they suspected…Schmitt left the, dare I say, mediocre Golden Apple guild and went straight to the Divine Dragon Alliance, the biggest guild on the front line. That's basically unprecedented without some kind of extremely fast-paced leveling or a sudden influx of much better equipment…"

"Yes, the DDA has very strict recruitment requirements. But does that mean he was the one responsible for the incident with the ring? Did he kill Griselda and steal the ring…?"

Asuna had met Schmitt several times, given her role in organizing strategy meetings. She stared at me, her eyes tense.

But with the image of the lancer in the back of my mind, I couldn't exactly give a straight answer.

"…I don't know. There's room to suspect him…but if you asked me whether or not he struck me as red…"

Murderers in *SAO*, otherwise known as "red players," tended to be unhinged in one way or another. That made sense, in a way. Killing other players here solved nothing but making beating the game more difficult. All red players, in some way, were essentially saying they didn't care if they ever got out of *SAO*. Some of them probably wished that the death game would continue forever.

Such dark desires always made their way to action at some point. But I didn't sense that red madness from Schmitt. Not with the way he quaked in fear of the black-robed reaper and even asked us to escort him back to his guild building.

"…I can't be sure, but I'm fairly certain that we can say he had something to do with it," I muttered. Asuna nodded in agreement.

She leaned back against the chair pointed toward the window, all thought of watching the pub gone. Her gaze traveled over the town to the sky.

"...In either case, Schmitt's at the end of his wits now. He believes there's someone out to get vengeance on him, and he finds no safety in town...even in his own guild room, I suspect. I wonder how he'll react."

"If he had an accomplice, he'll probably be making contact. Yolko and Caynz will be attempting the same thing. But if Schmitt doesn't know where to find his old accomplice, then... Hmm. If it were me..."

What would I do? If I had given in to temporary greed and killed a player, then regretted it later, what could I do?

I hadn't directly taken the life of another player before. But I'd known friends who had died because of me. I still bitterly regretted the loss of my old guildmates, who were all wiped out due to my stupid, ugly desire to stand out. I chose to make a small tree in the backyard of the inn we called our "home" into their grave marker. I went there from time to time to leave drinks and flowers, knowing it was no solace to them. So Schmitt, too, probably...

"...If Griselda has a grave, he'll probably go there to beg forgiveness."

Sensing the change in my tone of voice, Asuna turned to look straight at me and smiled gently. "Yes. That's what I would do, too. At the KoB headquarters, we have a grave for all of those who were lost in boss fights...In fact, I'm certain that both Yolko and Caynz are there, too...At Griselda's grave. Waiting for Schmitt to arrive..."

She fell silent, her expression darkening.

"...What's wrong?"

"Nothing...I just thought of something. What if Griselda's grave is outside of town? If Schmitt goes there to apologize... would Yolko and Caynz just forgive him? I don't want to imagine it, but what if that's where they want to have their revenge...?"

This chilling thought took me by surprise, crawling up my backbone.

I couldn't rule it out. Yolko and Caynz hated whomever orchestrated the ring incident enough to put on this complex, ingenious safe-haven "murder." They had already used two teleport crystals and possibly a corridor crystal. That was a huge expense, given their level. After all the trouble they'd gone to, would they be satisfied with a simple apology...?

"Uh...but...I see..."

But then something occurred to me, and I shook my head from side to side.

"No, they wouldn't. They're not going to kill Schmitt."

"How can you be so sure?"

"You're still registered friends with Yolko, right? And you haven't seen any notice that she's dissolved the friendship?"

"Oh...now that you mention it, that's right. I just assumed that it'd automatically been undone after she died, but if she's alive, we should still be registered."

Asuna waved her left hand to bring up the menu, then hit a few buttons.

"Yes, we're still registered friends. If I'd realized this sooner, we could have gotten to the bottom of the trick sooner...But that makes me wonder, why did Yolko accept a friend request from me in the first place? Didn't she realize it could have ruined her whole plan?"

"I'm guessing..." I started, closing my eyes and imagining the woman with the dark blue hair, "it was a gesture of apology for lying to us, and also because she trusted us. She trusted that if we noticed the friend registration was still active, we might figure out their true plan, and wouldn't get in their way with Schmitt. Try to check on her location right now, Asuna," I said, opening my eyes.

Asuna nodded and hit a few more buttons. "She's out in the field on the nineteenth floor right now. On a small hill near the main town. So this must be..."

"The grave of Griselda, leader of Golden Apple. And Schmitt and Caynz must be there, too. If Schmitt dies there, then we'll know that they killed him. So I doubt they'd do that."

"So…what about the reverse? What if Schmitt decides to kill them, to prevent them from telling anyone they know he was involved with the ring incident? Can we be sure that won't happen?"

I gave Asuna's troubled questions some thought, then shook my head again. "No. We'd find out about that, and he wouldn't be able to stand losing face among the front-liners for being an orange or red player. So I don't think there's any concern about either one killing the other. Let's just let them handle it. Our role in this case is over now. Sure, we played the patsy for Yolko and Caynz, just as they hoped…but it doesn't really bother me."

Asuna considered this for a moment, then smiled.

But at the time, neither of us was seeing even half of the truth of the matter.

The case was still ongoing.

11

Again, a story I heard afterward.

Schmitt stared back and forth at the faces of the two players who emerged from the black robes, forgetting to breathe in his shock.

The reapers he'd assumed were Griselda and Grimlock turned out to be Yolko and Caynz. But that didn't change the fact that his two assailants were dead. He had only heard the story of Caynz's death, but he'd just seen Yolko perish before his eyes only hours earlier. She was pierced by a black dagger flying through the window, then fell down into the street and burst into pieces.

For an instant, he was about to faint in the presence of a ghost, but it was what she had said before revealing herself that saved Schmitt's consciousness from fleeing him altogether.

"R…recor…ded…?" he rasped from a dry throat. Yolko pulled her hands out of the robe and showed them to him. She was holding an octagonal crystal, glowing light green—a sound-recording crystal.

A ghost would not use an item to record a conversation.

Meaning that Caynz's and Yolko's deaths were faked. He couldn't begin to guess how, but they had produced their own deaths in order to create a fictional agent of vengeance to terrify a third party who was deserving of that vengeance. Now they had a recording of that third man, admitting his crime and begging for mercy. All in order to reveal the truth of a murder that had taken place in the distant past.

"...Oh...I see..." Schmitt muttered in a voiceless sigh, finally understanding the truth. He flopped forward helplessly. He'd been totally fooled, and there was even proof of that, but he was not angry. He was simply numb at Yolko's and Caynz's tenacity—and their reverence for Griselda.

"You...you did all of this...for the leader...?" he mumbled.

Caynz quietly nodded. "Didn't you, too?"

"Huh...?"

"You didn't do it because you hated her, did you? You were fixated on the ring, but you never bore her any ill will. Isn't that true?"

"Of...of course. It's true, please believe me," Schmitt said, bowing his head repeatedly, face twisted with desperation.

He was probably stronger than the two of them combined. But the thought of drawing his weapon and using it to silence them forever never even occurred to him. As a red player, he couldn't remain in the guild or the front-line group as a whole, but even more importantly, if he killed Yolko and Caynz, he knew he would never regain his sanity.

So even knowing that the recording crystal was still active, Schmitt repented for his past crime.

"All I did...was sneak into the leader's inn room and save a portal exit there. Of course...the money I got from doing that helped me get the gear to pass the DDA's entrance standards..."

"Is it true that you don't know who gave you the note?" Yolko demanded. He nodded vigorously.

"I-I still don't know. Out of the eight members of the guild, it's probably one of the three left over after me, you two, the leader, and Grimlock...But I haven't contacted anyone since then. Have you got any ideas?" Schmitt asked. Yolko shook her head.

"All three of them joined other mid-level guilds like Golden

Apple afterward, and they have normal lives now. No one's bought fancy gear or a player home. You're the only one who leaped up in a big way, Schmitt."

"...I see..." he mumbled, looking down.

After Griselda's death, the sack of col delivered to his room was a fortune beyond anything he could imagine at the time. It was enough that he could go to the auction house and buy up all of the ultrapowerful gear at the top of the list at once, where he could only dream of owning such things before.

It would take steely self-control to toss that money into storage without using it. But more importantly...

Schmitt looked up, forgetting his plight momentarily, and asked something that popped into his head.

"B-but it doesn't make sense...If they weren't going to use it, why would they go to the trouble of killing the leader to steal the ring...?"

Yolko and Caynz pulled back a bit, stunned. There was virtually no benefit to leaving money stored up in one's inventory. The value of a col was maintained at all times by the Cardinal System's drop rate fine-tuning, so there was no inflation or deflation in the currency. An expensive sword or set of armor, if treated properly, could one day be sold for essentially the same price. There was no value to col that wasn't spent. Which meant...

"The person...who sent the note..." Schmitt started, his mind working feverishly.

But because he was concentrating so hard, he failed to notice what was happening.

"Sch...!"

By the time he heard Yolko's hoarse rasp, the little knife had stretched around toward his neck from behind and stuck into the spot between his breastplate and gorget. It was a sneak attack making use of the small-piercing-weapon skill, Armor Pierce, and the nonmetal armor skill, Sneaking.

After a moment of shock, the reflexes honed by life on the front line kicked in, and Schmitt tried to leap backward. Even being slashed across the throat was not instant death here. The damage would be significant, given that it was a critical area, but even that was miniscule in comparison to Schmitt's considerable HP total.

However.

Before he could spin around, his legs lost feeling, and Schmitt rolled helplessly to the ground. There was a blinking green border around his HP bar—the paralysis effect. As a tank, he naturally had a high anti-poison skill, but this poison was so high level it was not affected by it. Whose could it be?

"One down," said a childishly excited voice. Schmitt craned his neck, trying to look upward.

The first thing he saw was a pair of black leather boots with sharp studs on them. Then a thin black pair of pants. Tight-fitting leather armor, also black. In the right hand, a narrow knife gleaming green, and the left hand stuck inside a pocket.

A black mask that looked like a sack covered the player's head. Round eyeholes were cut out to see through, and just as he noticed the nasty gaze of the player, a player cursor appeared in Schmitt's view. It was not the usual green but a brilliant shade of orange.

"Ah...!"

He heard a gasp from behind him, and Schmitt glanced the other way to see that Yolko and Caynz were being threatened together by another player. This smaller one was dressed in black as well, but rather than leather, it was a cloth-scrap-like material that hung from all over. There was a skull-shaped mask on the figure's face, with small red eyes that gleamed in its dark depths. In his right hand was another estoc like the barbed one Yolko had, but the way the metal gleamed bright red spoke to the overwhelming power of its stats. This player's cursor was also orange.

The man in the skull mask reached out with his left hand and crudely yanked Yolko's estoc away. He glanced over the weapon, then spoke in a voice like scraping friction.

"The design's, not bad. I'll add it, to my, collection."

Schmitt knew these two. But he'd never seen them in person. He recognized them from the sketches of dangerous players displayed on the guild's bulletin board.

They were red players, the front line's most dire foes—even more than bosses. And these men were senior officers of the worst and deadliest guild of them all. The one with the poisoned dagger that had paralyzed Schmitt was Johnny Black, while the man with the estoc threatening Yolko and Caynz was Red-Eyed Xaxa.

Did that mean…*he* was here?

It couldn't be. Please no. It had to be a joke.

But Schmitt's silent pleas fell on deaf ears as he heard the approach of new, scraping shoes. He turned in terror to catch sight of the very image of the greatest danger in Aincrad.

A black matte poncho that hung to just above his knees. A deep, concealing hood. In his dangling right hand, a large, thick dagger as rectangular as a cleaver and as red as blood.

"…PoH…"

Schmitt's lips trembled with fear and despair.

It was Laughing Coffin, the murderer's guild.

The guild had formed a year after the start of *SAO*. Until then, the orange players had stuck to ganging up on solos or small teams and stealing their col and items. But then a number of them grew more extreme and idealized in their actions.

Their philosophy: It's a game of death, so killing is allowed and expected.

There was no method of legal murder in modern Japan, but it was possible in Aincrad. All the players' bodies were in a full dive in the real world—simply comatose, unable to move a finger on command. Under the purview of Japanese law, any player who was "killed" by losing all HP was the victim of Akihiko Kayaba, the creator of the NerveGear, and not the player who eliminated the HP.

So let's kill people. Let's enjoy the game. This is an equal right of every player.

And the one responsible for the poisonous agitation that seduced some of the many orange players, brainwashing them and driving them to fanatical PK activity, was the man with the black poncho and the cleaver, PoH.

In contrast to his humorous name, the tall man exuded an icy cruelty as he strode purposefully toward Schmitt.

"Flip him over," he ordered.

Johnny Black wedged his boot tip under Schmitt's downcast stomach. Once Schmitt was rolled over to face upward, the man in the poncho stared down at him from above.

"Wow...this *is* a big haul. A leader of the DDA, in the flesh."

His strong, silky voice was beautiful, but something alien lurked in the intonation of the words. His face was hidden within the hood of the poncho, but there was a lock of rich, wavy black hair hanging in sight, swaying in the breeze.

Despite knowing that he was trapped in a very deadly situation, half of Schmitt's mind was occupied with questions: why, what, how?

Why would they show up here and now? The top three members of Laughing Coffin were both the symbol of fear in the game and its most wanted criminals. They would not be hanging around in the overworld map of a lower floor like this without good reason.

That would mean they knew they'd find Schmitt here, and attacked.

But that didn't add up. He didn't tell anyone at the DDA where he was going, and Yolko and Caynz wouldn't have let that intel slip, either. Besides, both of them were pale with fear at the threat of Red-Eyed Xaxa's estoc. Even if they'd been hanging out by coincidence and saw Schmitt walk through the town alone, it was all too sudden for them to have informed PoH.

Was it simply some act of massive misfortune that all three of these players had happened across them on this random floor for a totally different reason? Was this sheer coincidence the vengeance of the late Griselda...?

PoH looked down indecisively at the prone, loglike Schmitt, who was trapped in a tangle of his own confused thoughts.

"Well...Normally this is the time for my 'It's Showtime' slogan...but first, how to play with them?"

"Let's do that one thing, Boss," came Johnny Black's cheery, high-pitched voice. "The game where they kill one another, so only the winner gets to survive. Of course, with these three, we'll need to set a handicap."

"Yeah, but remember how last time, we killed the winner after all?"

"Oh, c'mon! You're gonna ruin the game if you tell them that before it starts, Boss!"

Xaxa hissed with laughter at the lazy and horrifying chat, still holding up his estoc.

At this point, the honest danger and despair of the situation settled in, crawling up Schmitt's back. He instinctually shut his eyes. Without the ability to move, the heavy metal armor that covered him was nothing but a weight holding him down. Very soon, they would finish their pre-meal appetizer and bare their bloody, greedy fangs. PoH's large dagger, Mate-Chopper, was a rare monster drop that had greater stats than the highest quality items a player-blacksmith could create at present. It was an evil thing that would easily pierce through his full plate armor.

Griselda, Grimlock. If this is your vengeance, then I suppose I deserve to die here. But why would you involve Yolko and Caynz? They put all of this tremendous effort into revealing the true culprit of your murder. Why would you do this?

As Schmitt's despairing thoughts popped from his mind like short-lived bubbles, he sensed faint vibrations through the ground pressing against his back.

The rhythmic beat approached, *da-da-dum, da-da-dum*, growing louder and more insistent. Eventually, the dry, deep sounds hit his ears as well.

PoH sucked in a sharp breath and warned his two followers. Johnny jumped back, holding up his poisoned dagger, while

Xaxa jabbed his estoc even closer toward Yolko's and Caynz's throats.

Schmitt made use of what little neck mobility he had to catch sight of a white light approaching from the direction of the town.

The light bobbed up and down and, several seconds later, was revealed to be cold flame licking at the hooves of a black horse so dark, it melted into the night. On the steed's back was a rider, also in black. This person, who appeared like some undead knight from Hell, was bearing down on them and blazing a trail of white flame behind him. The sound of the hooves turned into a rumbling roar, soon joined by the whinnying of the horse.

The steed reached the foot of a little hill and bounded to the top in a few leaps, then reared up on its hind legs, spraying a white cloud of steam from its nostrils. Johnny took a few nervous steps back, and the rider pulled back hard on the reins—and promptly toppled backward off the horse.

The figure fell onto its butt and hissed a sharp "Ouch!" in a voice that Schmitt recognized. The man got up, rubbing his backside, and, still holding the reins to the massive black steed, turned to look at Schmitt, Yolko, and Caynz. In an easy, carefree tone, he said, "Looks like I made it just in time. You'll have the DDA expense the taxi fare, I hope."

There were no itemized mounts in Aincrad. But certain towns and villages had NPC-run stables where players could rent riding horses or cattle for transporting massive belongings that didn't fit into an inventory. But because they required considerable technique to master and cost an arm and a leg to rent, very few players bothered with them. There were only so many people in this deadly game with the time and wherewithal to bother practicing horseback riding.

Schmitt let out the breath he'd been holding in and looked up at the new arrival: Kirito the Black Swordsman, solo player.

Kirito tugged on the reins to turn the horse around and patted its rump. The rental service was disengaged, and the black beast began to run off, accompanied by Kirito's relaxed voice.

"Hey, PoH. Been a while. Still sticking with that ugly fashion sense, huh?"

"…Bold words, coming from you," went PoH's reply, his voice sharp with unmistakable lethality.

On its heels, Johnny Black darted forward a step and shrieked hysterically, "You freak! Quit actin' like you got this under control! You know what's happening here?!"

PoH silenced his follower's poison knife with a gesture, then tapped his shoulder with the butt of his own cleaver.

"He's got a point, Kirito. Flashy entrances are all well and good, but surely you don't think that even *you* can handle three of us at once."

Schmitt clenched his left hand, the only part of him that was capable of moving. PoH was right: Even Kirito, with his attack power near the top of the front-line gang, couldn't possibly defeat three officers of Laughing Coffin at once. Why hadn't he at least brought the Flash along?

"Yeah, I guess not," Kirito said calmly, his left hand on his waist. "But I've taken a poison-resistance potion, I've got a bundle of healing crystals, and I can hold out for a good ten minutes. That's enough time for the cavalry to arrive. Surely you don't think that even *you three* can handle thirty front-line vets," he teased, throwing PoH's challenge right back into his face.

The leader clicked his tongue in irritation, while Johnny and Xaxa looked around at the darkness nervously.

"…Shit," PoH swore, and drew back his right foot. He snapped his fingers, and his followers retreated several yards backward. Freed from the red estoc, Yolko and Caynz both fell unsteadily to their knees.

PoH held up his cleaver, pointed it straight at Kirito, and growled, "Black Swordsman. I swear that I will make you taste dirt. One day you will roll in an ocean of your precious friends' blood, and then you will regret this."

And with that, he spun the heavy cleaver nimbly in his fingertips and returned it to the holster at his side. The black leather poncho whirled around and he descended the hill, his two lack-eys scrambling after him.

Johnny Black was especially quick in his pursuit, worried about the imminent approach of the front-line guilds, but Red-Eyed Xaxa, he of the ragged attire and estoc, turned back after a few steps, his skull mask's eyes gleaming at Kirito.

"You think, you're so cool. Next time, it'll be me, chasing you, on a horse."

"...You'd better practice, then. It's not as easy as it looks," Kirito replied.

Xaxa let out a hiss of breath, then vanished in pursuit of his companions.

12

Even after the three shadows descended the hill and melted into the darkness, their orange cursors remained, thanks to the Search skill.

I'd encountered and exchanged words with PoH, leader of Laughing Coffin, on a previous occasion, but his two confidants were new to me: the poison knife–wielder with the childish attitude and appearance and the eerie estoc fencer with the ragged clothes. Naturally, their names hadn't appeared on their cursors, so I considered checking with Schmitt about them, then decided against it. The next time I faced them, it would turn into a fight for real. And I didn't want to know the names of the people I'd cross blades with in a battle to the death.

Instead, I just watched the cursors as they began to blink at the limit of my Search range. As a flat rule, criminal players were not allowed to enter towns and settlements protected by the Anti-Criminal Code, the "safe havens" of Aincrad. The instant they did, powerful NPC guardians would appear and attack en masse. And the teleport gates were all located in the Code's zones, so for the trio to move to other floors, they'd either have to designate tiny villages outside of the Code with their teleport crystals, use expensive corridor crystals, or climb and descend the labyrinth towers that had already been cleaned out—the long way.

It was probably the first of the three, but using six crystals for the round trip had to be a ridiculous expense for them. Despite my cocky parting statements, I couldn't help but breathe a sigh of relief when the three cursors were gone from sight. It was a much more dangerous group than I had been expecting. Somehow, the trio had known that Schmitt—front team leader for the Divine Dragon Alliance and the man with the highest defense and HP of any front-line player—would be at these coordinates.

The source of that info would be clear very soon.

I tore my gaze away from the dark landscape to look at my window and type up a quick message to Klein, who was approaching with his dozen-or-so friends, that "Laughing Coffin ran off, so wait in town."

Next, I took an antidote potion from my waist pouch and put it in Schmitt's left hand, watched to make sure the large man awkwardly drank it down, then looked at the other two people present.

When I spoke out to the would-be grim reapers in their black robes, I couldn't keep the note of irony out of my voice.

"It's nice to see you again, Yolko. And I guess…this is a 'nice to meet you,' Caynz."

The woman who had vanished before my eyes into a cloud of polygons a few hours earlier looked up at me and put on a tiny smile.

"I was planning to give you a proper apology when all was said and done…but I don't suppose you'd believe me now."

"Whether I believe you or not depends on how good the meal you buy me tastes. And no fishy-looking ramen or unidentified fried food will do."

Next to the stunned Yolko, the simpleminded-looking Caynz, original "victim" of the safe-haven murders, pulled off his robe and bowed his head.

"It's actually not our first meeting, Kirito. Our eyes met for just an instant, if you recall," he said in a deep, relaxed voice. Then it hit me.

"You know, that's right. It was right as you died—er, as you teleported and your armor broke, wasn't it?"

"Yes. When I saw you, I had a momentary feeling that you might see through our faked-death trick."

"You thought too much of me. I was completely fooled."

It was my turn to frown. With the atmosphere a bit looser now, Schmitt sat up, his armor clanking loudly. He turned on me, his voice still tense.

"Kirito…I must thank you for saving me…but how did you know that those men would attack us here?"

I looked back into his desperate, searching eyes and chose my words carefully.

"It wasn't that I *knew*. I just thought it might be possible. If I'd known it was PoH from the start, I might have freaked out and run for safety."

There was a reason I was playing this a bit aloof. What I was about to say was bound to deliver a huge shock to these three—particularly Yolko and Caynz. They had written their own scenario, engineered and starred in it to seeming perfection—but they didn't realize that there was a hidden producer lurking in the shadows of the entire incident. I took a deep breath and tried to speak as quietly and calmly as I could.

"…I only noticed that something was wrong about thirty minutes ago…"

The incident was over. The rest was up to Yolko, Caynz, and Schmitt now—or so I told Asuna, leaning back in my chair on the second floor of the inn overlooking the little pub on the twentieth floor.

They wouldn't kill one another. Let the players of the ring incident that had started this all take care of the business themselves, I said. Asuna nodded and agreed.

But in the silence that followed, I couldn't help but feel a tiny little thorn in my chest that would not come out cleanly.

There was something I needed to consider. I knew it was there, but I didn't know what it was or how to remember it.

The root of this sensation lay in something that Asuna said

while we were in this room, staking out the pub. Before I realized it, I was calling out to her.

"...What is it?" the vice commander of the KoB said, looking at me. About 80 percent of my mind was fixated on the sensation of wrongness, so the thoughtlessness of the question that followed could be blamed on that.

"Asuna, have you ever been married?"

Her answer was an icy, murderous glare, a clenched fist, and a preparatory attack stance.

"No, I mean, not that, forget it!!" I cried before she could slug me. I shook my hands and head in defensive panic, quickly adding, "No, what I mean is...you were saying something about marriage before, right?"

"I did. What about it?" she asked, fixing me with a steely gaze.

I trembled even harder, desperately running my mouth. "Um, w-well...gosh, what was it—something about how it was romantic, or plastic, or something-tic..."

"Nobody said anything remotely resembling that!"

She kicked me in the shin just soft enough not to set off the Code, then filled in the blanks for me. "I said it was romantic and *pragmatic*! And in case you've never opened a dictionary, pragmatic means practical and sensible!"

"Practical...? Marriage in *SAO*?"

"Yes. I mean, it doesn't get much more brutally faithful than shared inventory, right?"

"Shared...inventory..."

That was it.

That was the source of the thorn that was still stuck in my chest.

Married players completely shared all of their items. The carrying limit expanded to the total of both players' strength combined, so while it was extremely convenient, it also came with the danger of marriage fraud, where a spouse stole all the best items and disappeared.

What was it about this system that stuck out to me?

Unable to reach the root of this overwhelming frustration,

I asked, "Th-then…what happens to the items when you get divorced?"

"Huh…?"

Asuna looked at me in surprise, her eyes round. She inclined her head in wonderment, bringing her punching fist up to stroke her slender chin.

"Let's see…I believe there are a few options. There's automatic distribution, taking turns choosing an item at a time, and a few other methods that I don't remember…"

"I want to know more. How do we find out? Oh hey, what if we—"

That I didn't finish that question was either a brilliant decision or a stroke of good luck.

The Flash grinned at me, her left hand on the scabbard of her Lambent Light, several times the previous hint of murder in the air.

"What if we *what*?"

"…Wh-what if…weeee…write a question to Heathcliff right now?"

A minute later, he wrote back with a concise and accurate description of what happens to inventory space upon a divorce. The man was a walking game manual.

Asuna had already mentioned the automatic and by-turn methods of dividing items. It was also possible to set up an automated system that worked on designated percentages, rather than down the middle. That meant that alimony payments were essentially possible as well. Yes, very pragmatic.

As Asuna read off the message, my mind worked rapidly. These options had to be decided upon by both parties at the moment of divorce, of course. In other words, you could not legally divorce unless you both agreed to an asset-splitting scheme. But in reality, an amicable agreement couldn't be reached in every case. So what would happen if you wanted to get divorced but couldn't see eye to eye with your partner? There was no domestic affairs court in Aincrad.

The answer to that question was in the very last sentence of Heathcliff's reply to Asuna.

"'...Incidentally, an unconditional divorce is only possible if one sets their own item allotment to zero percent, with the partner receiving one hundred percent of the shared inventory. In that case, any items the partner cannot carry at the point of redistribution will be dropped at his or her feet. If Kirito is afraid of the imminent possibility of divorce, I would recommend staying in a private room at an inn'...he says." Asuna finished reading, closing the window with an unpleasant expression.

As I idly gazed at her face, I repeated one phrase from the message over and over.

Zero for you, hundred for partner. Zero for you...hundred for partner...

"Ah..."

The thorn of suspicion that remained firmly jammed into my chest suddenly twinged sharply. It was a small thing, but it started to grow and grow, from hesitation to doubt, to conviction and then shock, then all the way to fear.

"Ah...aaaah!!"

I stood up with a bolt, my chair rattling, and grabbed Asuna's shoulders. The Flash pulled away in startled disbelief and gaped, "Wha...what are you...You're not really expecting to..."

But I wasn't taking in any information. I husked, *Hundred for you, zero for your partner. There's only one way to ensure that happens.*"

"...Huh...? What are you talking about...?"

I kept a firm grip on her shoulders, drawing her petite face closer to mine, and whispered, "*Death.* The moment your spouse dies, your inventory returns to its original size, and the items you can't hold drop at your feet. Meaning...meaning..."

My throat convulsed and swallowed.

"Meaning...that in the instant of the murder of Griselda, leader of Golden Apple, that ultra-rare and powerful ring, which was kept in her item storage, went not to the killer...but into the inventory of her husband, Grimlock, or materialized and dropped at his feet."

The hazel-brown eyes, just inches away, blinked once, then twice. The disbelief in her eyes suddenly turned into stark horror.

So the ring...wasn't stolen...? she mouthed silently. But I couldn't answer right away. I let go of her shoulders, straightened up, and leaned back heavily against the window frame.

"No...that's not true. It *was* stolen. Grimlock stole a ring that was already in his inventory. He's not the one responsible for this fake safe-haven murder case. He's the mastermind of the ring incident from half a year ago."

The rapier sheath fell out of Asuna's hand and thudded heavily on the floor.

"...I only noticed that something was wrong about thirty minutes ago...Caynz, Yolko, how did you get these two weapons? The barbed short spear and dagger," I asked.

Yolko and her partner shared a glance, then she said, "In order to pull off a fake safe-haven PK, we needed a piercing weapon that would cause damage over time. We looked through all the weapon shops we could find, but there were no specially designed weapons with that feature...And if we had a blacksmith make one for us, his name would stay on the weapon. Then anyone could ask him and he'd reveal that it was paid for by the victims of the case, and the mystery would be over."

"So without a better option, we reached out to contact the leader's husband, Grimlock, for the first time since the guild disbanded. We explained our plan so that he would make us the piercing weapons we needed. We didn't know where to find him, but we were still registered as friends," Caynz continued for Yolko. At the mention of that name, all of my nerves honed in on my ears to listen.

"At first, Grimlock didn't seem very enthusiastic about it. His first response said to just let her memory sleep in peace. But we kept pleading with him, and he finally relented and made us two—no, three weapons. And we got them just three days before the moment of Kains's 'death.'"

This, at least, made it clear that Yolko and Caynz believed that Grimlock was the first and foremost victim in the murder of his wife. I took a deep breath, steeling myself to utter the words that I was certain would bring them much shock and pain.

"...I'm sorry to say that Grimlock wasn't against your plan for Griselda's sake. He was afraid that if you went to the trouble of an eye-catching PK inside the safe haven, someone was going to notice. Notice what happens to the items in a shared inventory when a marriage is dissolved because of death, rather than divorce."

"Huh...?"

Yolko stared at me, totally baffled.

I couldn't blame her. Even very close couples in Aincrad seldom made it to the stage of marriage, but divorces were even more rare, and couples split apart by death even more so. Both Asuna and I had totally believed that when Griselda died, the ring had dropped as loot for the one who killed her.

"Listen...everything in Griselda's possession simultaneously belonged to Grimlock. You couldn't steal that ring even by killing her. It would automatically teleport to Grimlock the instant she died. You got a reward of money for taking part in the scheme, right, Schmitt?" I asked. The big man sitting cross-legged on the ground shook his head in disbelief.

I continued. "It would have taken the sale of the ring to put together a fortune of that size in the first place. Only Grimlock could have done that once he got the ring, and he knew that Schmitt was an accomplice in the plan. Meaning..."

"Grimlock did this...? You're saying he was the one who sent the note...and actually took Griselda out of the town to kill her?" Schmitt mumbled, his voice cracking. I considered this possibility.

"No, he wouldn't have dirtied his hands directly. She might wake from her sleep while being portal-ed out of her bedchamber. If she saw his face, he'd never be able to cover it up. He probably paid some red players to do the dirty work of the killing. That doesn't decrease his crime in the slightest, of course..."

"…"

Schmitt simply gazed into empty space and said no more. Yolko and Caynz also looked as though their souls had temporarily left their bodies. A few seconds later, she shook her head, dark blue hair swaying, the motion growing fiercer over time.

"No…it's not true. It can't be! They were always together… Grimlock was always smiling happily at her side and…Besides! R-right?—If he was the true culprit, then why did he help us in our plan?! We couldn't have done a thing if he hadn't crafted those weapons for us, and the ring incident would never have been dug up again. Isn't that right?"

"You explained the entirety of your idea to him, didn't you?" I asked abruptly. She shut her mouth for a moment, then nodded. "Meaning that he knew what would happen in the end if your plan was successful. Wracked by guilt, Schmitt would visit Griselda's grave, to be accosted by you and Caynz, dressed as the dead. That would make it possible to permanently bury the ring incident forever. He could eliminate his accomplice, Schmitt, and you two searching for resolution, all at once."

"…I see. So…that's why *they* were here…" Schmitt mumbled. I looked in his direction and nodded, feeling gloomy.

"That's right. The top three members of Laughing Coffin showed up here because Grimlock fed them information. That a major officer of the DDA would be here without a security detail…He probably had connections to them ever since he paid them to kill off Griselda…"

"…I can't believe it…"

Caynz had to hold out his hand to keep Yolko from falling straight to the ground. But his face, too, was obviously pale, even in the dim light of the moon.

As she clung to Caynz's shoulder for support, Yolko whispered dully, "Grimlock was…trying to kill us? But…why…? And… why would he kill his own wife just to steal a ring…?"

"I can't possibly conjecture about a motive. But I'm guessing that while he stayed in the guild base the night of the murder for the sake of an alibi, he couldn't have helped coming to keep tabs on this one. Especially knowing that getting rid of you three would make the end of two criminal incidents. So...let's ask him for the real scoop."

At the end of my sentence, two sets of footsteps could be heard climbing the west face of the hill.

The first thing to come into sight was a knight's uniform of brilliant white and red, clearly visible through the night. This was, obviously, Asuna the Flash. In her right hand hung a rapier with a crystal-pure platinum blade. It was the most graceful and beautiful sword that I knew in Aincrad and also one of the fiercest and most efficient at breaking through defenses.

Its fierce point and owner's sharp gaze were keeping a man walking ahead of her. He was very tall, with a long-sleeve and loose-fitting leather jacket and a wide-brim hat. In the shadow beneath it, something occasionally reflected the moonlight—glasses, probably. He looked less like a blacksmith than a hit man from some Hong Kong movie. It was hard for me to avoid that preconception, for understandable reasons.

Both of their cursors were green. Realizing that if he tried to escape, Asuna might temporarily become an orange player in halting him, her green status was a relief to me—though I was prepared to undergo the annoying quests needed to restore one's good alignment alongside her, if necessary. As the man approached, however, I steeled myself properly to face him.

Behind his round, silver-framed glasses was a face that looked gentle and soft, if anything. His face was thin, and his slightly drooping eyes were kindly. But there was something in his small black pupils behind the lenses that set off my sense of caution.

The man stopped about ten feet away and looked first at Schmitt, then Yolko and Caynz, and lastly, at the mossy grave marker.

"Well...hello again, everyone," he said, cool and calm.

Several seconds later, Yolko responded, "Grimlock...Did...did you really..."

Kill Griselda and steal the ring? And try to erase three people here to ensure that the entire matter was covered up permanently?

The words were never spoken aloud, but everyone heard them. Grimlock the blacksmith, former sub-leader of Golden Apple, did not answer at once. When Asuna had returned her rapier to its sheath and moved to stand at my side, he smiled slightly.

"...You have the wrong idea. I was only on the way here under the belief that I had a responsibility to see this series of events to its conclusion. The reason I obeyed that scary woman's commands was because I wanted to clear up the misunderstanding."

He's going to deny it? I thought, closing my eyes. Sure, we had no proof that he'd passed the information to PoH, but when it came to the ring incident, there was no way for him to weasel out of the systematic evidence.

"Liar!" snapped Asuna. "You were hiding in the bushes. If I hadn't been able to reveal you with my Search skill, you'd have stayed put the whole time!"

"That's not my fault. I'm just a blacksmith. As you can see, I am unarmed. Can you blame me for not jumping out into the open with those terrifying orange players out and about?" he replied pleasantly, spreading his gloved hands.

Schmitt, Caynz, and Yolko listened to Grimlock's words in silence. They were still having trouble believing it. Accepting that your former sub-leader had paid bloodthirsty killers to knock you off was a huge leap, and one they didn't consciously want to make.

Asuna started to retort again, but I stilled her with a hand and spoke at last.

"Hello there, Grimlock. My name is Kirito and...well, I'm an outsider in this matter. I'll be honest: I don't have evidence linking your presence here to the attack by Laughing Coffin. They certainly won't be offering testimony to us."

Of course, if we had Grimlock make his menu window visible so we could check his friend list or sent messages, we would certainly find the name of whatever player handled the assassination business for Laughing Coffin. I just didn't know what that name was.

But while the matter of the attempted murders here might not be solvable, I knew that the other matter was undeniable.

"But the ring incident last fall that caused the breakup of Golden Apple...You are absolutely involved with that—you orchestrated it, in fact. Because whoever actually killed Griselda, the ring would have stayed in your possession, thanks to your shared inventory. You hid that fact, secretly liquidated the ring, then gave half of the amount to Schmitt. Only the culprit could have done this. So your only motive for getting involved in this safe-haven incident was to silence the people involved with the past and cover it up. Am I wrong?"

A heavy silence filled the open air on the hill. The pale moonlight falling upon the scene cast Grimlock's face into shadowy contrast. Eventually his mouth twisted in an odd way and he spoke again, slightly cooler this time.

"This is a very fascinating line of logic, Detective...But sadly, you have missed one thing."

"What?" I asked automatically. Grimlock reached up with a black glove and pulled the brim of his wide hat lower.

"It's true that Griselda and I had a shared inventory. So your assertion that when she was killed, all of the items within her storage remained with me is true. However..."

The tall blacksmith's sharp gaze traveled through the moonlight-reflecting glasses to pierce me. In a flat voice, he continued. "What if the ring wasn't being kept in her inventory? What if it was materialized as a physical object, equipped on her finger...?"

"Ah..." Asuna gasped.

I was just as taken aback. I had completely failed to take that possibility into account.

Materialized items always dropped at the spot of a player's death, if killed by a monster or another player. So if Griselda were equipping the ring in question, it would fall into the murderer's hands rather than staying in Grimlock's possession.

Realizing that he now held the advantage, Grimlock's mouth

curled into a grin. But that smile vanished as he put his fingertips to his forehead and shook his head in a display of mourning.

"...Griselda was a speed-type swordsman. Surely it's not that surprising that she'd want to just get a little taste of the massive agility boost from wearing the ring before it got auctioned off, right? Yes, when she was killed, all of the items that were in our shared inventory stayed with me. But the ring was not among them. It's the truth, Detective."

I suddenly realized I was clenching my teeth. I tried searching for some means of tearing apart his argument, but the only person who could testify as to whether she was wearing the ring in question at the moment of her death was the killer—most likely, a member of Laughing Coffin.

As I held my silence, Grimlock lifted up the brim of his hat. He swung a look over the other four and gave a sanctimonious bow.

"And now, I will be on my way. It's a shame that the ringleader in Griselda's murder wasn't caught, but I believe that Schmitt's repentance will surely soothe her soul."

With another tip of his hat, the blacksmith turned around. Amid the silence, Yolko's voice over his shoulder was full of something fiery.

"Please wait...No—*stop*."

He came to an abrupt halt and turned back just a bit. Those kindly looking eyes behind the glasses glimmered with something dangerous.

"Is there more? Please don't bother me with your emotional, unfounded accusations. This is a holy place to me," he said smoothly and haughtily. Yolko took a step farther. For some reason, she raised her hands in front of her and glanced down at them for an instant. When her dark eyes faced forward again, there was a fierce power in them that I hadn't seen in her before.

"Grimlock, you're claiming that the leader was wearing the ring at the time. So the killer stole it without you having it. But... that's impossible."

"...Oh? Based on what evidence?" Grimlock asked, turning smoothly.

Yolko tore into him. "You remember when the guild had that meeting to decide what to do with the ring? Me, Caynz, and Schmitt said that we should use it to strengthen the guild, rather than sell it. Caynz actually wanted to use it himself, but he decided to stick with the leader. He said she was the strongest fighter in Golden Apple, so she ought to equip it."

Next to Yolko, Caynz looked somewhat guilty. But she merely gestured and continued. "I still remember every last word of her response. She smiled and said, 'You can only wear one ring on each hand in *SAO*. On my right hand is the guild leader's sigil... and on the left is my wedding ring. So I can't use this.' Understand? There's no way she would secretly take off either of those rings to try out that new one's bonus!"

When her harsh shriek died out, everyone present held their breath.

It was true that there was only one ring slot for each hand on the equipment mannequin in the menu. If both were already full, a new ring could not be equipped. But...it was still weak.

No sooner had the thought entered my mind than Grimlock quietly pounced. "What do you mean? She would never do that? If you're going to use that logic, I would never kill Griselda—she was my wife! You are leveling unfounded accusations against me, nothing more."

"No," Yolko whispered. I held my breath as the petite woman slowly, firmly shook her head. "No, you're wrong. There is proof...Whoever actually killed her left behind every item they judged to be worthless, right out in the open where they did the act. Fortunately, the player who discovered them knew the leader's name and delivered her leftover articles to the guild home. That's how, when we chose to make this grave marker her resting place, we were able to leave her sword here, until it eventually disintegrated. But...that wasn't all. I didn't tell anyone...but there was another memento of hers that I buried here on my own."

Suddenly, she spun around, knelt behind the little grave nearby, and began to dig in the dirt with her bare hands as everyone else watched and waited. When Yolko stood up again, she held out her hand to show what she was holding. Despite being freshly dug up from the soil, the little box shone silver in the moonlight.

"Oh…a Permanent Storage Trinket!" Asuna gasped. As she noted, it was the box of permanence that only master-class craftsmen could fashion. At maximum, they could be about four inches to a side, so they couldn't hold large items, but a few small accessories could fit inside. Even if left out in the open, no item inside here would ever suffer the natural degradation of its durability.

Yolko reached out with her left hand and pulled up the lid of the silver box.

Sitting on the white silk liner were two gleaming rings. She picked up one, a larger silver ring. On its flat tip was a carving of an apple.

"This is the Golden Apple sigil, which she always wore on her right hand. I still have my own, so it will be very easy to compare and confirm."

She put that ring back and picked up the other one—a narrow golden band.

"And this is the ring that she never took off the ring finger of her left hand—your wedding ring, Grimlock! It has your name carved on the inside! The fact that these rings are here is unshakeable proof that at the moment she was taken through a portal outside of town and murdered, she was wearing them! Am I wrong?! If I am, then explain it to me!!" she finished in a tearful scream. She thrust the glittering golden ring right at Grimlock, large teardrops rolling down her cheeks.

No one spoke for several moments. Caynz, Schmitt, Asuna, and I held our breath, eyes wide, watching the confrontation.

The tall blacksmith, his lips pursed, stood frozen in place for over ten seconds. Eventually, one corner of his mouth twitched, then tensed.

"That ring…You asked me about this on the day of her funeral,

Yolko—if I wanted to keep Griselda's wedding ring. And I told you to let it fade away, like her sword. If you'd just said you wanted it…"

Grimlock's head was downcast, his face hidden behind his wide-brim hat. He fell to his knees, as though the string holding him upright had snapped.

Yolko put the golden ring back into the box, closed the lid, and clenched it to her chest. She looked skyward, her damp face scrunched up, and whispered, in a voice now dull and soft, "Why…why, Grimlock? Why would you kill the leader…your own wife, just to turn the ring into money?"

"…Money? Money, you say?" Grimlock rasped from his knees, chuckling. He brought up his left hand to open the menu. With a few short operations, he produced a large leather bag. He lifted it up, then hurled it onto the ground. The heavy thud contained the clear sound of many metal items scraping. Just the sound alone made it clear to me how much col was contained within.

"This is half of the money I got from liquidating the ring. I haven't spent a single coin."

"Huh…?" Yolko said, her eyebrows crossed in confusion.

Grimlock looked up at her, then the rest of us, and said in a dry voice, "It wasn't for money. I…I just had to kill her. While she was still my wife."

The round glasses turned to the mossy grave for a moment, then came back. The blacksmith continued his confession.

"Griselda. Grimlock. It's no coincidence that our names sound similar. We always had the same names, going back to the games we played before *SAO*. And if the game featured it, we were always married. After all…after all, she was my wife in the real world, too."

My mouth fell open in shock. Asuna sucked in a sharp breath, and the others' faces were portraits of stunned surprise.

"She was the ideal wife for me; I had no complaints. She was the very picture of the sidekick wife: cute, sweet, obedient. We never once had a fight. But…once we got stuck in this world… she changed…"

He shook his head, hidden beneath the hat, and let out a low breath.

"I was the only one who quaked and shivered in fear at being trapped in here. Where did she hide all of that talent? In fighting ability, decision-making, and everything else, Griselda—no, Yuuko—was greater than me. And more than that, she overrode my complaints to create the guild, recruit members, and start training. She was far more alive here than even in real life...and more fulfilled...Watching her up close, I had to admit that the Yuuko I loved was gone. Even if we someday beat the game and got back to reality, the well-behaved, subservient wife I knew would not return."

The shoulders of his long-sleeve jacket trembled. Whether it was in self-mocking laughter or sobs of distress, I couldn't tell.

His whispering continued. "Can you understand my fears? If we got back to the real world...and Yuuko asked for a divorce...I couldn't bear that disgrace. So...so it was best to act while I was still her husband. While I was still here, with a legal method of murder at my disposal. Can anyone blame me...for wishing to keep my memories of Yuuko pure and pristine?"

After his long and ghastly confession had finished, no one spoke.

I heard the hoarse voice emerge from my throat, though I wasn't even aware I was doing it at first.

"Disgrace...*disgrace*? Your wife wouldn't listen to you...and that's why you killed her? She was strengthening herself and your friends to help escape from here...and might have one day stood among the ranks of those advancing us through the game...And just for that...?"

I had to use my left hand to hold down my right to keep it from instinctually drawing the blade on my back.

Grimlock looked up lazily, the lower frame of his glasses glinting, and whispered, "*Just* for that? It was plenty enough for what I did. Someday you will understand, Detective, once you have found love and are about to lose it."

"No, Grimlock. You're wrong about that."

It was not me who bit back at him, but Asuna. Her beautiful features were cast in an expression I couldn't read as she quietly stated, "What you felt for Griselda wasn't love. It was possession. If you still love her, then take off your left glove. But I'm sure that you've already cast aside the wedding ring that Griselda never removed even to the moment of her murder."

Grimlock's shoulders trembled, and in a mirror image of what I had done moments before, grabbed his left hand with his right.

But he stopped there. The blacksmith silently held his grip, not removing the glove. The silence that followed was broken by Schmitt, who spoke up at last.

"…Kirito. Can you allow us to determine his fate? We will not execute him ourselves, of course. But he must pay for his crimes."

His calm voice contained none of the terror that had gripped him until just minutes earlier. I looked up at the tall man in his clanking armor and nodded.

"Okay. He's all yours."

He nodded back and grabbed Grimlock's right arm, pulling him to his feet. With the slumping blacksmith firmly under control, he said to me, "I appreciate this," and descended the hill.

Next to leave were Yolko and Caynz, after she had buried the silver box back where it belonged. They passed by us, bowing deeply, then shared a look.

Yolko offered, "Asuna, Kirito. I don't know how to apologize to you…or to thank you. If you hadn't come to our aid, we would have died tonight…and never succeeded in exposing Grimlock's crimes."

"No…it's thanks to you for remembering about the two rings at the end. It was a brilliant closing argument. You should be a lawyer or a prosecutor if we ever get back to reality."

She chuckled and shrugged. "No…You might not believe me, but at that very moment, I swear I heard her voice, telling me to remember the rings."

"…I see…"

They bowed again and descended the hill after Schmitt as Asuna and I watched. Eventually all four cursors had vanished in the direction of the town, leaving only the blue moonlight and gentle breeze on the lonely hilltop.

"...Hey, Kirito," Asuna said abruptly. "If you were married to someone...and later on, you found out she had a side you never knew about, what would you think?"

"Uh..."

I hadn't expected this question and didn't have a quick answer. I had only been alive for fifteen and a half years. I had no way to understand a life like that. But after giving it some good, desperate thought, I came up with an answer, shallow though it was.

"I guess I'd think I was lucky."

"Huh?"

"I...I mean, being married means you already love the sides of her you've already seen, right? So if you find a new side of her and fall in love with that...it's t-twice as much to love."

It was hardly worthy of being called intelligent, but Asuna thought it over, tilted her head, and grinned a bit.

"Hmm. That's weird."

"Uh...weird...?"

"Whatever. More importantly...all this activity has got me starving. Let's get something to eat."

"G-good idea. Then...let's go get that Algade specialty, the one that looks like a fried pancake, only without the savory sauce it's supposed to have..."

"Rejected," she stated flatly. I started to trudge along, when she suddenly grabbed my shoulder from behind.

I turned around with a start and witnessed an inexplicable sight for the nth time since the safe-haven incident occurred.

In Aincrad, all sensory information was nothing more than coded digital data. That meant that ghostly phenomena could not exist.

So what I was seeing was either a bug in the server or an illusion that my biological brain was producing.

On the north face of the hill, a slight distance away, next to the grave marker that stood solitary next to the foot of the gnarled tree, stood a female player, translucent and glowing a pale gold.

Her skinny body was wrapped in the minimum of metal armor. There was a narrow longsword at her waist and a shield on her back. Her hair was short, and her face was stately and beautiful, but her eyes were brimming with a strong light that I recognized from several other players I knew.

They were the eyes of a conqueror, of one with a strong will to bring this game of death to an end with her own sword. The woman watched Asuna and me silently with a smile on her lips, then, as though offering something, stretched out her open right hand.

I, like Asuna, held out my right hand in return and, when I felt something warm in the palm of my hand, clenched it tight. The warmth passed through my body and lit a fire in my chest, only to leave through my lips in the form of words.

"We will carry on...your will. One day, we'll beat this game and free everyone."

"Yes, we promise. So please...watch over us, Griselda," Asuna continued, the whisper reaching the lady warrior on the night breeze. Her translucent face split in a wide grin.

And in the next moment, there was no one there.

We let our hands drop and stood in place. Eventually Asuna squeezed my hand and grinned.

"C'mon, let's go. We've got a lot of work tomorrow."

"...That's right. Gotta clear this floor before the week is over."

We turned and walked down the little hill in the direction of town.

Calibur

§ Alfheim
§ December 2025

1

"Look at this, Big Brother."

With dull, sleepy eyes, I stared at the tablet Suguha was holding out to me.

I'd gotten plenty of sleep last night, but I felt like my dreams were exceptionally long. So when I got to the kitchen table, it was the sort of situation where I had to force my recalcitrant mental gears to turn via a strong cup of coffee. But even with that mental fog, the warning light in a corner of my brain was flashing as I took the tablet from her.

After all, the last time she had handed me something under similar circumstances, it was two weeks ago, when she had proof of my secret shame—that I had converted my character from *ALfheim Online* (*ALO*), the fantasy flight-based VRMMO, to *Gun Gale Online* (*GGO*), a sci-fi gunfighter of the same medium. At first I wondered if she'd uncovered some other misdeed of mine and hastily tried to think of what I'd done recently. But Suguha only chuckled and reassured me. "I'm not trying to string you up this time, Big Brother. Just look at it!"

I hesitantly took the tablet she offered me and examined it. Just like the printed copy she'd shown me last time, it was a news article from MMO Tomorrow, the country's biggest VRMMORPG website. But this time, it was not categorized as *GGO* news, but

ALO. The first thing that caught my eye was the screenshot in the article, which was not a player avatar but a landscape shot. So the spriggan in black truly hadn't gotten himself into trouble this time.

Relieved, I read the lead paragraph of the article. Almost instantly, I was hit by a different kind of shock and couldn't stop myself from shouting. "Wh-what?!"

The article read, *The Holy Sword Excalibur, most powerful of the legendary weapons, found at last!*

My fatigue completely forgotten now, I tore through the rest of the article and let out a long groan.

"Hrrrrmmm...So they finally found it..."

"Personally, it was a lot longer than I expected." Suguha pouted, spreading blueberry jam on her toast from her seat across the table.

The Holy Sword Excalibur.

It was the one weapon in *ALO* said to be able to overpower the Demon Blade Gram, weapon of the salamander general Eugene. Its existence was long known, thanks to its tiny description and picture on the official website's index of weapons, but the means of finding it in the game had remained a mystery.

Though technically, there *were* three—no, four players who knew about it. Suguha, Asuna, Yui, and me. We'd found it at the very start of this year: January 2025. Today was December 28th, so Excalibur's secret had stayed hidden for an entire year.

"Aww, man...If I'd known this was going to happen, I'd have given it another shot," I grumbled and stuck a spoon in the jar of homemade jam, scooping out a huge dollop of the gelatinous material and dropping it onto my toast. Next, I added a blast of whipped butter, spreading it until the two toppings were marbled. Suguha, who'd been watching her calories recently, looked back and forth between the toast in her hand and what I was doing with mine. Eventually, she lost the saving roll against temptation and silently pulled the butter container over to herself.

Her meager resistance came in the form of taking a more reasonable amount of butter. Once she'd taken a bite of her toast, she pointed out, "Read it closer; they only just found it. They haven't figured out how to get it yet."

"What?"

I stopped myself in the middle of another huge bite and squinted at the tablet again. The article said that Excalibur's location had been identified but there was no information about any player acquiring it. Now that I thought about it, if someone had found the prize, the screenshot would have been of the lucky winner holding the golden blade aloft.

"Man, don't scare me like that..." I sighed in relief, finishing the bite I'd started. Suguha smiled at me, picked up the carton of milk, and filled my glass.

It was nine thirty in the morning on Sunday, December 28th, 2025. Winter vacation started today for the both of us, so it was a late breakfast. Our mom still had a few proofs to clear up before the end of the year, so she'd bolted out the door with another piece of toast earlier. Just because digital publishing didn't need to worry about the status of the printer didn't mean there weren't challenges of its own.

As usual, my dad was busy on assignment in New York, and the last message we'd got from him said he'd be home on the thirtieth. So Suguha and I ate alone, which meant that our conversation naturally turned to the subject of *ALO*.

After my first slice of toast, I decided on the tuna spread for the second, at which point a thought occurred to me.

"But how'd they find it, then? You can't fly in Jotunheim, but Excalibur's location is up high enough that you can't see it without flight."

One year ago, Suguha (as Leafa) and I (as Kirito) were traveling from sylph lands to the center city Alne, and just as the World Tree came into sight, we got gobbled up by a giant earthworm and traveled through its digestive tract to the underground realm of Jotunheim.

We were making our way around the subterranean map,

avoiding the unbeatable, enormous Deviant God monsters as we sought a stairway back to the surface, when we came across a very odd sight. A humanoid Deviant God with four arms was fighting with another Deviant God with countless tentacles and a long nose, like a cross between an elephant and a jellyfish.

When Leafa begged me to help save the one being picked on, I somehow managed to pull the four-armed monster to a nearby lake, where the jellyphant took advantage of the watery conditions to win. When the winner—which Leafa nicknamed "Tonky"—proved to be helpful rather than hostile, we got to ride on its back to the center of Jotunheim. Tonky cocooned and subsequently hatched with wings, flying us up to a passage in the ceiling that took us back to the surface. But on the way, we saw an upside-down pyramid dungeon tangled in the giant roots of the World Tree and, trapped in crystal at its very tip, the gleaming golden sword.

As Suguha revisited the memories of that adventure, she looked up and grinned.

"You were really torn at the time, weren't you? You didn't know whether to stay on Tonky and travel to the surface or jump over to the dungeon and go after Excalibur."

"W-well, yeah, I was torn...But if you ask me, anyone who doesn't at least entertain the thought isn't a true online gamer!"

"That didn't sound as cool as you thought it did." Suguha grinned, snarky. But then she looked down in serious thought—and not about what to spread on her second piece of toast; her hand was already reaching for the tube of tuna paste.

"...Tonky's not going to come unless you or I call for him... and I haven't heard anything about people discovering a way of flying in Jotunheim. So maybe someone else saved another jellyphant Deviant God the way we did and succeeded in enabling the quest..."

"I suppose so...It's hard for me to imagine another weirdo—er, charitable soul like you wanting to save such a gross—er, unique monster that way."

"They're not gross! They're cute!" argued my little sister, who turned sixteen this year. She continued. "But in that case, it's only a matter of time before someone clears that dungeon and succeeds in getting the sword. It wasn't discovered until today because the conditions for unlocking the quest were well hidden, but it's been a year now, and there was that update that added sword skills, so the difficulty of the dungeon isn't what it once was."

"Yeah…I guess…" I mumbled, and took a drink of milk.

It had been this January that we spotted Excalibur. Since then, *ALO*'s management had passed from RCT Progress to its current group of venture capitalists, and they'd added the floating castle Aincrad to the game—in all, it had undergone a massive renovation. Once that upheaval settled down in June, I had joined Leafa, Yui, and Asuna for another ride on Tonky's back to attempt winning the legendary Excalibur.

We failed spectacularly. The hanging-pyramid dungeon was packed with the four-armed Deviant Gods that had bullied Tonky, only big-daddy versions of them, so powerful that it immediately made me want to give up. We challenged the dungeon as a party of three (plus one companion) as a reconnaissance run before a true attempt, but it was so clearly out of our league that we called it off early and decided to try again when we were much stronger.

But when Aincrad was installed and the first ten floors made available to play, followed by the second ten in September, we switched over to that part of the game. We'd go back to Jotunheim to farm materials and hang out with Tonky every now and then, but there was no rush to deal with Excalibur—no one else could even spot the thing, much less succeed at reaching it.

The thing about MMORPGs is that no item stays hidden forever. Now that the location of the sword was published online, even in a vague form, a swarm of players was bound to descend on Jotunheim. Some of them might even be in the dungeon as we spoke.

"…What should we do, Big Brother?" Suguha asked, lifting her glass of milk with two hands now that she was done with her second piece of toast.

I cleared my throat and answered. "Sugu, chasing after legendary items isn't the only pleasure to be had in a VRMMO."

"...Yeah, I know. Getting a weapon with better stats doesn't mean—"

"But I think that we owe it to Tonky for showing us where the sword is. I'm pretty sure that deep down, he wants us to beat that dungeon. I mean, we're pretty much best friends with him, aren't we?"

"...You just said he was gross," my sister said with a piercing glance. I summoned my most dazzling smile for her.

"So, you doing anything today, Sugu?"

"...Well, the club's on break, too."

I smacked a fist into my palm in triumph. With that decided, my mind was now in full-on tactical planning mode.

"I'm pretty sure seven is the most you can fit on Tonky's back. That means me, you, Asuna, Klein, Liz, Silica...and one more. Agil's got his business...Chrysheight's too unreliable, and Recon's going to be in sylph territory..."

"...Why not invite Sinon?"

"Ooh, that's it!"

I snapped my fingers, pulled out my cell phone, and started scrolling through my contacts list.

Earlier this month, I converted my character Kirito into *Gun Gale Online* as part of an ongoing investigation and met a girl named Sinon there. After the case was solved, Sinon became friends with Asuna, Liz, and the rest, and created a new character in *ALO* to play with us.

It was a brand-new character, just two weeks old, but given the skill-based nature of *ALO*, numerical stats carried less weight than most games. With Sinon's talent, even a high-difficulty dungeon wouldn't be out of her reach.

While I typed up a message at maximum speed, Suguha nimbly stacked the plates and glasses and carried them to the kitchen. I couldn't help but notice a bit of a bounce to her step as she did so. She had to be thinking the same thing as I was from the moment she showed me the news.

We were going to fly into an alternate world with good friends and tackle a challenging but thrilling mission together. Few things could possibly be as exciting and fun.

Once I was done sending the invitation to Sinon and the other four, I practically skipped over to the kitchen to assist Suguha with the cleaning.

Even on a Sunday, getting seven players together so quickly at midmorning at the end of the year was quite a feat, only made possible through the personal respect I commanded—or more likely, the online gamer instincts roused by the allure of the Holy Sword Excalibur. Compared to when we challenged it as a group of four half a year ago, we had more people with better stats now.

We met up at the workshop of the famous Lisbeth Armory on the main street of Yggdrasil City, where the leprechaun black-smith took turns sharpening our weapons. It was common prac-tice to refill your gear's durability to maximum before tackling a major quest.

Sitting on a bench against the wall and slugging from a bottle of liquor "for atmosphere"—though naturally, there wasn't a sin-gle drop of alcohol entering his actual body—was Klein the sala-mander. Next to him, the cait sith beast-tamer Silica, complete with fluffy sky-blue dragon on her head, asked, "Are you already on New Year's vacation, Klein?"

"Yep, since yesterday. Even if I wanted to work, there's just no business this time of year. And the stupid boss tries to spin it by saying that we're a worker-friendly company, since we get a whole week off over the holiday!"

In real life, Klein was an employee at a small import company. He often complained about his boss, but in reality it must have been a good company, because they looked after his needs dur-ing his two-year imprisonment in *SAO* and instantly returned his position to him when he got out. Klein clearly felt some debt to them in return, as evidenced by the fact that he was working hard on a new remote presentation system for their clients using the Seed package and mobile cameras. Given all the help I provided in modifying the cameras, a single all-you-can-eat Korean BBQ meal seemed insufficient, but I was willing to overlook it if he helped out with this quest.

At that moment, Klein looked over as I leaned against the wall, considering my plan.

"Hey, Kirito, if we manage to actually strike gold and win Excalibur today, you gotta help me go get the Spirit Katana Kagutsuchi."

"Aww, man…That dungeon's so freakin' hot…"

"Yeah, and Jotunheim's so freakin' cold!"

Our childish bickering was interrupted by a soft comment from the left.

"In that case, I'd like the Bow of Light, Shekinah."

I looked over, feeling my breath catch in my throat. Leaning back against the wall like me, her arms crossed, was a cait sith with short, pale blue hair and pointed, triangular ears. If Silica was a cute, friendly munchkin cat, this cait sith was a cool, aloof Siamese—or perhaps even a vicious wildcat.

"Y-you made your character two weeks ago, and you're already after a legendary weapon?" I asked. The wildcat's long, thin tail swished.

"The bow Liz made me is wonderful, but I could use a bit more range…"

At the worktable in the back, restringing the very bow in question, Lisbeth looked up with a pained expression and called out, "Just so you know, bows in this world are basically somewhere between spears and magic spells in terms of range! You can't normally use them to hit a target a hundred yards away!"

The wildcat shrugged coolly and smirked. "If I could, I'd go for twice that range."

Knowing that most of her experience was as an expert

ultra-long sniper who could shoot a target two kilometers away in *GGO*, the best I could do was smile uncomfortably. If she actually found a bow with that kind of range, she'd be able to win any duel without an area restriction; she could dart out of sword range and fill her opponent with arrows like a pincushion.

The blue-haired wildcat—my new friend, Sinon, who had just come to *ALO* two weeks ago—had picked up the bow, one of the trickier weapons in the game to use, and mastered it in the span of just a day. In *ALO*, the speedy sylphs could use shortbows and the powerful, burly gnomes could shoot down foes with their heavy ballistas, but she had overturned the usual tropes and gone for a long-distance longbow build as a cait sith, which had the best eyesight of all nine fairy races. At first I was skeptical, but I decided to let her have her fun. When Sinon started dispatching monsters before they began approaching, well beyond the range of even fire magic, I had to rethink my opinion.

Bows in this world got the same accuracy correction that spells did, but beyond the bounds of that system assistance, the effects of wind and gravity kept arrows from flying where you wanted. But given that Sinon had played so much in *GGO*, which shared the same engine, she was already trained to take those factors into account. It was the same thing that happened when I went to *GGO* and was able to use my knowledge of "reading eyesight" successfully. Perhaps traveling among the many worlds of the Seed Nexus carried a meaning that I hadn't considered before—

The door to the workshop crashing open to my right interrupted my thoughts.

"We're here!"

"Thanks for waiting!"

It was Leafa and Asuna, who had gone out to buy potions and other supplies. They had just flown here straight from the market without bothering to store their purchases in their inventory, so the supplies from the baskets they were carrying quickly stacked up on the table in the middle of the room—colorful bottles of liquid, various seeds, and so on.

A tiny navigation pixie named Yui flitted off of Asuna's shoulder and flew over to plop onto the top of my head. My spriggan version of Kirito had featured spiky hair for a long time, but at Yui's request, my hairstyle was closer to the old look now. She claimed it was easier to sit on this way.

From atop my head, Yui's little bell-chime voice tinkled, "We were gathering some intelligence on our shopping trip, and it seems like no players or parties have yet reached the hanging dungeon, Papa."

"Ahh...Then how did they find out about the location of Excalibur?"

"Apparently they found another quest, separate from the hidden Tonky quest we discovered. As a reward for that quest, an NPC pointed out the location of Excalibur."

Asuna turned away from sorting the potions, her special undine-blue hair swaying, and grimaced. "And it sounds like this other quest was pretty vicious. It wasn't an errand or protection quest, but the slaughtering kind. So now Jotunheim's pretty decimated, with people fighting over pop spots."

"...Yeah, that sounds messy," I opined.

Slaughter quests were, as the name suggested, your typical RPG quest to "kill X number of X monsters" or "collect X items dropped by X monsters." Because you had to go and whack every one of those monsters you could find, that meant that parties on the same quest in the same small area often found themselves at odds as they competed for the "pop" point—the place where the monsters repopulated.

"Don'tcha think it's weird?" Klein said, wiping his lips after he'd finally drained the last of his bottle of fire whiskey. "Excalibur's sealed at the very bottom of a floating dungeon packed with all kinds of terrible monsters, right? Why would the *location* be a quest reward?"

"That's a good point," Silica piped up, stroking Pina against her chest. "I would understand if the reward was the means of getting to the dungeon, but not that..."

"Well, I'm sure we'll find out when we get there," said Sinon coolly from my left. No sooner had the words left her mouth than Lisbeth shouted from the back of the workshop.

"All right! Everyone's weapons are at full capacity!"

"Thank you very much!!" we all chorused. We grabbed our beloved swords, katanas, and bows, sparkling as though they were brand-new, and equipped them. At the table, Asuna had called upon her experience as a battle planner to expertly divvy up seven different potion portions. We packed them away in our pouches, storing any that couldn't be held as physical objects in our inventories.

The clock readout in the lower right of my vision said it was still eleven o'clock. We'd probably have to stop at some point for a lunch-and-bathroom break, but we could probably reach the first safe spot in the dungeon before then.

Once the seven players, one fairy, and one dragon were fully equipped, I surveyed the group and cleared my throat.

"Thank you for answering my abrupt summons today, everyone! You have my word that I will pay you back for your assistance— emotionally! And now…let's kick some ass!"

It was probably just my imagination that there was a note of exasperation in the cheer that followed. I spun around, opening the workshop door directly beneath Ygg City and on the way to Alne, to reveal a secret tunnel entrance that would take us down to the underground realm of Jotunheim.

2

The door was at the end of a long route through Alne that was not found on any map; it wound through tiny alleys, up and down stairs, and even through backyards.

It was just a normal, totally unremarkable round wooden door. It looked more like a decorative detail than a functioning door, in fact. But when Leafa pulled a small copper key from her belt pouch and twisted it inside the lock, there was a dry click. The key had simply appeared in her inventory after Tonky flew us up to the bottom of the tunnel that led to this door. In other words, the door would not open unless you had come through it from the other side first.

I pulled the round iron knocker, and the wooden door split into two sides, revealing a staircase leading down. The seven of us filed in one at a time, and when Klein closed it at the end, it automatically locked itself again.

"Yikes…How many steps are on this thing?" moaned Lisbeth. I couldn't blame her; the stairs in the six-foot-wide tunnel, lit only by the small pale lamps on the walls, continued down as far as the game engine would display.

"Hmm, I'd say it takes us down about the length of an entire labyrinth tower from Aincrad," Asuna said from the lead position.

Liz, Silica, and Klein all grimaced. I couldn't help but chuckle, and explained the benefit of the tunnel.

"Listen, first of all, if you want to get to Jotunheim via the normal route, you have to travel to one of the staircase dungeons a few miles away from Alne, fight monsters all the way down, then defeat a boss at the end just to get there. It'll take a single party at least two hours to do that, but this is just five minutes of walking! If I were Leafa, I'd start a business charging a thousand yrd per person to use these stairs."

"Big Brother, you know that once you get down there, unless Tonky comes up to the platform, you'll just fall down into the hole in the middle of Jotunheim and die," Leafa said exasperatedly, and she was right.

In the center of the vast cave that was Jotunheim was a bottomless pit about a mile across known as the Great Void. The hanging pyramid dungeon housing Excalibur jutted out of the earth directly over said Great Void. The stairs we were descending now let out in the air above the Void, close to the dungeon. So jumping off the bottom of the staircase just meant you would fall into the Void, die, and be respawned at the save point on the surface above.

I cleared my throat loudly to cover up the greedy statement I'd just made and formally intoned, "Well, at any rate, I should think that you will thank each and every step with all of your heart as we descend, boys and girls."

"As if you built them," Sinon muttered from the spot in front of me. She was always quick with a sharp comment, but in this case, I was glad for it.

"Thanks for the feedback," I said, and grabbed the light blue tail waving in front of me by way of a handshake.

"*Fgyaa!!*"

The wildcat archer leaped up with an incredible screech. She spun around and, running backward down the stairs, held up her hands as if she meant to scratch my face with her nails.

The cait sith's triangular ears and tail were organs that humans

didn't possess, of course. But somehow, they had a physical sensation when you played as one, apparently. When someone suddenly grabbed them, a player still getting used to the sensation would feel something "very weird" (according to Silica), which meant their reactions were always entertaining.

"The next time you do that, I'm shooting a fire arrow in each of your nostrils," Sinon snorted. Over her shoulder, Leafa, Liz, Silica, Asuna, and Yui all shook their heads in perfectly synchronized exasperation. Behind me, I heard Klein murmur in admiration, "I gotta say, man, you know no fear."

As expected, the party reached the end of the staircase tunnel that passed through the mantle of Alfheim in less than five minutes. A pale light appeared ahead.

At the same time, the virtual air dropped in temperature. Tiny little ice crystals began to sparkle around our faces. A few seconds later, we breached the earth and caught sight of the entirety of Jotunheim. The stairs, carved into a massive tree root, continued out into open air until they stopped at a point fifty feet ahead.

"Wh-whoaaa!!"

"Incredible…"

It was the first sight of Jotunheim for the two cats, Silica and Sinon. Even little Pina flapped her wings wildly atop Silica's head.

The world below us was a cruel but beautiful realm of endless night, covered in thick snow and ice. The only light source was from the faint glow of mammoth crystal pillars extending from the earthy ceiling, carrying a dim remnant of the light from the surface. Here and there were Deviant God castles and fortresses, lit by eerie fires of purple and green. At the center of the map, the span from the floor to the ceiling was over half a mile, so we couldn't see the countless Deviant Gods milling about from here. Directly below was the bottomless pit that sucked in all light: the Void.

When I tore my eyes away from that hole and looked forward, I was met by another stunning sight.

Entangled in countless writhing roots—coming straight through the earth from the World Tree that loomed over all of Alfheim—was a gigantic mass of sky-blue ice crystal, jutting out like an upside-down pyramid. It was the hanging dungeon that was our destination. Its base was about a thousand feet to a side, and the height of the crystal was about the same. From this distance, it was clear that the interior of the ice was carved out with many rooms and hallways—filled with large, prowling shadows.

Lastly, I glanced down at the sharp tip of the pyramid at the very bottom.

My spriggan eyes, gifted with an advantage to night vision, could only make out the occasional tiny glint of golden light. But the richness of that light exerted a powerful pull of desire on me. It was the Holy Sword Excalibur, the most powerful of *ALO*'s legendary weapons, sitting right there.

Once we were done confirming the basics, Asuna raised her right hand and smoothly chanted some spellwords. Our bodies were briefly shrouded in pale blue light, and a small icon turned on above the HP gauge in the top left of my vision. Soon the chill receded, and it felt like I was wearing a thick down jacket. She had buffed our resistance to cold.

"Okay," Asuna said, and Leafa put her fingers to her mouth and whistled loudly. A few seconds later came a distant sound among the wind, moaning, *Kwooo...*

When I looked down, a white shadow was visible against the backdrop of the Great Void. From the sides of its main body, which was flat like a flounder or a rice ladle, were four sets of white wings that resembled fins. On the underside of the body hung a mass of tentacles like vines. And on the head were three black eyes to either side of a long nose. It was Tonky the Deviant God, who had evolved from its jellyphant look into this eerie and beautiful form.

"Tonkyyyy!" Yui called out from Asuna's shoulder. The bizarre creature let out another long moan. With a flap of its powerful wings, it began to ascend in a spiral pattern. As it got closer, the sheer size of the beast caused those of us who hadn't seen him yet to back away.

"No worries, he's an herbivore," I reassured them. Leafa turned around and beamed.

"But when I brought him a fish from the surface earlier, he ate it in a single slurp."

"...O-oh."

Klein and the others took another step back, but there wasn't much room left on the narrow staircase. Once Tonky was right in front of us, he examined the party with his still-elephantine face, then extended his long trunk and, with the hairy tip, ruffled Klein's spiky hair.

"*Ubyorhu?!*" Klein exclaimed bizarrely. I pushed him.

"He says to get on his back. It's all you."

"Y-yeah, but...My gramps had one piece of advice for me before he died: never ride American cars or flying elephants..."

"Last time we were at Dicey Café, you gave us his homemade dried persimmons! Get us some more, next time you visit him!" I scolded, and shoved him again. Klein's momentum took him a step onto Tonky's shoulder, which he quickly crossed to the flatter part of the back. Next was Sinon, who was always fearless, and Silica, who decided that her love of animals extended to cover Tonky as well. Lisbeth crossed next with a very unladylike shout, and then Leafa and Asuna, who were familiar with riding Tonky. Lastly, I scratched the root of his trunk and leaped onto the back of the thirty-foot-long Deviant God.

"Okay, Tonky, take us to the entrance of the dungeon!" Leafa called from her seat right behind his neck. Tonky lifted his long snout and trumpeted again, then started flapping his eight wings in a pattern from front to rear.

Including the times I did it just for fun, this was my fifth ride on Tonky's back. I never spoke it out loud, but there was a thought that crossed my mind each and every time. It was...

"...Hey, what happens if you fall off?" said Lisbeth from behind me, giving voice to that exact thought.

As a basic rule, fairy flight did not work in Jotunheim, and the normal rules of fall damage applied. Damage would start occurring from a fall of just thirty feet, depending on one's skills, and at about a hundred feet, death was unavoidable.

At the present moment, Tonky was floating nearly half a mile in the air. There was no question what would happen if we fell. Perhaps there was some safety mechanism—say, his stomach tentacles grabbing us if we fell off—but I was certainly in no mood to test it out.

Everyone else was grappling with the same concerns. The only ones enjoying the flight were Leafa the speedaholic in the front; Yui, who was now sitting on Leafa's head; and Pina, in Silica's arms.

The answer to Liz's question came from Asuna, who was sitting next to her. Despite the concern in her face, she smiled at me and said, "I'm sure that fellow over there, who once tried to climb the outer pillars of Aincrad to reach the next floor, will find out the answer for us."

"...When it comes to falling from heights, I'd think that felines are best suited for the task."

Instantly, the two felines in the party shook their heads.

As we chatted, Tonky continued to flap his four sets of wings in a flowing pattern, gliding through the air. It was taking us to the terrace that served as entrance to the hanging dungeon of ice. Hopefully the trip would be smooth and safe—

No sooner had the thought occurred to me than Tonky folded his wings and entered a precipitous dive.

"Aaaaaah!!" bellowed the two men in the group.

"Eeeeeek!!" screamed the women.

"Yahoooo!" cheered Leafa.

I gripped the thick hair covering the creature's back in an effort to fight against the terrific wind pressure. We were practically vertical; the ground far below was visibly coming closer. But why would he do this? The times we rode him before, he just made gentle, relaxing tours from the root staircase to the ice terrace.

Was he getting sick of being used as a taxi? Or had the fish Leafa fed him last time given him a stomachache?

My pointless questions aside, the texture of the ice-laden ground came into sharper detail as Tonky headed us toward the southern lip of the Great Void. It was the very spot where Leafa and I had rescued Tonky from a raid party of undine hunters.

Suddenly, extreme deceleration g-force hit my body, slamming me flat against the Deviant God's back. Tonky spread his wings again, hitting the brakes on his speedy fall. Relieved that he at least wasn't going to toss his cargo flat against the ground, I straightened up.

Now that his back was horizontal again, I had the presence of mind to survey the ground, which was now under two hundred feet away. The surface was clearly detailed, unlike the previous aerial scale model view. Dead trees hung sharp icicles from their branches. Rivers and lakes, frozen solid. And…

"…Huh?!"

It was Leafa, stretching forward to look over Tonky's head. She pointed at a spot on the ground and practically screamed, "Big Brother, look at that!!"

The other five and I obeyed, looking ahead and to the left, where she was pointing. Instantly, I caught sight of a quick succession of bright flashes in the darkness. A bit later came a tremendous, low-pitched rumble. It was the signature of a wide-area attack spell.

Tonky cooed sadly. I understood why at once.

The target of the attacks was a large monster with a dumpling-shaped body, long tentacles, an extended nose, and large ears, somewhere between an elephant and a jellyfish. It was the same type of monster as Tonky, before he cocooned and hatched.

The attackers were a large raid party of over thirty members.

Based on the vibrant array of sizes and hair colors, they were clearly a mixed-race team. In that sense, it was a typical Deviant God hunting party. But what was shocking to us was that it wasn't just players attacking the jellyphant.

Standing six or seven times taller than the tallest gnome was a humanoid shape, but with four arms and three stacked faces in a column. Its skin was as pale as steel, and the eyes burned red like hot coals.

Just as unmistakable as the jellyphant, this was one of the humanoid Deviant Gods who we saw trying to kill Tonky on our first encounter. Each arm held a crude sword like a rebar, and it was slamming the practically blunt weapons against the jellyphant's back. When the hard surface cracked and liquid spilled forth, the players would attack those weak points with magic, arrows, and sword skills.

"Wh-what does that mean? Did someone tame that humanoid Deviant God?" Asuna gaped.

Silica shook her head furiously and said, "That's impossible! Even with the skill maxed and a full boost from specialized equipment, the taming rate on Deviant Gods is zero percent!"

"Then that means," Klein grunted, spiking up his red hair to its proper height again, "they're just…piggybacking? When the four-armed giant was attacking the elephant thing, they jumped in to help it out…?"

"But would it be that easy to manage the aggro levels?" Sinon wondered calmly. She had a point. Given the aggressive behavior patterns of the Deviant Gods, even if the spells and skills weren't causing it damage, using them so close nearby would most likely cause it to target the players instead.

As we watched in bafflement and concern, the jellyphant's body shook and fell sideways onto the snow with a great crash. A storm of swords and spells wracked its sensitive underbelly.

"*Hrroooo…*"

The jellyphant let out a dying wail and burst into a massive swarm of polygonal shards.

"Kwooo," mourned Tonky. Riding on his head, Leafa's shoulders trembled, and atop *her* head, Yui drooped sadly.

I had no comforting comments to offer them, so instead I looked down at the raid party below. Almost immediately, my eyes bulged with fresh shock.

The four-armed giant, who was neither tamed, agitated, nor bewitched, bellowed victoriously, and the dozens of players at its feet cheered and hollered. Then the two sides set off together in search of a new target.

"Wh-why aren't they fighting now?!" I gasped, but Asuna raised her head with a start, noticing something.

"Ah…look over there!"

She was pointing out a distant hilltop on the right. There were more flashes of battle over there. I squinted to see another large party, this time assisted by a pair of the humanoids, hunting a Deviant God who looked like a many-legged crocodile.

"Well, I'll be damned…What the hell's going on here?" Klein said in a daze.

"Maybe these are the slaughter quests that Asuna said they'd discovered in Jotunheim? Teaming up with the humanoid ones to wipe out the animalistic ones…" Lisbeth suggested.

"…!"

Everyone else sucked in a sharp breath.

That had to be it. Fighting alongside normally hostile mobs to complete a specific quest wasn't particularly uncommon. But what did it mean that the reward for that quest would be Excalibur? The sword was sealed away in the hanging dungeon that was the humanoid Deviant Gods' base. You'd assume that the way to get it was to kill the humanoid ones instead…

Instinctually, my gaze swung to the huge ice pyramid overhead. But it was interrupted partway, as at the very rear of Tonky's back, where no one was sitting, particles of light were floating and coalescing into the figure of a person.

It was wearing a long robe. Blond hair flowed from its back down to its feet. The unearthly beauty of the figure marked it as female.

But the unthinking comment that escaped from Klein's and my mouths was hardly the kind of thing one was supposed to say to a beautiful woman.

"She's…"

"…freakin' huge!"

We couldn't be blamed. Even a conservative estimate of the woman's height put her over ten feet tall, which was twice our size.

Fortunately, she did not seem bothered by our rudeness. She serenely opened her mouth and spoke in a voice modulated with a grand effect that further distinguished her from an ordinary player.

"I am Urd, queen of the lake."

The enormous blond lady continued. "Little fairies who have aligned yourselves with my kindred."

Kindred? I wondered. If she were speaking of Tonky, who was still hovering with us on top of him, then that would mean this beautiful lady was friends with the animal-type Deviant Gods of Jotunheim…

At that point, I noticed that the "queen of the lake" was not actually entirely human in shape herself. The blond hair that stretched to her feet actually ended in writhing, translucent feelers, and the feet peeking out from her long robe were covered in pearly gray scales. It made me imagine that she was another bizarre creature like Tonky, except she chose to assume a humanoid form.

"My two sisters and I have a request of you. Please save this land from the attack of the frost giants."

The next thing I wondered was exactly *what* she was, systemwise. Given that there was no color cursor when I focused on her, she couldn't possibly be another player transformed by illusion magic. But whether she was a harmless event NPC, a trap set by a spontaneous quest mob, or a human GM role-playing within the game was unclear to me.

Suddenly, I felt a slight weight on my left shoulder, accompanied by Yui's sweet little whisper.

"Papa, she's an NPC. But something's odd. She doesn't seem to be speaking using ordinary fixed-response routines like other NPCs. She's interfacing with a language engine module very close to the core program."

"...Meaning she's an AI?"

"Right, Papa."

As I pondered the meaning of what Yui had just said, I lent my ears to the woman's speech. Urd, queen of the lake, beckoned a pearly hand toward the vast expanse of the underground realm.

"Like your Alfheim, Jotunheim was once under the blessing of Yggdrasil the World Tree, and it flowed with clean water and lush greenery. We hill giants lived here peacefully with our kindred beasts."

As she spoke, the environment of snow and ice silently wavered and faded. Superimposed over them were the very trees, flowers, and flowing water that Urd was describing. The image was even lusher than the gnome and salamander territories up on the surface.

Even more surprising, Urd revealed that the bottomless Great Void behind us was not a simple hole in this other vision. It was a wide lake full of crystal-clear water. And the roots of the World Tree that dangled from the ceiling now were once thicker and stronger, reaching all the way down to the lake in all directions.

Atop the thick root bursting through the surface of the water were little log cabins—no, entire towns. The whole image was very similar to Alne, the city on the surface.

Urd lowered her arm, and the vision disappeared. The familiar sight of icy Jotunheim returned, and she surveyed it with a glance that was both impassive and somehow mournful.

"Below even Jotunheim is Niflheim, the realm of ice. One day, Thrym, king of the frost giants there, turned himself into a wolf and snuck into this land, where he cast the sword that cuts all steel and wood, Excalibur, forged by Wayland the blacksmith god, into the Spring of Urd in the center of the world. The sword severed the World Tree's most vital root, and in that moment, Jotunheim lost the blessing of Yggdrasil."

This time, Urd raised her left arm. The image screen appeared again, and I was silenced with wonder by the overwhelming sight contained within it.

The roots of the World Tree that stretched all around the Spring of Urd suddenly rose and began to shrink upward toward the earth ceiling above. The towns resting upon them were shattered and destroyed in their entirety.

Meanwhile, all the trees' leaves fell, the grasses dried up, and the light faded. The rivers froze, frost descended, and blizzards raged. The unfathomable amount of water that filled the Spring of Urd froze instantly, and the withdrawing roots of the tree pulled the titanic ice block upward. The enormous creatures that resided within the lake fell out of the massive iceberg, spilling down into the abyss. I spotted what looked like the same jellyphant types as Tonky.

The roots eventually rose up into the ceiling of Jotunheim—the ground level of Alfheim—and wedged the block of ice halfway into the soil. There was no doubt now that the iceberg was none other than the upside down ice pyramid that loomed over Jotunheim today. The very bottom of the iceberg, sharpened like an icicle, contained a tiny glint of gold. It was Excalibur, the very sword that King Thrym of the frost giants had used to sever the physical connection between the World Tree and Jotunheim.

With all of the water gone, the once-beautiful lake had turned into a bottomless hole.

Urd lowered her hand and the screen disappeared again. But this time there was no big change in the background behind it. At most, the block of ice overhead had been reshaped into its current dungeon shape. Leafa and I had seen for ourselves that Excalibur was still locked at the bottom of the pyramid.

"A great horde of King Thrym's frost giants spilled forth from Niflheim into Jotunheim, building fortresses and castles and enslaving us hill giants. He built his own castle, Thrymheim, within the ice block that was once the Spring of Urd, and he ruled over this land. My sisters and I survived at the bottom of a spring that froze over, but our former power is lost."

Urd lowered her eyelids, her story approaching its end. We were all listening with rapt attention, largely forgetting that she was an NPC relating a game quest.

"The frost giants were not satisfied with just this, and they continue to attempt to wipe out our kindred beasts, who still survive in Jotunheim. If they succeed, my power will be entirely lost, and Thrymheim, the land of the pyramid, will be able to ascend into Alfheim above."

"Wh-whaaat?! But that'll totally destroy Alne!" Klein bellowed indignantly, lost in his own full dive within the fairy tale we'd just heard. Urd, who was more of an AI than just an NPC with a few speech routines, nodded.

"King Thrym's goal is to lock Alfheim under ice as well, and invade the branches of the World Tree Yggdrasil. That is where he will find the Golden Apple that he seeks."

For a moment, I tried to recall such an item, and then it hit me. There was an area near the top of the tree guarded by an impossibly powerful eagle type named mob. Perhaps that was where this golden apple could be found.

"Angered by the continued survival of our kindred beasts, Thrym and his frost giant generals have decided to use the strength of the fairies to achieve their goals. They promise Excalibur as a reward, to convince you to help slaughter our kindred. But Thrym would never give that sword to another. If Excalibur leaves Thrymheim, the blessing of Yggdrasil will return to this land, and his castle will melt into water once more."

"So...so Excalibur being a reward is all just a lie?! What kind of quest is that?!" Lisbeth squawked.

The queen replied regally. "I believe that when Wayland, the blacksmith god, was forging Excalibur, he made one impure strike and cast aside his failure. This false blade, Caliburn, which is otherwise indistinguishable from Excalibur, is what I believe he intends to give away. It is very strong on its own but does not contain the true power of the holy sword."

"N-no way…He's a king, and he's just going to lie about that?" Leafa muttered. Urd nodded and took a deep breath.

"That craftiness is Thrym's greatest weapon. But in his haste to wipe out my kindred beasts, he made one mistake. In order to help the fairies he tricked with his honeyed words, he summoned most of his followers from Thrymheim down to the surface below. The defenses of his castle are now but a shadow of their normal strength."

At last, I glimpsed the outcome of this quest—of the queen's plea.

Urd, lady of the lake, gestured to Thrymheim above with a massive arm.

"Fairies, will you infiltrate Thrymheim and draw Excalibur from the keystone pedestal?"

3

"…This is all getting pretty crazy…"

Asuna was the first to speak after Queen Urd disappeared back into golden droplets and Tonky began to fly back upward—at a much more reasonable pace this time.

Next, Sinon's light blue tail whipped back and forth as she wondered, "This is…a normal quest, right? It just seems way too *big* for that…What did she say—that if all the animal Deviant Gods get wiped out, the frost giants will take over the surface?"

"…She did," I muttered, my arms crossed. "But do you think the developers would really do something like that without an update or an event notification? Other MMOs have events all the time where a boss comes to invade a town, but they at least warn you about it a week ahead of time…"

Everyone in the group nodded in agreement. Then Yui leaped off my shoulder to hover in the air, shouting at a volume loud enough for everyone to hear, "Well, I have a conjecture, although I'm not one hundred percent certain about it…"

She blinked slowly, processing how best to say it, then continued. "There is one aspect of *ALfheim Online* that makes it very different from other VRMMOs based on The Seed. The Cardinal System that runs the game is not the scaled-down version the others use but is a full-scale replica of the processor used in the old *Sword Art Online*."

She was right about that. Though I hated to remember it, *ALO* started as a wholesale copy of the *SAO* server so that one power-mad lunatic could perform illegal experiments on a small subset of the old *SAO* victims. So the Cardinal System that controlled the game world had the same power as that of the original *SAO*.

Yui looked at her rapt audience and went on. "The original Cardinal System had several features that were taken out of the shrunken version. One of them is an automated quest-generation function. It absorbs legends and myths from cultures worldwide using the network, then repackages and remixes the proper names and story patterns to generate an infinite number of quests."

"Wh-what th' hell?" Klein gasped, his scraggly chin dropping open. "You're sayin' that all those quests we busted our asses to beat in Aincrad were just generated outta thin air by the system?"

"...No wonder there were so many of them. By the seventy-fifth floor, the quest database of the intel agents had easily over ten thousand individual quests listed," said the former vice commander of the KoB, who had diligently taken on as many quests as she could to help line the coffers of the guild's operating budget.

Meanwhile, Silica looked into the vacant distance and mumbled, "Plus, the stories were weird sometimes. Around the thirtieth floor, I think, there was a quest to beat some weird ogre with a mask and a saw, and no matter how many times you killed it, the quest would always reappear on the bulletin board the next week. Wonder what legend that was based on..."

There were plenty of other examples I could think of, but I didn't want this to devolve into an Aincrad-griping marathon all the way until we arrived at the pyramid of ice, so I steered us back to the original topic.

"So Yui, you're saying that the Cardinal System automatically generated this quest?"

"Based on the actions of that NPC, I believe it is highly likely.

Perhaps the developers have caused the inactive quest-generation function to start running again," she said, her face dark. "But if that is the case, then it's quite possible that the effects of the quest will play out as the story goes. That ice dungeon could float up to Alfheim, Alne will fall, and those Deviant Gods will begin to pop into the surrounding areas. In fact…"

The little AI's lips shut for a moment, and her features took on a note of fear. "According to my archived data, the Scandinavian mythology that forms the basis for this quest, and *ALO* as a whole, includes an apocalyptic war. It won't just be an invasion of the frost giants from Jotunheim and Niflheim, but also flame giants from the realm of fire Muspelheim, even farther down, and they will burn down the World Tree…"

"…Ragnarok," muttered Leafa, who loved myths and legends and had a number of books about them in her room back home. Her emerald green eyes shot open and she cried, "But…I can't possibly believe that the game system would totally overwrite and destroy the maps that it's charged with managing!"

That was true. But Yui just shook her head.

"The original Cardinal System has the right to completely destroy the entire world map. After all, the final duty of the old Cardinal was to obliterate Aincrad."

"…"

This time, I had no response.

The next to speak was Sinon, who had been listening in silence until now.

"So…let's say this Ragnarok really does happen. If it's not what the developers intended to have happen, can't they just rewind the server status?"

"Oh…yeah, yeah, that's right," Klein muttered, nodding.

Rolling back a server by overwriting the current state with a backup version was something that happened from time to time, when programmer error or bugs caused players to gain undue advantages. Alfheim being reduced to a wasteland might not have any effect on individual players' levels or gear, but nobody actually wanted the entirety of the fairy realm to look like the burned land in the east of salamander territory.

However, Yui did not immediately confirm this suggestion.

"It will be possible if the developers manually backed up all data and saved them to physically isolated media...But if they're using Cardinal's automatic backup function, depending on the settings, the best they can recover will be player data but not the original environment maps."

"..."

Everyone was silent for two seconds. Then Klein abruptly shouted, "I've got it!" and opened his window. Then he hung his head and shouted, "Never mind!"

"...What was that about?" Lisbeth asked, and the would-be samurai turned to her with a pitiful look on his face.

"I thought I'd just call a GM and ask to check if they realize what's going on. But it's outside of normal user support hours..."

"Morning on a Sunday at the end of the year," I sighed, and looked up into the darkness.

The giant ice pyramid was just in front of us now. If that structure, a thousand feet to a side, burst through the surface above, Alne would certainly panic—and worse. Half of its population had moved to Yggdrasil City atop the World Tree, but the city was still quite busy on weekend nights, both as a base of operations for the high-level dungeons in the Alne plains and as a central trading hub for the various fairy races. It was a very memorable city for me.

"...I think we have no choice but to do this, Big Brother," Leafa said, holding up a large medallion dangling from her right hand. Queen Urd's gift to them was embedded with a large, exquisitely cut gemstone. But over 60 percent of the facets were pitch-black and did not reflect the light.

When the gem was entirely black and every last animal Deviant God was hunted to extinction, Urd's power would be lost entirely. That moment would mark the beginning of King Thrym's invasion of Alfheim.

"…I agree. After all, I gathered you here today so we could tackle that dungeon and get Excalibur. If their guard is down, even better."

I opened my window and fiddled with my equipment mannequin. Hanging on my back were both my long sword special-ordered from Lisbeth and a sword I earned from the fifteenth-floor boss of the New Aincrad.

Seeing that I was back to my two-sword ways again, Klein smirked and crowed, "Awright, it's the last big quest of the year! Let's whup some ass and get on the front page of *MMO Tomorrow*!"

Sure, the reasons were a bit crass, but Lisbeth had no complaints this time. The whole group cheered in unison, and even Tonky beat his wings and crooned.

As the flying Deviant God picked up his ascent speed, he circled around the ice pyramid and sidled up to the entrance placed at the top. When Leafa was last to hop off onto the terrace, she rubbed his massive ear and said, "Wait for us here, Tonky. We're gonna make sure you get your country back!"

The sylph girl turned and drew a gently curved longsword from her waist. With all of our weapons in hand, we faced the tall double doors of ice that greeted us.

Normally you would have to fight the first guardian at this point, but as Urd said, the door opened right away today. We took on a formation of Klein, Leafa, and me in the front; Liz and Silica in the middle; and Asuna and Sinon bringing up the rear. The group headed across the icy floor into the giant palace of Thrymheim.

The maximum limit of a single party in *ALO* was the slightly irregular number of seven.

In most games it was six or eight, and no official reason had been given for the choice of seven. That meant the max for a raid party was forty-nine, from seven parties of seven. It was a good thing there was an automatic redistribution option for money, because dividing it among seven members would be very annoying.

When trying to construct a full party of just close friends, there were five of us always present: Asuna, Liz, Silica, Leafa, and me. We were all in high school—four of us in the same school—and two of us lived together, so it was easy to coordinate activities.

For the sixth and seventh slot, it usually rotated between Klein the adult worker, Agil the café/bar owner, Chrysheight the busy government agent, and Leafa's real-life friend Recon, according to whoever was free at the moment. Recon was in school, too, but in the Battle for Yggdrasil months ago, Sakuya the sylph leader had taken a shine to his bravery, and he was now permanently stationed in Swilvane as a staff member in her mansion. We could only hang out with him when Aincrad was hovering over sylph territory.

In this case, we were happily able to welcome the archer—more like sniper—Sinon from my time in *GGO*, but that still left one problem with our party arrangement.

We didn't have enough magic. Our only member who regularly used magic skills was Asuna the undine, and because half of her ability was put into the Rapier skill, she had only mastered support and healing spells. Leafa was a magic warrior, too, but all she could use was in-battle obstruction spells and light heals. Silica had some magic skill, too, but she was primarily support, and Liz's specialty was, of course, blacksmithing. A third of Agil's skills were mercantile, and Klein and I were muscle heads who put everything into close combat. Not one of us was any good at attacking spells.

When our seventh slot was filled with either Recon, who played a very odd sylph build of daggers and high-level dark magic, or Chrysheight, whose ice magic attacks commanded even the respect of his racial leader, our attack strategies were much richer and varied. So if there was one weakness in this particular lineup, it was the lack of magical firepower.

But that couldn't be helped—we were transfers from *SAO*, a game of swords without any kind of real magic. My longsword, Asuna's rapier, Liz's battle hammer, Silica's dagger, Klein's katana, Agil's ax, and no doubt Leafa's sword and Sinon's bow were not just simple weapons, but something like our proof of existence. We couldn't just give up on the skills we'd honed and pick up magic. Whether it was inefficient or not, we stuck to our physical-damage-heavy combat style because that was where our pride lay…Until now.

But even then, there were times when we faced a truly sticky situation.

"This is a sticky situation, Big Brother! The golden one has too much physical resistance!" Leafa hissed on my left.

I only had time to nod before the "golden one" lifted up its impossibly huge battle-ax.

"Two seconds to shock wave! One, zero!" called out Yui from atop my head, as loud as her tiny body could muster. At the countdown, the five members in the front and middle rows leaped to either side. The hurtling ax blade and the resulting shock wave passed right where we had formerly stood, blasting against the far wall.

Twenty minutes had passed since we entered Thrymheim, the palace of ice. As Queen Urd said, the density of enemies in the dungeon was much thinner than usual. There were essentially no encounters with ordinary mobs in the hallways. The mid-bosses on each floor were half gone. But the staircase guardians on the way to the next floor were still present, and the unfair, overwhelming power that once drove us off on a previous attempt was still on display.

Still, we somehow managed to defeat the Cyclops-type boss of the first floor that had crushed us before, and we raced through the second floor to the next boss chamber.

What awaited us there was a bull-headed man, a Minotaur-type monster. And not one—two. The one on the right was all black, and the one on the left was all gold. The axes they carried had blades the size of a dinner table.

They didn't use any attack spells, so at first they seemed easier to beat than the icicle-dropping Cyclops, but there was a problem. The black one was incredibly resistant to magic, while the golden one was incredibly resistant to physical damage.

Naturally, we decided to focus our attacks on the black Minotaur to finish him off, then whittle away at the golden one, but the two beasts had a very close personal bond, and whenever we knocked the black one's HP down, the golden one would ignore its aggro hate and rush to protect his partner. In the meantime, the black Minotaur would curl into a ball and use some kind of meditation power to rapidly heal his HP.

After the first time, we considered blasting the golden Minotaur while the black one meditated, but his physical resistance was so high that we could barely put a scratch on him. Meanwhile, we could dodge the insta-kill attacks, but the splash damage of their area effects was tearing huge chunks of HP away from us, and it was clear that Asuna's heals on their own would not hold up over an extended battle.

"Kirito, at this pace I'm going to run out of MP within one hundred and fifty seconds!" Asuna cried from the back. I held out my right-hand sword by way of response.

In these battles of attrition, a healer running out of MP signaled the doom of the party—the dreaded wipe. If at least one person survived, the Remain Lights could be collected and revived one by one, but that took quite a lot of time and effort. And if we wiped out, we'd all start over from the save point in Alne. The problem was whether we had enough time to suffer a setback like that...

Leafa sensed my concerns and whispered, "The medallion's over seventy percent black now. We don't have time to die and try again."

"Got it," I said, and sucked in a deep breath.

If this were the old Aincrad, I'd give an order to retreat. Betting on probabilities there was not an option. But *ALO* was not a game of death. Whether the Cardinal System burned all of Alfheim to the ground or not, our only goal here was to "enjoy the game." Part of that was trusting in the ability of my companions and myself.

"At this rate, there's just one thing we can do!" I shouted, dodging the golden Minotaur's ax and checking on the black one's gauge as it recovered HP toward the rear. "One way or another, we have to beat down the golden one with concentrated sword skills!"

Sword skills: the one feature that truly made *SAO*, *SAO*. When the developers of *ALO* put in the Aincrad update this past May, they also included the old sword-skill system. But there were a few new modifications. One of them was the addition of elemental damage. Now, high-level sword skills inflicted not just physical damage like a normal attack, but one of the magic properties of fire, water, earth, wind, darkness, or light. That should ensure that the physically resistant golden Minotaur would take damage.

This was risky, of course. With the long combination-attack sword skills, there was naturally a long delay period afterward. One direct hit from that battle-ax while immobilized and we would be dead. A wide-range swiping attack would completely obliterate the front and middle rows.

But my companions took that into account and agreed immediately.

"Hell yeah! That's what I've been waitin' for, Kiri-my-boy!" bellowed Klein, holding his katana aloft on the right wing. On the left, Leafa held her longsword at her waist. Behind me, I could sense Liz and Silica assume positions with their mace and dagger.

"Give us bubbles on my count, Silica! Two, one—now!" I shouted, timing the golden Minotaur.

Silica cried, "Pina, Bubble Breath!"

Normally, even a master beast-tamer's orders to a pet were not successful all the time. But I had never once seen Pina ignore an order from Silica. As expected, the little dragon fluttering above her head opened its tiny mouth and blew a rainbow stream of bubbles.

They flew through the air and popped right at the nose of the golden Minotaur as it was about to unleash an ax attack. The magic-weak boss fell under a bewitchment effect—just for a second, but long enough to stop it in its tracks.

"Go!" I screamed.

Every weapon aside from Asuna's glowed and began to fly forth in a variety of colors.

Why had Akihiko Kayaba, creator of the floating castle Aincrad, implemented the system of "unique skills" that veered so far from the normal bounds of the game? I felt as though I still hadn't discovered the full truth of his intent.

If it were just the Holy Sword skill that he kept to himself, that would make sense. As the leader of the Knights of the Blood, strongest guild in the game, and holy paladin whose cross shield had blocked every sword drawn against him, he would have been the greatest and deadliest final boss of any RPG in history, once he'd executed his stunning ninety-fifth-floor role reversal as planned.

That moment would be the very incarnation of the paradox of an MMORPG in which the players wrote the main story. Aincrad was "An INCarnating RADius"—which was supposed to mean "an embodying world." In order to carry out his goal of creating a new world, he had to continue being the almighty paladin—even if that meant relying on the unfair advantages of the Holy Sword, immortality, and system assistance.

But in that case, Holy Sword was the only unique skill the game needed. In an MMO, there was no need for a lone hero to fight the big baddie. Such a hero could not exist. Of course, differences in player skill were inevitable, but there had to be a basic foundation of fairness to prop up the game.

Yet he gave players the Dual Blade skill, as well as several other unique skills, most likely. He must have known that granting powers outside of the rules would tilt the balance of game resources and twist the story the world should have followed. In fact, if I hadn't had Dual Blades when I challenged Heathcliff to a duel for Asuna's right to leave the guild, he would have won without using the system's help. If I hadn't noticed that instant of wrongness, I wouldn't have discovered Heathcliff's identity there on the seventy-fifth floor. But because he gave me that unique skill, the story that he envisioned ended three-quarters of the way through.

On the rare occasion that I used two swords in *ALO*, a little part of my brain always returned to the question: *Why?*

At the same time, there was a tiny twinge of guilt. Of course, I had no regrets about defeating Heathcliff—being *able* to beat him—on the seventy-fifth floor. If I hadn't beaten the game then, the number of victims from his crime would surely have risen. Perhaps people I cared about would have been among them. Perhaps even me.

But I still couldn't eliminate that thought, that wonder if it was really the right decision. Should I have continued climbing to the hundredth floor of Aincrad and fought Heathcliff the demon king there? No, not "should" I have; it was my own desire and personal fixation to do so. It was the worst kind of egotism, and why I always hesitated to use my dual blades in Alfheim.

But at the very least, there were no unique skills in *ALO*. The wise new developers of the game combed through the vast number of sword skills by hand, removing those few with suspicious effects from the system—rumor said it was ten in all.

So I couldn't use my original Dual Blades skills like Double Circular or Starburst Stream anymore. As a matter of fact, I'd 99 percent succeeded at recreating the movements of those skills without the system's assistance, but they were sadly pointless here. Recreating those skills by hand didn't provide the magic effects that I needed to hurt this golden Minotaur.

But using a one-handed sword skill with two swords equipped carried one distinct advantage: something Leafa claimed was "a hundred times worse than using an illegally weighted bamboo shinai."

*   *   *

Pina's bubble breath stopped the golden Minotaur from unleashing a major attack, stunning it for one second. We charged it en masse: me from the front, Klein on the right, Leafa on my left, and Liz and Silica at the far wings.

"Raaaah!"

We all roared, starting the most powerful sword skills we knew. Klein's katana raged with fire, Leafa's longsword flashed and brought gusts of wind, Silica's daggers sprayed droplets as they cut, and Leafa's mace growled with lightning. From the rear came a series of arrows glinting with icy arrowheads, piercing the weak point on the bull's nose.

For my part, I swung the orange-glowing sword in my right hand with all my might. A series of five quick thrusts, then slices down and up, and finally a ferocious overhand swipe: the eight-part longsword skill, Howling Octave. This did 40 percent physical damage, 60 percent flame damage. It was one of the biggest attacks in the one-handed sword arsenal. Naturally, that meant it also had a very long skill delay. However…

"…!!"

With a silent scream, I disconnected my consciousness from the right hand that was about to deliver the final blow. It was like cutting all movement commands from my brain to the AmuSphere for just an instant. My next command was only to my left hand.

The system assistance carried my right hand through its final overhead swing. But at the same time, my left hand pulled its sword back. That blade shone with a brilliant blue glow.

The right-hand sword drove deep into the giant Minotaur's exposed belly. This was the point where the delay would kick in, freezing my avatar. But the parallel left-hand sword skill overwrote that delay. A horizontal swipe leaped out and dug into his right flank.

It was an extremely bizarre sensation to feel the two sides of my body—no, my brain—acting independent of the other. But if I tried to combine them into one, the skill would stop. I let the skill automatically wrap up my right hand and focused only on my left.

The sword, still stuck in the enemy's body, made a ninety-degree rotation. My hand pushed the hilt up, and the sword ripped upward through the Minotaur's stomach. It came loose, then swung downward from the top. This was an effective three-part skill against larger monsters called Savage Fulcrum: half physical, half ice.

Just before my left hand completed that final blow—

I shunted my brain output again.

If I were just a moment too soon or late, the skill would fail, and my avatar would freeze. My window of opportunity was less than a tenth of a second. When I noticed this odd skill combination effect by coincidence three months ago, I underwent a lot of practice I didn't care to think about, but my success rate was still under 50 percent. I started to move my right hand, essentially praying it would work.

"Kh...aah!" I grunted, my blade blazing light blue. It was a vertical slice, a high-low combination, and then a full-power downward chop: the high-speed four-part skill, Vertical Square.

At this point, the total attack number of my combo was at fifteen, close to the highest Dual Blades skills. Because I was choosing attacks with a high knock-back effect, I could keep the foe in a delayed state as long as my attacks kept landing. No need to worry about defense.

As my Vertical Square initiated, the others were recovering from their own delay.

"*Zeryaaaa!*" Klein thundered, and a second wave of attacks assaulted the golden Minotaur. The floor of the dungeon rumbled, and the boss's massive HP gauge began losing large chunks.

Just before the final slice, I attempted another "skill connection," expecting failure for sure this time.

I couldn't just use any old one-handed sword skill. The movement of the non-attacking arm had to match up perfectly with the starting motion of the new skill.

While my right arm was busy with Vertical Square, my left arm stayed folded, drawn up to the shoulder. A simple twist of my body would complete the proper form: sword cradled on the

shoulder, other hand outstretched. The sword in my left hand took on a deep red glow. The rumbling of a jet engine approached from behind and burst my left arm forward at light speed. This was the single-hit heavy attack, Vorpal Strike: three parts physical, three parts flame, four parts darkness.

Zwamm! My blade punctured the enemy's lower belly to the hilt with a tremendous shock. The Minotaur's massive body, five times my height, shot back violently. The second round of team sword skills was finishing up. This time, I was going to suffer a long skill delay with the others.

The golden Minotaur's HP gauge descended toward the left edge of the bar, turning red—and stopped at just 2 percent left.

The bull head with massive horns grinned fiercely. The enemy recovered from its delay first and swung its mammoth ax backward for a horizontal slice. The high-speed rotating swing meant instant death for anyone caught within it. My mind commanded me to flee backward, but my body wouldn't obey. The ax glowed wickedly, and a whirlwind flared from his feet…

"*Yaaaah!*"

A piercing scream erupted. A blue blur shot past my right side. The rapier jabbed five times at eye-blurring speed, the high-level rapier skill with the quickest release, Neutron. The damage, 20 percent physical and 80 percent holy, silently stole the very last of the golden Minotaur's HP before it could swing its ax.

The Deviant God stopped still. Beyond him, the black Minotaur lifted its ax gleefully, its HP fully recovered through meditation. But the next moment, the partner who had been keeping him safe emitted a high-pitched shriek and, with a hard shattering sound, burst into pieces.

…*Huh?* the black Minotaur seemed to be thinking, eyes bulging. Meanwhile, the seven of us had recovered from our delays and turned to this fresh target.

"…Sit your ass down right there, cowboy," Klein warned, grinding his exposed teeth at high speed.

4

When our samurai finished taking out all of his pent-up frustrations on the hapless black Minotaur, he ignored the impressive list of dropped loot as its avatar exploded, and he turned to bellow at me.

"'Ey, Kirito! What the hell was that about?!"

He was referring to the combination of sword skills I pulled off by equipping two one-handed swords, but it would be very exhausting to explain it all from the start, so I put as much honest disgust on my face as I could and grumbled, "...Do I *have* to explain?"

"Bet your ass you do! I've never seen anything like that!"

I pushed Klein's insistent, stubbled face out of my own and reluctantly replied, "It's a non-system skill of mine. Skill Connection."

Liz, Silica, and Sinon murmured in admiring surprise, while Asuna pressed her fingertips to her temple and groaned, "Wow... why do I feel like I just got wicked déjà vu?"

"Just your imagination," I grumbled. I reached over and gave a pat on the back to our healer, whose blazing attack from the back row had saved us in the nick of time. "But there's no time to sit around and relax. How much time do we have left, Leafa?"

"Oh, right."

Leafa loudly sheathed her sword and lifted the medallion hanging about her neck. Even from several steps away, it was clear that the gemstone in it had lost most of its light.

"...At this rate, we might have an hour left, but not two."

"I see. You said this is a four-level dungeon, Yui?"

The little pixie riding on my head promptly answered, "Yes, the third floor is about seventy percent the size of the second, and the fourth is essentially just the boss chamber."

"Thanks."

I reached out and rubbed her tiny head with a finger as I considered the situation.

Right now, on the map of Jotunheim far below, the players undertaking the frost-giant-faction quest would be picking up steam in their extermination of the animal-type Deviant Gods. If anything, the number of players involved would only increase over time, not decrease. Factoring that into account, we'd be lucky to still have a full hour. The final boss—likely King Thrym himself—might take thirty minutes to finish, which meant we had another thirty minutes at best to clear out the third and fourth floors.

If we had a bit more time, I might have entertained the idea of explaining the full situation to the players down on the ground, so they would abandon their quest and help us out, but we didn't have time to go back down there now. I wanted to send messages to friendly leaders like Sakuya and Alicia Rue for backup, but by the time they arranged parties in their distant mountain homes, reached the Alne Highlands, finished the staircase dungeon, and finally reached Jotunheim, it would already be nightfall.

In other words, our only option was for the seven of us to face nearly impossible odds. Otherwise, it was quite possible that Cardinal's automatic quest-generation system already had a massive quest campaign for Ragnarok prepared, in the event that we failed Queen Urd's quest and Thrymheim ascended to destroy Alfheim. If that were true, Cardinal had most certainly inherited the twisted personality of its creator.

But in any case…

"Well, I don't know much about this Deviant God king or whatever, but our only choice is to rush him and win!" Lisbeth shouted, slapping me on the back. The rest of the party chorused in agreement. I had to wonder from where these people got their recklessness.

"Everyone's HP and MP fully recovered? Let's go clean out that third floor, then!"

We all roared again and charged for the icy staircase at the very back of the boss chamber.

As Yui said, the third floor was clearly smaller than the one above. That made sense, as we were descending an inverted pyramid, but that meant the halls were smaller and more crowded. In a normal dungeon crawl, we'd get lost and deal with traps here and there, but I had a navigation pixie who would put any other intelligent nav system to shame.

For this one special occasion, we lifted our ban on Yui reading the map data, so she could offer us the fastest possible route through the floor. All of the puzzles with levels, gears, and foot switches were a breeze when you knew exactly what to do. If any impartial observer had been watching us, they'd assume we were doing a speed run.

Even with two minor boss fights on the way, we reached the third-floor boss in just eighteen minutes. The creature was an extremely unpleasant giant, nearly twice the size of the Cyclops and Minotaurs, with dozens of centipede-like legs on its elongated lower half, but its physical resistance was nothing serious. In exchange, it had whopping attack power, and both Klein and I had our HP in the red several times as we kept pulling aggro. Knowing that if either of us died it was the end of our run, the nine minutes of battle were practically ulcer inducing.

But with the help of Liz, Silica, Sinon, and Pina severing the giant's legs one by one, I was able to use my Skill Connection to do a long combo on the immobilized boss to finish it off. As we headed toward the staircase in the back, ready to barrel onto the fourth floor and pound King Thrym back to Niflheim, one particular feature gave us pause.

It was a cage against the wall, made from narrow icicles.

Beyond the bars of ice that hung from ceiling to floor like stalactites was a humanoid figure. It was not giant-sized. As the person was crumpled on the ground, it was hard to tell, but it seemed to be about Asuna the undine's height.

The prisoner's skin was as white as freshly fallen snow. The long, flowing hair was a deep golden-brown. The bust volume peeking out from the meager cloth covering her body was, not to be politically incorrect, on a class far above all five women present. Crude ice shackles bound her soft limbs as well.

As we stopped still, stunned by this sight, the kidnapped woman lying facedown twitched, then raised her head, rattling blue chains.

Like her hair, her eyes were also golden-brown. Assuming she was a player, her facial features were so finely chiseled that she was either astronomically lucky or astronomically rich enough to keep buying accounts until she got a face this beautiful. On top of that, there was a Scandinavian regality to her beauty that was quite rare for this game.

The woman blinked, long lashes trembling, and said in a frail voice, "Please…free me…from this place…"

The samurai lurched toward the ice cage, but I grabbed him by the back of his bandanna and pulled hard.

"It's a trap."

"That's a trap."

"Totally a trap."

The latter two comments were from Sinon and Liz.

Klein turned back around, his back arched. He scratched his head with a very doubtful look on his face.

"Y-yeah…it's a…trap. Um…I guess?" he mumbled reluctantly. I prompted Yui to explain, and the pixie instantly obliged.

"She's an NPC. She is connected to the same language-engine

module as Urd. But there's one difference. This person has an HP gauge enabled."

Normally, quest NPCs had no need for an HP gauge and couldn't be harmed. The only exceptions were the targets of escort quests, or…

"Absolute trap."

"Definitely a trap."

"I think it's a trap," offered Asuna, Silica, and Leafa in unison.

Klein made a truly bizarre face with his eyebrows hanging, eyes bulging, and mouth puckered. I clapped him on the shoulder.

"Of course, it might not be a trap, but we don't have the leeway for some trial and error right now. We've got to get to Thrym as soon as we can."

"Y…yeah. Of course. Right. For sure."

Klein kept nodding rapidly and tore his gaze away from the cage of ice. But after the group took a few more steps toward the stairs in the back, the voice came again.

"…Please…someone…"

In all honesty, I wanted to help her, too. NPCs weren't just moving objects automatically generated by the game system; they were residents of this world. If we were on a normal quest and we saved her, took her along, then at the climax of the quest story, she turned on us with a "Fwa-ha-ha, you fools!" then that would be part of the fun. But now was not the time to take on needless risks. Klein had to know that.

One of our perfectly synchronized footsteps went sour, scraping on the icy floor.

I turned to see the tall, skinny samurai standing still, his hands clenched, facing downward. A low murmur emerged from his unkempt mouth.

"…It's a trap. I know it's a trap. But…even as a trap, even knowing it's a trap…"

He bolted upright, the liquid pooling in his eyes most definitely not an illusion.

"Even then…I can't just leave her here! Even if…we fail the

quest…and Alne is ruined…saving her here is the right decision, according to my way of life—the samurai code!"

He bolted around and stomped toward the cage of ice. As I watched him go, two conflicting emotions came to my mind.

…*What an idiot.*

And—

You're awesome, Klein!

I would probably never know which of the two was stronger.

Klein called out, "I'll save you now!" to the imprisoned woman, who was propping herself up now. He grabbed the katana at his left side, and in the next moment, his quick-draw sword skill Tsujikaze erupted, severing the icicle bars in one horizontal swipe.

Fortunately, the beautiful woman did not transform into an enormous monster and attack us the moment she was saved.

With four more slices, Klein's katana cut all of the ice shackles loose. The woman looked up and said weakly, "Thank you…fairy swordsman."

"Can you stand? Are you hurt?"

He was fully absorbed in the role, kneeling down and offering his hand to her. Of course, we were in the middle of a VRMMO quest, so personal investment in the story was the point. I myself was in the middle of a desperate quest to help Queen Urd by stopping the plot of King Thrym of the giants, so I couldn't act like Klein's behavior was beyond the pale. He was within his rights. But still…

"Yes…I'm fine," the blond woman insisted, but she faltered as soon as she got to her feet.

He put a chivalrous hand on her back to steady her and asked, "It's a long way to the exit. Can you make it there alone, madam?"

"…"

The beautiful woman looked down, saying nothing.

Put in simple terms, the Cardinal System's automated conversational language engine module was an extremely complex version of a list of patterns: the player says A, the NPC responds

B. With its advanced predictive and learning ability, the engine allowed any NPC calling upon it to have remarkably lifelike—but still artificial—conversations with players.

A breakthrough version of the module that had also gained human emotion and nearly human-level intelligence was riding on my head at this very moment, in the person of Yui the pixie. But the automated-response NPCs were far from Yui's level at present. It was still a night-and-day difference between them and the fixed-response NPCs who only repeated their written lines, but there were still times where they had trouble identifying player speech, which left the players to search for the "proper" question to elicit the answer they wanted.

I suspected at first that the woman's silence was one of these pauses, but to my surprise, before Klein could phrase his question a different way, she looked up and said, "I cannot simply escape from this castle right away. I snuck in here to steal back a relic of our people that King Thrym stole from us, but the third guardian spotted me and imprisoned me. I cannot return until I have the treasure. Will you please take me to Thrym's chamber with you?"

"Uh...um...hmm..."

For some reason, the man who lived by the samurai code mumbled and murmured awkwardly. As we watched from several yards away, Asuna whispered to me, "Something about this doesn't seem right..."

"Yeah," I responded.

Meanwhile, Klein turned away from the woman and gave me a pathetic, pleading look.

"Hey, Kiri, my man..."

"...All right, fine, fine. I guess we're stuck on this story route until the end. And we're not a hundred percent sure it's a trap, I suppose," I said. Klein grinned and turned proudly back to the pretty woman.

"You've got a deal, madam! Diversity makes for strange bedfellows! And now, to face Thrym and rip off his balls!"

"Thank you, Sir Swordsman!" she said, squeezing his left arm. Meanwhile, as the party leader, I saw a window pop up asking if I wanted to include the NPC in the party.

"Don't get your sayings mixed up, or Yui will learn them by accident," I grumbled, and hit the YES button. At the bottom of the list of HP/MP bars for the whole party on the left side of my vision, an eighth gauge appeared.

The woman's name was *Freyja*. The name struck me as familiar for some reason. Both of her numbers were significant, but it was the MP in particular that was astronomical. She had to be a mage type.

If she stays with the party the whole while, that would be really helpful, I thought, glancing at the medallion hanging around Leafa's neck. The many-faceted gemstone was covered with black over 90 percent of its surface. As we predicted before, that left us with maybe half an hour. I sucked in a deep breath to give a speech.

"Based on the construction of the dungeon, we'll probably be heading right into the final boss's chamber once we're down those stairs. He's going to be tougher than the others, but we have no choice but to face him without any tricks. At first we'll focus on defense, until we get a hang of the boss's attack patterns, and I'll give the signal to fight back. And be careful, because his attacks are bound to change when his gauge goes yellow, and then again in the red."

With a look at the rest of the group to make sure they were all on board, I raised my voice and called out, "Let's blaze our way through this final battle!"

"Yeah!"

The third group cheer of this quest was joined in by Yui, Silica's pet Pina, and our blond bombshell NPC, Freyja.

The staircase downward widened partway through, giving way to pillars and decorative sculptures. The old Aincrad adage that the more complex the map data became, the closer you were to the boss chamber, still rang true.

At the very end stood doors of thick ice, carved with two wolves. It was the royal chamber of the king of the frost giants, no doubt. Once we were sure there were no tricks or traps around, we approached, still feeling cautious.

Once we got within fifteen feet of the doors, they automatically swung open. An even deeper chill and indescribable sense of pressure emanated. Asuna began to rebuff the party, and Freyja joined in, including a previously unknown buff that greatly boosted our HP.

When the spot under our HP/MP gauges was lined with buff icons, we all made eye contact. With a nod of purpose, we rushed in together.

The interior of the chamber was vast in both width and height. As before, the walls and floor were blue ice. Candleholders of ice featured eerie, rippling purple flames. A line of chandeliers hung from the distant ceiling. But the first thing to catch our eyes was the brilliant shine of countless lights reflecting along both walls.

Gold. Coins, accessories, swords, armor, shields, sculptures, even furniture, every last piece of it made of gold, piled high in countless amounts. The rear of the chamber was shrouded in darkness, making it impossible to estimate the total amount of treasure present.

"...How many yrd would all of this equal?" murmured Lisbeth, the only player present who actually ran a shop. As for me, all I could think was, *Why didn't I completely clear out my entire inventory for extra space first?!*

At the far right of our stunned group, Klein was driven by his samurai code (I assumed) to take a few uneasy steps toward the mountain of treasure. But before he got more than a few steps—

"...Little bugs, flitting about."

A deep, floor-rumbling voice emerged from the darkness in the back of the chamber.

"I can hear the buzzing of their obnoxious wings. I must crush them before they can get into trouble."

Thud. The floor shook. *Thud, thud.* As the vibrations came closer, I was almost afraid they were going to shatter the ice floor with their power.

Eventually, a shadow emerged into the light's range.

"Giant" wasn't enough to describe it. It was at least twice as tall as the humanoid Deviant Gods prowling the cave floor below, as well as the boss-level Deviant Gods here in the castle. The head was looming so far above us that I didn't even want to guess its height. Even my strongest jump would be lucky to reach the knee of this monster.

His skin was a dull blue, like lead. His arms and legs were covered in black and brown furs from some impossibly large animal. Around his waist was sheet-metal plated armor, each piece the size of a small boat. His torso was bare, but those rippling muscles looked strong enough to deflect any weapon.

A long blue beard draped over his bulging chest. The head sitting atop it all was unclear, shrouded in shadow. But the gold of his crown and the freezing blue of his eyes shone brilliantly in the darkness.

In the old Aincrad, a single floor was capped at just over three hundred feet high, and the boss chambers of each labyrinth tower weren't very tall, so every boss monster had a fairly hard height limit. In other words, I couldn't remember ever looking up this far to see an enemy. How could we fight this monster without being able to fly? The best we could do was prick his shins with our swords.

Meanwhile, the gigantic giant—a redundant description, but the only applicable one—took a step forward and laughed, his voice like a gong.

"Hah...hah...Insects of Alfheim, summoned here by Urd's pleas. Little ones, if you tell me where she is, you may take all you can carry of my gold. What say you?"

From his off-the-charts size, golden crown, and nature of his offer, there was no room to doubt that this was Thrym, king of the frost giants.

As we faced off against the giant, a fellow AI like Urd and Freyja, it was Klein who responded first.

"...Heh! A samurai would rather go hungry than give in to temptation! If you think I'd jump at a pitiful offer like that, you've got another think coming!"

He drew his beloved katana boldly, while the rest of the group sighed behind his back. But as if on signal, the other six of us brandished our weapons.

Although none of them were legendary weapons, they *were* all either unique-named ancient weapons or masterpieces crafted by Lisbeth herself, a master blacksmith. But the sight of them did not remove the grin from King Thrym's whiskered mouth. Of course, to him we might as well have been carrying toothpicks.

With a glare from his dark eyes far above, the king eventually settled upon the barehanded eighth member of our group.

"...Oho. Is that you there, Freyja? Since you are out of your cage, I suspect you must have agreed to be my bride at last?" his cracked bell of a voice tolled.

"B-bride?!" Klein yelped.

"Indeed. This girl was brought into the palace to be my bride, but on the night before the ceremony, I caught her sniffing around my treasure. I placed her in an icy cell for punishment. Hah! Hah!"

Things are getting a bit more complicated; I gotta figure this out...

The blond beauty named Freyja claimed earlier that she had snuck into this castle to take back a treasure that he had stolen from her people. But thinking realistically, it would be nearly impossible to sneak into a floating palace with only one entrance. So she pretended she would be Thrym's bride and passed right through the entrance, then snuck into the royal chamber at night in an attempt to steal the treasure. The guards then spotted her and chained her to that prison cell.

If this was true, it lowered the chance that she would back-stab us in the middle of the fight. But something still didn't add up with the story. It was too complex and tricky for an optional sub-route. And which of the nine fairy races in Alfheim was her "people"? What was the stolen treasure?

I noted that we should have asked these questions when we recruited her to join us, then remembered that we hadn't had the time for that to start with. Meanwhile, at the front left of the group, Leafa pulled my sleeve and whispered, "Big Brother, I think I read about this in a book…The story of Thrym and Freyja…and a stolen treasure. Let's see, how did it go…"

But before Leafa could recall the details, Freyja herself stood up and shouted, "Who would ever be your wife?! Instead, I shall battle you with Sir Swordsman and his companions and take back what was stolen!"

"Nwah-hah-hah. How bold you are. There is good reason your beauty and valor have reached all nine realms, Freyja. But it is the proudest flowers that are most tempting to pick…Once I have crushed these flies, I will enjoy showering you with the love you deserve, nwah-hah-hah-hah," King Thrym intoned, stroking his beard with massive fingers. His threat was toeing the line of acceptable dialogue for an all-ages game, which made me wonder if the quest generator really came up with this scenario.

While all the women present grimaced, Klein stood in front, waving his fist.

"H-h-how *dare* you! You'll never have her! The great Klein will ensure that you never lay a stinking finger on Freyja!!"

"I hear the buzzing of little wings. Perhaps I shall flatten you as a pre-celebration to my conquest of all of Jotunheim…"

The giant king took one rumbling step forward as a tremendously large HP gauge appeared in the upper right of my view. And it was a three-stack. It would take an incredible effort to grind that down.

But the menacing floor bosses of New Aincrad didn't even display HP bars, to break the spirit of those players who challenged them. At least here we could tell how quickly we were grinding him down.

"Here he comes! Listen for Yui's orders, and remember: dodge-only for this first part!" I shouted. Thrym lifted a fist like a giant boulder up to the ceiling—then brought it down swiftly, his skin wreathed in a storm of frost.

The final battle (I hoped) of Castle Thrymheim was, as expected, a fiercer fight than I could ever remember.

King Thrym's first round of attacks comprised of downward punches with both fists, a three-part stomp attack with his right foot, a straight line of ice breath, and a summon of ice dwarf adds, twelve at a time, rising from the floor.

The most troublesome of these were the dwarves, but the stunning accuracy of Sinon's arrows in finding the weak points from the back row cleaned them up in no time. As for the direct attacks, they could be dodged entirely as long as you paid close attention, so with the help of Yui's countdown, the three of us in front were able to continually evade damage.

Once we had our defense down, it was time to go on the attack, but if anything, *this* was the hard part. As I feared, our swords could reach no higher than Thrym's shins, and thanks to his thick fur leggings, they had significant damage resistance, if not as high as the golden Minotaur. I could do a three-part sword skill with perfect timing to get as much HP down as possible, but without going into attacks with longer delays, the damage was piddling. It felt wrong, like I was whacking away fruitlessly at an indestructible game object.

Under these circumstances, Freyja's lightning attacks were a wonderful boon. I needed to apologize to Klein afterward. As an NPC, her ability to coordinate with us was clumsy, but each time the purple bolt of light rained down, Thrym's HP took noticeable damage.

After more than ten minutes of battle, the first gauge was finally depleted, and the king of the giants let out a vicious roar.

"Watch out! His pattern's going to change!" I shouted.

From the side, I could hear Leafa's worried voice whisper, "This is bad, Big Brother. There are only three lights left on the medallion. We've probably got only fifteen minutes."

"..."

Thrym had three bars. But it took us over ten minutes to eliminate one of them. It was going to be a monumental task to knock out the other two within fifteen minutes.

And worse, spamming the Skill Connection trick I used against the golden Minotaur was not likely to work. Afflicting a monster with knock-back required high-damage blows within a combo. Thrym was not weak to either swords or magic, so putting four sword skills together in a row was not going to do major damage, given his vast total of HP.

As if sensing my moment of panic, Thrym suddenly puffed out his chest like a bellows and sucked in a tremendous breath.

The powerful pull of wind dragged the five of us in the front and middle rows toward the giant. This had to be the precursor to a major wide-area attack. The first trick to evading would be to neutralize the suction with wind magic. Realizing this, Leafa held up her left hand and began chanting a spell.

But I had a feeling that it wouldn't be in time unless she started from the moment his tell began.

"Leafa, everyone, defensive positions!"

At my command, Leafa canceled the spell, crossed her arms in front of her, and bent her legs. Everyone else assumed the same position.

Right then, Thrym's mouth emitted a diamond dust across a wide range, not at all like the linear breath attack he'd been using before.

We were enveloped in pale, glowing light. The chill pierced Asuna's buff and seemed to slice my skin. With sharp tingling noises, our five avatars began to freeze solid. I tried to escape, but the thick sheet of ice kept me in place. Leafa, Klein, Liz, Silica (with Pina held tight in her arms), and I were all turned to blue ice sculptures.

At this stage, my HP bar was still full. But that was little relief.

The longer an attack like this took, the worse the damage we would suffer.

Up front, Thrym was gradually lifting his enormous right foot. *Oh no, oh crap, oh shoot*, I screamed to myself.

"Nrrrn!"

He slammed his foot onto the floor with a bellow. The shock wave swallowed up the ice sculptures, rattling tremendously. With a stomach-dropping *craaash!* the ice that covered my body split apart. The shock nearly blinded me. I was thrown to the floor, visual damage effects flashing past.

At the top of my view, five of the eight HP bars shot down into the red at once.

Of course, the three in the back outside the range of Thrym's massive attack were not standing by as the rest of us were immobilized.

Just after we lost about 80 percent of our HP, a gentle blue light shone down, healing our wounds. It was Asuna's high-level full-party healing spell. The spell was perfectly timed, pre-cast so that it went off right after we took damage.

But most of the major healing spells in this game were heals-over-time, meaning they only healed a portion of the total each second and not all at once. If we took another attack now, it could easily wipe us out, even as the heal spell was working on us.

Thrym proceeded forward, ready to deliver the finishing blow as we got to our feet. Suddenly, a series of burning red arrows shot up at the beard covering his throat. They stuck in and burst. That was Exploding Arrows, Sinon's Two-Handed Longbow skill. The one-part physical, nine-parts flame-damage attack was to the frost giant's weakness, and his HP loss was visible.

"Mrrrn!" Thrym roared, changing directions. He was targeting Sinon now. It was usually an elementary mistake when low-defense, high-power attackers in the back earned too much hate with a major attack and pulled a boss's aggro away from the tanks in front, but that was not the case here. Sinon had used herself as bait to give us time to regroup and recover.

"Give us thirty seconds, Sinon!" I shouted, grabbing a healing potion out of my pouch. Nearby, the others were already pouring the red liquid into their mouths. Pina had just barely survived, thanks to her master's guarding skill. Unlike in Aincrad, there were pet resurrection spells here, but they took so long to cast, they were almost useless in battle.

I looked back and forth between the agonizingly slow refueling of my HP and the light blue cait sith barely evading Thrym's ferocious attacks. Sinon was new to *ALO*, but her reflexes were incredible. Since she played a sniper with no defensive skills in *GGO*, she must have built up a lot of experience darting out of the way when close-range attackers honed in on her.

"...Prepare to attack," I commanded my partners, seeing that my HP gauge was finally up to 80 percent. But just as I brandished my swords again and started a countdown, I was interrupted by a surprising voice.

"Sir Swordsman."

It was the eighth member of our party, Freyja, whom I'd assumed was still next to Asuna.

The AI-controlled NPC stared at me with her odd golden-brown eyes and said, "At this rate, we cannot defeat Thrym. Our only hope is the treasure of our people, buried somewhere in this chamber. If I get that back, my true power will return, and I can defeat Thrym."

"T-true power..."

For the span of an entire breath, I couldn't decide what to do.

Then my mind was made. There was no point in being afraid of Freyja using her regained power to join Thrym's side and wipe us out. At this rate, we would enter a battle of attrition and the quest would run out of time, if we didn't get destroyed first. We had to make use of any possibility we could.

"All right. What's the treasure?" I said, just slow enough so the

NPC would recognize my speech. Freyja spread her hands about a foot apart.

"It is a golden hammer, about this size."

"...Huh? A h-hammer?"

"A hammer," she repeated. I stared at her for half a second. Then I noticed that Sinon, trapped in the back right corner of the chamber, finally took some splash damage from one of Thrym's attacks, losing nearly a fifth of her health. I couldn't force her to hold his aggro any longer. I turned to Klein, Leafa, and the rest.

"Go and back her up! I'll catch up with you in no time!"

"You bet!" the samurai responded, then raced off shouting. In seconds, the sound of group battle resumed, and I looked desperately around the vast treasure chamber.

There were piles and piles of shining golden items against the walls of blue ice. And I was supposed to find one little hammer? Sure, finding the hidden item was a classic quest type, but this was like finding a needle in a haystack!

The quest had to have been designed for a raid party of at least thirty members. There was no way to find a single item out of all these without an excess of members like that.

"...Yui," I said, turning a wishful eye to the navigation pixie, but all she did was shake her head.

"It won't work, Papa. Map data don't include the locations of key items. I believe it was probably randomly generated when we entered the room. The only way to determine which one is the key is to give it to Freyja!"

"Great...uhhh..."

I wrung out my brain so hard, steam might as well have shot out of my ears. But this time, no idea was forthcoming. It seemed as though my only hope was to start digging through a nearby pile and hope I hit the jackpot...

Just then, Leafa looked over and shouted from the distant battle.

"Big Brother! Use a lightning-type skill!"

"L-light...?"

I was taken aback for a moment, but the next instant, I swung the sword in my right hand up high.

Since I had only learned the very basics of illusion magic, there was only one way for me to produce lightning damage.

"Seyaaa!"

I launched forward, doing a front flip in the air, and plunged the sword downward as I fell, holding it backhand. It was Lightning Fall, one of the few heavy-hitting area attacks in the One-Handed Sword category: three parts physical, seven parts lightning.

My blade plunged deep into the ground, accompanied by the dry crack of thunder. Purplish sparks raced in every direction from that point. I rose at once and did a quick spin, cutting across all the piles of objects with my eyes…

"…!"

I saw it. Deep in the mountain of gold, a quickly pulsing purple light, answering the call of my blast. I clenched my teeth and raced for the top left corner of the room. With Thrym's massive throne to my right, I dove completely into the mountain of treasure, ripping aside priceless items and hurling them behind me as I went.

"…Is this it?!"

A few seconds later, I reached out to what was one of the less impressive items in the treasure chamber. It was a small hammer with a golden hilt and a platinum head embedded with jewels. The moment I grabbed and lifted it, my avatar sank with a phenomenal weight. I roared and hoisted it up, turning to shout, "Freyja, here!"

And with that built-up momentum, I hurled it overhand. Then I panicked. What if this was interpreted as my attacking a friendly NPC? Fortunately, the curvaceous blonde simply held up a slender hand and caught the deadly heavy hammer with ease.

But the next moment, she crouched down into a ball, most likely due to the weight. Her long, wavy hair fanned out, and the exposed white skin of her back trembled.

…Wait, was that bad? Did I give her the wrong thing?
At that point, I heard Freyja's low-pitched murmur.

"…wing…"

There was a little crackle of electricity in the air.
"…flowing…I am overflowing…"
It struck me as an odd thing for a young, beautiful witch to say. Maybe the Cardinal System's language module made mistakes sometimes? But her voice was off, too. The glazed, husky voice from before was now deeper, cracking.

Bzzp, zapp. The sparks were growing fiercer. Her golden-brown hair rose up into the air, the hem of the thin white dress flapping upward.
"I am overflowing…*with POWERRRRR!!*"
The third scream no longer belonged to the old Freyja in any way. I was beyond a "fishy feeling" at this point and in full-on open-mouthed shock as the muscles of the beautiful woman's limbs and back bulged like ropes. Her white dress exploded into shreds and vanished.

No doubt making use of his secret ability Hyper-Senses, Klein turned away from the battle on the other side of the room at that very moment. When he caught sight of his beloved Freyja's utterly nude form, his eyes bulged. Then his jaw dropped.

I couldn't blame him. As the lightning crackled all over Freyja, she began to grow. Ten feet…fifteen…It wouldn't stop. Now her arms and legs were the size of tree trunks, her bust even brawnier than Thrym's. The hammer in her right hand had grown to match the size of its owner. It was already too large for even a heavy gnome warrior to wield, and it sprayed lightning in all directions.

And then, Klein and I spotted the detail that delivered the greatest, nastiest shock yet.

From the downturned face's rugged cheeks and chin fell a long, *very* long, golden—beard.

"She's…"

"A dude!"

Two male screams echoed on opposite ends of the room.

The captive beauty who had spurred Klein's samurai code into motion was nowhere to be seen now. The new giant with the stunning, rippling muscles looked like nothing other than a bodybuilder in his forties.

"Raaaaahhhhh!"

The giant dude unleashed a roar that rattled the entire chamber. He took a rumbling step toward the distant King Thrym with a thick leather boot that had appeared out of nowhere.

With dread, I looked over to the left to check the eighth name at the bottom of the list of party members, below all the HP and MP bars.

While it had read *Freyja* less than a minute ago, there was now a different name in its place.

Our new companion's name: *Thor*.

5

Even I, with my total lack of mythological knowledge, had heard that name before.

One of the most famous of Norse gods, alongside Odin and the trickster Loki, was Thor, god of thunder. The sight of him swinging a hammer that caused lightning to strike down giants was a visual motif found often enough in movies and games.

From what Leafa told me later, there was indeed a story in Norse mythology about Thor going to take his hammer back from King Thrym of the giants. In the story, Thor is disguised as the goddess Freyja and offers to be Thrym's wife. At the celebration, despite losing his cover several times, his true identity stays hidden through Loki's clever explanations, and when he finally gets his hammer back, he crushes Thrym and all of his giants one by one, a story as comedic as it was brutal. So it was most likely that Cardinal had collected that myth and rearranged it a bit to attach it to the quest as an optional sub-story.

In other words, if someone present actually knew the story, they would have realized as soon as the name appeared that Freyja was not a secret agent of Thrym's. I was still grateful to Klein's honest instincts and samurai code for saving her at the cell—regardless of how he felt after learning of Freyja's true identity.

"Rrrgh...Cowardly giant! You shall now pay for the theft of my precious Mjolnir!"

Thor the god of thunder held up the massive golden hammer in his right hand and charged across the thick floor so hard he seemed likely to break through it.

Thrym the frost king blew into his hands, producing a battle-ax of ice. He swung the weapon and shot back, "Treacherous god, you will rue this deviant lie! I will cut off your beard and send it back to Asgard when I'm done with you!"

Now that I thought about it, Thrym believed that Freyja was a real goddess and was looking forward to their marriage. He might've been the villain, but he had a right to be angry.

In the center of the chamber, the two bearded giants of gold and blue met, golden hammer and icy battle-ax clashing. The impact caused the entire castle to shudder. Meanwhile, the rest of us were still grappling with the shock of Freyja's growth—and sex change. At the back of the room, Sinon finished up her healing and called out to the group.

"Let's all attack while Thor's holding his attention!"

She was absolutely right. There was no guarantee that Thor would be helping us to the very end of the battle. I swung my swords and shouted, "All-out attack! Use all the sword skills you can!"

The seven of us leaped as one, bearing down on Thrym from every direction.

"Nraaaah!"

I felt as though something was sparkling from the ends of Klein's eyes as he charged with his katana overhead and a particularly fierce battle cry, but my warrior's mercy made me pretend not to see it. Ignoring the skill delay, we assaulted Thrym's legs with every sword skill of three or more hits we could. Asuna had switched out her wand for a rapier and was tattooing his Achilles tendon. Next to her, Lisbeth was beating the tip of a toe with her mace.

"Gr...rrgh...!"

Thrym grunted in pain, wobbled, and fell to a knee. A yellow effect was spinning around his crown—he was stunned.

"That's it!" I cried, and we all unleashed our biggest combos. Brilliant flashes of light enveloped his naked torso. From overhead fell a furious rain of orange arrows.

"*Hrrng!* Return to the depths from which you came, giant king!" roared Thor, bringing down his hammer right onto Thrym's head. The crown cracked and flew off, and the boss who had seemed completely untouchable fell face-first onto the ground.

His HP gauge was already gone. His massive limbs and the tip of his beard began to crackle and turn into ice.

The blue light that sparkled in his black eye sockets faded, vanishing. Just then, his tangled whiskers parted and emitted a deep voice.

"Nwa-hah-hah…Enjoy your triumph, little bugs. But you will see…You will regret trusting the Aesir…for they are the true pl—"

Zumm! Thor stomped down powerfully, his foot breaking through the ice giant. An End Flame animation of extraordinary scale erupted, and the frost giant blasted into countless shards of ice. We held our hands up against the pressure of the effect, taking a few steps back. From the heights above, Thor cast us a look with his golden eyes.

"…You have my thanks, fairy warriors. Now I have regained my honor after the shame of losing my treasure. You must have a reward."

He lifted his left hand to brush the hilt of the massive, beautiful hammer in his other hand. One of the gemstones embedded in it came loose, began to glow, and turned into a hammer sized for a human to use.

Thor tossed this golden hammer, a shrunken-down version of the original, to Klein.

"Use Mjolnir, Hammer of Lightning, for your righteous battles. And now—farewell."

The god waved his right hand, and a bolt of pale lightning

erupted throughout the chamber. We reflexively shut our eyes, and when they opened, no one was there. A small dialog box announced that a member had left, and the eighth set of HP/MP bars was gone.

On the spot where Thrym fell, a veritable waterfall of items was dropping and vanishing as they were automatically stored in the party's temporary inventory.

When the rain of loot abated, the light shone brighter in the boss chamber, driving away the darkness. Sadly, the mountain range of golden treasure lining the walls also vanished. On the other hand, I had a feeling that we were all packed to the limit with items and wouldn't have been able to take any of it with us anyway.

"…Phew…"

I walked over to Klein with a little sigh and placed a hand on his shoulder. "Congrats on the legendary weapon."

"…And here I am, without a single point in Hammer skills," the katana swordsman replied, face halfway between laughing and crying, holding the hammer as it glowed with a dazzling aura effect. I gave him a big smile.

"Well, I'm sure Liz would be delighted to have it. Oh, wait, she'll probably melt it down for ingots…"

"Hey! Even I wouldn't be that wasteful!" Lisbeth retorted.

With a straight face, Asuna pointed out, "But Liz, I hear you get an incredible number of orichalcum ingots if you melt down a legendary."

"What, really?"

"H-hey, I haven't said I'm giving it to her yet!" Klein wailed, clutching the hammer. A wave of laughs broke out from the group.

But at that very instant, a roar broke out that shook me to the core, the ice floor rattling and swaying.

"Aaaah!" Silica screamed, her triangle ears down.

Next to her, tail twisted into an S-shape, Sinon shouted, "We're…moving?! No, floating!"

I came to a belated realization.

The palace of Thrymheim was rising bit by bit, shuddering like a living being. But why—No—Unless—

Leafa looked at the medallion around her neck and yelped, "B-Big Brother! The quest is still going!!"

"Wh-what?!" wailed Klein. I shared his feeling. I assumed that beating Thrym, head of the frost giants, would be the end of the quest—but then I recalled the exact words of Urd, queen of the lake, when she gave us the mission.

Infiltrate Thrymheim and draw Excalibur from the plinth. Not "beat Thrym." In other words, that horrendous boss was only a single hurdle along the way...

"The last light is blinking!" Leafa nearly screamed.

Yui responded, "Papa, there's a downward staircase being generated behind the throne!"

"...!!"

No time for a response. I took off running for the royal throne.

It looked like a chair, but as Thrym's personal seat, it was really more like a shack. If it weren't such an emergency, we might have fun trying to see who could climb onto the seat portion, but on this occasion, I just ran around the left side.

Around the back, as Yui said, there was a small staircase leading downward in the ice floor. It was much too small for a frost giant but just large enough for a single human—er, fairy—to pass through. I plunged into the dark opening as the footsteps of my companions drew closer.

My mind worked furiously as I dove down the stairs, skipping three steps at a time. If we failed Urd's quest—meaning that the players down on the ground below succeeded in their slaughter quest—the ice palace of Thrymheim would rise up to the city of Alne above. But Thrym, the very king who sought to invade Alfheim, was no longer around. Maybe he would just come back to life as if nothing had ever happened. But given the Cardinal System's fixation on details, I couldn't imagine it going ahead with such a forceful story progression.

Meanwhile, as if she were reading my mind, Leafa's voice came over my shoulder as we ran down the stairs.

"...Listen, Big Brother. I only remember a few vague details... but I'm pretty sure that in the original Norse myth, Thrym wasn't actually the master of Thrymheim."

"Wait...what?! But the name..."

"Yeah, I know. But in the myth, it was Th...Th..."

While Leafa tried to pronounce the name, Yui must have connected to the outer Net and run a search, because she filled in, "Thjazi. In the myth, it was not actually Thrym who desired the golden apple Urd mentioned, but Thjazi. And within *ALO*, it seems that the NPC actually offering the slaughter quest in question is one Archduke Thjazi, found in the largest castle in Jotunheim."

"...Meaning the replacement was already there from the start..."

So if Thrymheim ascended to Alne, this Thjazi guy would probably come up and assume the throne above as the true last boss. I couldn't help but feel that Cardinal was actually trying to have the city destroyed and the Alne Highlands conquered, but I had no intention of giving up now. Not because I wanted Excalibur that badly but because I owed it to our friend Tonky. And if I happened to get a legendary sword out of the deal, I wasn't going to complain...

Meanwhile, the vibrations running through the castle were getting fiercer. At times there was a palpable shift in speed, making it clear that the palace was carving its way through the soil of Jotunheim. I held my breath and practically fell down the spiral staircase, I was running so fast.

"Papa, the exit is in five seconds!"

"Okay!" I shouted, racing pell-mell for the bright light coming into view.

It was an octahedral space carved into the ice—in other words, like two pyramids placed base to base. Essentially, it was a burial chamber.

The walls were very thin, such that the lower parts of them

offered a clear view of the map of Jotunheim below. Around us was a fall of rocks and crystals coming loose from the ceiling of the cave. The spiral staircase went through the center of the burial chamber and down to the deepest point.

And at the end, a deep, pure gleam of golden light.

It was the very same light I'd seen with Leafa when we first rode Tonky up to escape from Jotunheim, twinkling away at the base of the inverted pyramid of ice. After an entire year, I'd finally come to it.

The staircase ended at last, and the seven of us filed down to form a semicircle around it.

At the center of the circular floor was an ice pedestal about twenty inches to a side. Something small seemed to be trapped in the middle. When I looked closer, I realized it was a fine, soft-looking tree root. Countless delicate little fibers wound around each other, forming one thick root.

But after a point, the two-inch-wide root was cleanly severed. The cause of the cut was a thin, sharp blade detailed with delicate runes—a sword. The shining golden sword stretched straight upward, such that half of it was exposed out of the ice pedestal. It had a finely shaped knuckle guard and a hilt of smooth black leather. A large rainbow gemstone shone on the pommel.

I had once seen a sword exactly like this. In fact, I had held it myself.

The man who treated *ALO* like a tool for his own ambitions had tried to generate it using GM privileges to cut me apart. But those privileges had already transferred to me, so I created the sword instead and tossed it to him so we could finish our fight.

At the time, creating the world's strongest sword with a single command filled me with revulsion. I felt like I could never undo that action unless I someday sought that blade through the proper means. Yes, it might largely have been through coincidence, but the time had finally come.

…Sorry about the wait, I silently told the sword, and took a step forward to grab the hilt of the legendary blade, the Holy Sword Excalibur.

"…!!"

I tugged at it with all of my strength.

But the sword was totally immobile, as if fused with the pedestal—with the very pyramid castle itself. I got a two-handed grip, braced my feet against the ground, and heaved with all of my body.

"Hrng…gah…!!"

The result was the same. A nasty chill trickled down my back.

Unlike *SAO* and *GGO*, numerical stats like strength and agility weren't displayed in *ALO*. The requirements for equipping any weapon or armor were vague, no more detailed than ambiguous stages like "easy to use," to "a little tricky," to "not really under control," to "difficult even to lift." So more than a few players wound up with great weapons that were clearly too heavy for them but, too stubborn to give up, they kept using their over-weight gear and ultimately suffered as a result.

But given that it was a game and there had to be numbers underpinning everything, that meant they were simply hidden stats. Basic values determined by race and body size could be affected and pushed in different directions by skill boosts, magical gear bonuses, support magic, and so on. Looking just at base stats, a salamander like Klein would be a bit higher than a spriggan like me.

But as he used a katana and relied on sharpness and accuracy in his cuts, he leaned toward agility effects with his skills and gear. And since I liked using heavy swords, most of my adjustments affected my strength. As a result, out of the seven of us, I most certainly had the highest strength. Meaning that if I couldn't get the sword to budge, no one else would be able to pull it free. It was so obvious that nobody even offered to try.

Instead there came a voice from behind.

"Keep trying, Kirito!"

It was Asuna. Liz piped up with a "You're almost there!" Instantly, Leafa, Silica, and Klein joined in with their own cheers.

Sinon yelled, "Show me your spirit!" Yui cried, "Come on,

Papa," with as much volume as she could muster, and Pina howled, "Krurururu!"

As I was the one who recruited this party in the first place, I wasn't going to stop now. I had as much statistical buff as I could get, so the rest was down to enthusiasm and willpower. I had to believe that my stats weren't numerically insufficient; I just had to unlock the right amount with force and timing. The only answer was to pull with all of my muscle—all of my mental force of will.

My vision began to fade into white, lights flashed in front of my eyes, and I started to wonder if I'd soon cause the AmuSphere to auto-disconnect me due to abnormal brain patterns, when—

Something *cracked*. I felt a faint vibration in my hands.

"Ah!" someone shouted.

A powerful light began surging through the pedestal at my feet, blotting out my vision with gold.

Next, a crashing deeper and more tremendous than any sound effect I'd ever heard pierced my ears. My body stretched backward, and amid shards of ice that shot in all directions, the sword in my right hand traced a brilliant golden arc in the air.

My six companions reached out to steady me as my body flew backward. I looked up, struggling with the tremendous weight of the sword, and met their downward glances. Their mouths twisted and broke into smiles, ready to unleash raucous cheers—if it weren't for what happened an instant later.

The little tree root was freed from the ice pedestal. It rose up into the air and began to stretch, to grow. The fine little hairs spread downward before my eyes. A fresh growth emerged from the severed end of the root, racing directly upward.

A powerful roar was approaching from above. I looked up to see that something was rushing down through the hole we'd come from, disintegrating the spiral staircase as it went. It was more roots. The roots of the World Tree that were holding Thrymheim in place.

The thick roots tore through the chamber to touch the much smaller one freed from the pedestal. They wound together and fused.

Then, as if all the shaking we'd felt so far was just a precursor, a true shock wave rippled through Thrymheim.

"Wh-whoa! It…it's gonna split apart!" Klein roared, and we all grabbed hold of one another as a million tiny cracks spread through the ice walls around us.

There was a series of earsplitting explosions. Pieces of the thick ice walls as large as a horse carriage broke free left and right, plummeting downward toward the Great Void below.

"Thrymheim itself is collapsing! We must escape, Papa!" Yui bleated overhead. I looked to my right at Asuna, and she looked back.

Together we chorused, "But there's no staircase!"

The spiral staircase we descended into the chamber had just been destroyed without a trace by the onslaught of the massive roots of the World Tree. And even if we raced at top speed back the way we came, the best we could do was return to that open terrace.

"What about clinging to the roots?" Sinon asked, keeping cool despite the chaos. She looked up and shrugged. "Actually…never mind."

The roots affixed into the soil above stretched down halfway through the chamber, but even the little capillary roots closest to the circular disc we were standing on were a good thirty feet away. We couldn't jump that far.

"Hey, World Tree! This isn't very thoughtful of you!" Lisbeth shouted, brandishing a fist upward, but she was talking to a tree. What was it going to do, say sorry?

"Awwright…Time to check out the great Klein's Olympic medal–winning high-jumping skills!"

The samurai hopped to his feet and got a running start—but the circular platform wasn't even twenty feet across.

"No, you idiot, don't—"

But I couldn't stop him. Klein launched himself into a beautiful Fosbury flop of about seven feet high. Given the meager running start he had, it was actually quite impressive, but still far short of the roots. He traced a hard parabola in the air and crashed into the center of the floor.

The shock of that impact—or so we all believed—caused a fresh series of cracks to spider through the walls. The bottom of the chamber, the very bottom tip of Thrymheim, separated from the rest of the palace at last.

"K-Klein, you idiot!" cursed Silica, who hated roller coasters, and seven players, one pixie, and one pet entered free fall atop a small circular cylinder of ice.

If it were a slapstick manga, we could all sit down and enjoy a cup of tea during the scene.

But falling from heights in a VRMMO was actually quite terrifying. Sure, we got to fly among the clouds in Alfheim, but that was thanks to our trusty wings. A player in a flightless situation, such as a dungeon, would get quite the scare from a jump of even fifteen feet. Even I didn't like to do them.

So the seven of us all clung to the circle of ice, screaming for all we were worth.

In the air around us, other massive chunks of ice that came loose at the same time as us were colliding violently and bursting into smaller pieces. Up above, massive Thrymheim seemed to be breaking into pieces, each crack freeing more of the World Tree's roots to swing loose.

At last, I hesitantly peered over the edge of the circle to what lay below.

Three thousand feet below—less than that by now—loomed the surface of Jotunheim, the Great Void yawning wide. The disc we were riding on was heading straight for the center of the hole.

"I wonder what's down there," Sinon wondered.

"M-m-maybe it's like Urd said, and it g-g-goes down to N-Niflheim!" I managed to respond.

"I hope it's not too cold…"

"I-I-I bet it's absolutely f-freezing! It's the h-home of the f-f-frost giants!"

The conversation gave me a bit of willpower at last, so with

Excalibur still clutched in my hands, I turned left to ask Leafa, "H-h-how goes the slaughter q-quest?"

The sylph girl, her ponytail sticking straight upward with the acceleration of the fall, instantly stopped screaming—I suspected she might have been shrieking with delight—and glanced at the medallion around her neck.

"Oh…w-we made it in time, Big Brother! There's still one light left! Oh, good…"

She beamed wholeheartedly, spreading her arms wide to hug me, and I rubbed her head.

Since the World Tree was regaining its former state, that meant that Queen Urd and her kindred would be regaining their power, and the humanoid Deviant Gods would no longer hunt them. That would mean that even if we fell into the Great Void and died partway or plunged all the way down to Niflheim, our sacrifice wouldn't be in vain.

The only worry on my mind was Excalibur, held tight in my hands. The big question was if I could actually earn the right to own the sword if I hadn't yet completed the quest. I probably needed to meet up with Urd alive and ensure that the quest completion switch was flipped.

Behind Leafa's back, I tried to open my window and stash Excalibur inside anyway. As I suspected, the sword resisted my attempt to stick it into the menu.

Hey, I got the sword in my hands legitimately. That's all that matters. If I don't get to keep it, well, this gaudy, golden legendary look isn't really my style to begin with, I told myself, a weak sour-grapes defense.

Suddenly, Leafa pulled back from her grip around my neck.

"…I heard something."

"Huh…?"

I put all of my concentration into listening, but all I heard was the rushing of the wind. The ground level was much closer now. We had maybe sixty seconds at best before we smashed—er, plummeted—into the Void.

"There it was again!" she cried, and managed to carefully stand up on the falling disc.

"H-hey, be caref..." I started to shout, when I heard it.

It sounded like a distant wailing: *Kwooo...*

I looked around with a start. Beyond the falling chunks of ice around us, in the distant southern sky, a small white light was approaching. As it swung closer, I made out a fishlike body, four pairs of wings, and a long nose.

"Tonkyyyyy!" Leafa called, her hands around her mouth. It wailed in response again. That sealed it. It was Tonky, the flying Deviant God who delivered us to the entrance of Thrymheim. Now it seemed all too obvious: He gave us a ride there, so it made sense he would pick us up. If only he would hurry...

"Th-this way, this way!" Liz cried, and Asuna waved, too. Silica timidly looked up from Pina's feathers, where her face had been buried, and Sinon swung her tail in annoyance.

Still sprawled out in the same position that he had landed from his ultra-high-jump, Klein finally looked up, grinned, and gave a thumbs-up.

"Heh heh...I knew this would happen...Knew that guy would come and save us at the last second..."

Liar! I thought furiously, and I suspected everyone else joined me on that one. In fact, we'd all forgotten about him. The dutiful, heroic Deviant God glided closer and closer, with plenty of time to scoop all of us up before we crashed.

Because of all the falling ice around the disc, Tonky couldn't sidle up directly next to us; instead, he pulled into a hover about five yards away. But even a heavily weighted player could make that jump.

Leafa was the first to effortlessly leap over onto Tonky's back, practically humming as she did so. She held out both hands toward us and shouted, "Silica!"

Silica nodded, clutched Pina's legs with both hands, and made an awkward running start before she jumped. Pina was left essentially dangling Silica below her, and she flapped her wings to boost the airborne time. That was a privilege only a tamer with a flying pet could boast. She flew over and landed safely in Leafa's arms.

Next to leap was Lisbeth, with a bold *"Traaah!"* and Asuna following with a graceful long jump. Sinon even showed off with a double spin before landing near Tonky's tail.

Klein looked at me nervously and I waved him onward.

"Awwright, get ready to see my beautiful—" he started, preparing his timing. I whacked him on the back. The jump at the end of his flailing head start was coming up a bit short, but Tonky reached out his trunk and caught Klein in midair.

"Wh-whoaaaa?! Ohmygod!!" he screamed.

I ignored him and looked down below. Beyond the translucent disc of ice, the Great Void threatened to swallow my entire view. I looked forward, started a quick run—then came to a horrifying realization.

I couldn't jump.

Or to be precise, I couldn't jump five yards with the tremendous weight of the Holy Sword Excalibur clenched in my arms. It felt like my boots were biting into the ice just standing here.

Over on Tonky's back, everyone else seemed to pick up on my concern.

"Kirito!" came their impassioned cries. My head downcast, I grappled with a powerful, momentary doubt.

I had two choices—fall to my death holding Excalibur or discard it and live. Was this five-yard gap a test of my greed and fixation as a player, really just a coincidence? Or was it a trap laid by the Cardinal System…?

"Papa…" Yui murmured worriedly above my head. I nodded back.

"…Damn you, Cardinal!" I swore, grimacing.

The next moment, I cast aside the sword in my hand.

Suddenly, my body felt light as a feather. The golden shine glittered as it spun out of my field of view.

I took a short lead, tensed, and leaped, turning around in midair. For all of its weight, Excalibur fell slowly, like a feather fallen from a phoenix's wing, glittering into the endless hole.

The moment I landed backward on Tonky, his eight wings spread wide. I felt myself pressing into his back with deceleration. The creature had been falling with the disc so we would remain level, and now it switched to a hover, stopping our fall.

Asuna came over and patted me on the shoulder. "We can go back and get it sometime."

"I will get a lock on its coordinates!" Yui reassured me.

"Yeah...good idea. I'm sure it'll be waiting for me somewhere in Niflheim," I muttered, ready to say a silent farewell to the world's strongest sword, which I had once held in my hands.

But that was cut short by the blue-haired cait sith who stepped in front of me, pulling her enormous longbow off of her shoulder and nocking a narrow silver arrow.

"Two hundred meters," she muttered, chanting a quick spell. White light wreathed the arrow.

As we watched in disbelief, the archer/sniper Sinon drew her arrow back.

At a forty-five-degree angle, far below the plummeting Excalibur, she let it fly. The arrow shot off, leaving a strange silver line in the air behind it—Retrieving Arrow, a spell common to archers of any race. It essentially stuck an extremely elastic, sticky thread to the arrow. It was a useful spell, allowing you to retrieve arrows that would normally be lost and pulling distant objects within reach, but the thread threw off the arrow's arc, and there was no homing ability, so it was only accurate at close range.

Finally realizing what Sinon was intending, I couldn't help but think, *Even you couldn't...*

Even she couldn't do this. That distance was twice the effective range of the bow Liz crafted for her. And even within range, there were plenty of negative factors: unsteady footing, falling ice, a moving target.

But—but, but, but.

The falling point of golden light and the descending silver thread, as if pulling toward the other, grew closer, closer...

And collided with a little *thack*.

"Hah!"

Sinon yanked on the magic thread connected to her right hand. The golden light abruptly slowed, then came to a stop and began to ascend. The little point of light steadily grew larger and longer, until it resembled a sword again.

Two seconds later, the legendary weapon that I had just given an eternal farewell stuck right into Sinon's palm.

"Wow, it's heavy," the cait sith grunted, using both hands to secure it before turning to the group.

"S…S…S…"

Seven voices chimed in perfect unison.

"Sinon's so freakin' cool!"

She responded to the group's adulation with a twitch of her triangular ears, as her hands were full with the sword, then looked at me last and gave a slight shrug.

"Don't look so pathetic. You can have it."

Apparently I'd had a giant message reading *Give it to me!* in magic marker on my forehead. I looked off in an attempt at innocence, but Sinon grunted, holding out the sword.

I felt a slight bit of déjà vu. Two weeks earlier, Sinon had given me something with the exact same gesture at the end of the battle-royale final round of the Bullet of Bullets tournament in *GGO*.

I had taken it automatically, a plasma grenade that would wipe out all of my HP in one blast, and the two of us had held it between us so we could die together—a bit of an ominous end, I had to admit. I was too scared to look up how the rest of the Net had reacted to that scene.

But this time, the sword wasn't going to explode. I hoped.

"Th…thanks," I said, holding out my hands to accept the sword—which was pulled back at the last second.

"But promise me one thing first."

And with a dazzling smile, the biggest she'd worn since

coming to *ALO*, the blue-haired cait sith dropped a bomb ten times more destructive than that plasma grenade.

"Every time you draw this sword, think of me."

Crackle.

The air went icy cold, and the golden blade Excalibur passed from Sinon's hands to mine. But the virtual sweat running down my back was so vivid, I didn't even feel its unearthly weight.

"Ooh, it's tough being a real playe—"

Klein started to say unhelpfully, but I cut him off with a stomp on his foot and tried to keep my voice as calm as possible.

"…Yes, I will think of you, and be grateful. Thank you. Your aim was simply superb."

"You're welcome," Sinon replied with a saucy wink, then turned and moved in the direction of Tonky's tail. She pulled out a peppermint stem from her quiver, stuck it in her mouth, and sucked on it. Sinon was trying to pull off the super-cool, hotshot sniper aloofness, but I didn't miss the trembling in the tip of her tail. That was the sign she was holding in belly laughter. *She got one over on me!* I groaned, but there was nothing to be done about the suspicious glances from the women now.

To my surprise, the first one to come to my aid this time was Tonky.

"Kwoooo…" he trumpeted, drawing out the sound and powerfully flapping his eight wings to ascend. I looked up and saw what was probably the last and biggest spectacle of the entire quest commencing before my eyes.

Thrymheim palace, jammed deep into the ceiling of the cavernous realm of Jotunheim, was beginning to fall.

The bottom part had crumbled without a trace, but the rest of the structure was still intact. We'd always assumed it was an upside-down pyramid, but there had been an identical mass of the same size hidden above it. In total, Thrymheim was a pyramidal octahedron, just like the chamber that contained Excalibur.

The length of each side was exactly three hundred meters. Which meant the distance from top point to bottom point was the same as the diagonal of a square: 300 times $\sqrt{2}$ made 424.26 meters. The special viewing deck of the Tokyo Skytree was 450 meters high, so it was nearly that size. I was glad that we didn't need to travel *up* through the dungeon before going back down.

As my brain was busy with those pointless calculations, the palace of ice began to fall with a cracking like thunder. As the wind pressure hit it, the ice began to crumble faster. Glacier-size crevasses began to form up and down the structure, breaking it into several large chunks.

"...So we got to go on one little adventure in that dungeon, and now it's gone forever..." Liz murmured. Silica clutched Pina in her arms and chimed in.

"It's a bit of a shame, isn't it? There were plenty of rooms we didn't even go in..."

"Our mapping percentage was only 37.2 percent," Yui added sadly from atop my head.

"Yeah, it's a real waste...But I had a lotta fun," Klein said gravely, hands on his hips. Then he thought of something and swiveled around, and in an odd voice, he asked, "Hey, Leafa. So, erm...that Freyja's still a real goddess somewhere, right? One that ain't that Thor guy in disguise?"

"Yeah, that's right," Leafa said.

He smirked. "Ah, great. So if I go around lookin', I might just meet her someday."

"...Maybe you will."

It was an act of kindness on Leafa's part that she didn't point out that Asgard, realm of the gods, did not exist in *ALO*. I thought back to King Thrym's final words before Thor finished him off for good. He seemed to be saying something about the Aesir being the true...*something*. What was it?

But that fragment of memory was wiped out by the dying wail of Thrymheim, the deafening crash of its utter annihilation at last.

The tremendous icebergs falling through the sky passed so near to Tonky that I practically could have reached out to touch them. They tumbled down into the Great Void below and vanished into endless darkness.

…Actually, that wasn't quite right.

I could see some kind of light at the bottom of the hole. A flash of wavering blue, glimmering just like…water. It was the surface of water.

From the depths of the seemingly endless pit came a different kind of rumbling as a mass of water swelled up higher and higher. The tremendous deluge of ice was swallowed by the liquid, melting and adding to the water level.

"Oh…up above!" Sinon motioned, mint stem still poking out of the corner of her mouth.

Following her lead, I looked upward, to be met by yet another astonishing sight.

With the collapse of Thrymheim, the roots of the World Tree shriveled into the ceiling of Jotunheim were freed at last, thickening and writhing like massive animals. They tangled together and stretched downward, in search of something. It was like a giant had just dropped a mass of wooden stakes. As we watched in silence, the roots reached down into the pure water surface that filled the former Great Void, sending huge concentric waves rippling outward. They spread across the vast lake like a net, until they splashed against its shores.

It was the same sight as Queen Urd had shown us. The roots of the World Tree, now thick enough that they looked like an extension of its massive trunk, finally stopped moving and seemed to be emitting powerful waves of some kind. They felt like pure adulation, the rejoicing of a desert wanderer who arrives at the oasis at last.

"Look…there are buds coming from the roots," Asuna whispered. Indeed, all over the sprawling roots, tiny buds were popping up and sprouting green leaves—though from this distance, it was clear that each were in fact huge trees of their own.

A breeze picked up.

Not the bone-chilling rattle that had always swept through

Jotunheim. A warm, gentle wafting of spring. At the same time, the light filling the realm grew several times brighter. I looked up again to see that the dim crystals embedded into the ceiling of the cave were each shining as powerfully as a tiny sun.

Kissed by the breeze and the light, the snow choking the ground and thick ice covering the brooks and rivers began to melt before our eyes, replaced by fresh green buds on the damp black earth. The Deviant God fortresses and castles here and there were quickly covered in greenery and turned into ruins.

"Kwoooooh..."

Tonky suddenly spread his eight wings and wide ears, lifting his lengthy nose for a long, loud trumpeting.

Seconds later, similar responses echoed back from every direction. Emerging from the springs, rivers, and the massive lake in the center of the world were more jellyphants, like giant dumplings with tentacles. And that wasn't all. Many-legged crocodiles, two-headed leopards—a variety of animal-type Deviant Gods were emerging from the ground and water to roam the land again.

In fact, amid the beautiful greenery, they were no longer "Deviant Gods" at all. They were simply pleasant, gentle inhabitants of the land, soaking in the breeze, the flora, and the sunlight. Even if they were a bit...bigger than most. No matter how hard I looked, there was no sign of any humanoid Deviant Gods to torment them.

Tonky had lowered himself enough that here and there were tiny raid parties visible below, standing still in shock. They had to be absolutely stunned. After hours of frantic work for Archduke Thjazi on his slaughter quest, just before they were about to succeed, their ally giants vanished and the environment around them underwent a dramatic change. No wonder they were shocked.

As Klein had said before we started, we might need to explain what exactly happened to an *MMO Tomorrow* reporter for anyone to understand the full story, but he could fulfill that role and soak in the glory, I decided.

Leafa sat down promptly and began to brush the silky white fur on Tonky's broad back, whispering, "...I'm glad. I'm so glad for you, Tonky. Look at all of those friends. There...and there... and there...All around us."

Even antisocial me had trouble keeping down a rise of emotion at seeing the large tears dripping down her cheeks. Silica joined in and embraced Leafa, heaving with sobs, as Asuna and Liz wiped their eyes. Klein, arms folded, turned away so that no one could see his face, and even Sinon seemed to be blinking rapidly.

Lastly, Yui leaped off of my head and landed on Asuna's shoulder to bury her face into the long blue hair. For some reason, she didn't like my seeing her cry recently. I wondered whom she got that habit from...

And then I heard a voice.

"You have succeeded gloriously."

I faced forward with a start.

Beyond Tonky's large head was a floating figure amid a backdrop of golden light.

It hadn't even been two hours since I last saw it, but the sight was practically nostalgic for me. It was none other than the ten-foot-tall blond bombshell, Urd, queen of the lake, the source of our quest.

But unlike last time, where she was faint and translucent, now she was clearly full-bodied and real. She must have escaped from the spring that she'd been hiding in to keep away from Thrym's grasp. The pearly scales on her limbs, the golden hair that ended in tentacle tips, and the light green robe that covered her body were all glittering in the fresh new light.

Her mysterious turquoise eyes narrowed serenely, Urd spoke again.

"With the removal of Excalibur, blade that cuts all steel and wood, the spirit root severed from Yggdrasil has returned to its mother tree. The tree's blessing fills the land again, and Jotunheim has regained its proper form. This is all thanks to you."

"Aww…shucks. If it weren't for Thor, I doubt we'd have ever beaten Thrym," I mumbled, and Urd nodded.

"I felt the lightning god's power as well. But…be cautious, fairies. The Aesir may be the enemies of the frost giants, but that does not make them your friends…"

"Um…Thrym was trying to say something like that himself. What does that…?" Leafa asked, wiping her tears away as she got to her feet. But the Cardinal System didn't seem to understand the vague question, and Urd silently ignored it, rising slightly.

"My sisters wish to thank you as well."

Urd's right side rippled like water, and a figure emerged.

It was slightly smaller than her older sister—but still tall enough to tower over us. Her hair was blond as well, but a bit shorter than Urd's. Her robe was a deep blue. If Urd's features were "regal," hers were "refined."

"My name is Verdandi. Thank you, fairy warriors. It is like a dream to witness Jotunheim green and verdant once again…" she whispered blissfully. Verdandi waved a willowy hand, and a wave of items and sacks of yrd fell before our eyes, flowing into our temporary item storage. As a party of seven, we had plenty of room, but I was starting to worry about hitting even that limit.

Then, on Urd's left side, a little whirlwind burst into life, bringing with it a third silhouette.

This one was in full armor. Long wings stretched from either side of her helmet and boots. Her blond hair was tied tight, hanging on either side of her beautiful, bold face.

And this third sister had a very striking feature of her own. She was human—er, fairy—sized. Compared to Urd, the eldest, she was not even half as large. Klein's throat made a strange *glumph* sound.

"My name is Skuld! You have my thanks, warriors!"

Her clear, clipped voice rang out, and she swung her arm in turn. There was another treasure-fall of loot. A warning about imminent space shortage began to blink in my message area on the right side of my view.

The two younger sisters backed away, and Urd strode forward again. If she gave us a similar windfall, we would absolutely run out of space. If that happened, the leftover items would be materialized as objects, to pile up on Tonky's back. But, for better or for worse, Urd merely smiled at us.

"And I shall grant you that blade. Be careful not to hurl it into Urd's Spring."

"N-no, I won't," I replied, all childlike obedience.

The legendary blade Excalibur, which I'd been clutching in my hands all this time, vanished. It was now in my inventory, of course. I wasn't childish enough to scream and holler in joy, so I kept my exultation to a single pump of a fist.

The three women floated to a distance and intoned in unison.

"Thank you, fairies. May we meet again."

In the center of my vision, a system message in an exotic font appeared. When the notice that we had completed the quest faded, the three spun around and made to leave.

Before they could go, Klein raced up front and screamed, "S-S-Skuld! How can I get in touch with you?!"

What happened to you and Freyja?! An NPC isn't going to give you her e-mail address!!

Unable to decide whether to hit him with the former or the latter, I froze in place. Only...

My goodness.

The two elder sisters vanished abruptly, but the youngest, Skuld, turned around with what almost looked like an expression of amusement and waved. Something shining flew through the air and landed in Klein's hand.

Then the warrior goddess did indeed disappear, leaving only silence and a faint breeze behind.

Eventually Liz shook her head and muttered, "Klein, at this very moment, you have my utmost respect."

I agreed. I just had to agree.

In any case...

Our grand quest, starting spontaneously on the morning of December 28th, 2025, ended just like that, shortly after noon.

"…Hey, you feel like having a party-slash-year-end celebration?" I suggested.

Looking tired, Asuna smiled back at me and said, "I'm in."

"Me, too!" said Yui on her shoulder, thrusting her tiny hand into the air.

6

I wasn't sure whether to hold our spontaneous celebration in the forest cabin on the twenty-second floor of New Aincrad or in a real-life location.

In *ALO*, we had the absolute participation of Yui, who played a huge role in our success. But for a week starting from the 29th of December, Asuna would be at her family's Kyoto home, so if we missed today, I wouldn't see her again until next year.

Recognizing this, our "daughter," Yui, suggested it be held IRL, and so our year-end party was slated for Dicey Café at three o'clock in the Okachimachi neighborhood. After we waved fare-well to Tonky at the landing of the hanging staircase, we raced up the long stairway to the city of Alne, which was still as lively as when we started the quest—they'd apparently felt some shaking when Thrymheim began ascending. A quick trip to the inn, and we all logged out.

As soon as I woke up on my bed, I called Agil with the story. He grumbled about not having enough food on short notice, but he said he would have his famous spare ribs and baked beans ready by then in ample supply. The man was a model business owner.

The forecast called for snow in the evening, so Suguha and I took the train into the city rather than my motorcycle. We had big luggage to bring this time, so my rickety old 125cc and its cramped trunk wouldn't do.

Tokyo residents like Klein often treated Kawagoe in Saitama Prefecture like the ends of the earth, but if you got on an express train, it took less than an hour to reach Okachimachi. By the time we opened the doors of Dicey Café just after two, only Sinon was there, and she lived practically down the street.

After greeting the owner, who was busy cooking the meal, I got out the hard case I'd brought along. It contained four cameras with moving lenses and a notepad PC control station.

"What is that?" Sinon asked curiously. She and Suguha helped me set up the cameras in four different locations around the room. They were ordinary webcams with onboard mics that we'd upgraded with high-capacity batteries and Wi-Fi connections, so four of them were enough to cover just about all of the small room.

Once all the cameras were talking to the notepad and working properly, I connected to my high-spec desktop back home over the Internet and put on a small headset.

"How is it, Yui?"

"*...I can see. I can see and hear everything, Papa!*" came Yui's clear voice through both the earbud in my ear and the notepad's speaker.

"Okay, try some slow movement."

"*Sure!*" she piped up, and the nearest camera's small lens began to move.

Yui would have a makeshift 3D model of Dicey Café in real time now, which she could fly inside like a pixie. The picture quality was poor and the system slow to react, but compared to the passive view she'd gotten from my cell phone camera before, this was a much more liberating glimpse into the real world for her.

"...I see. So those cameras and mics are kind of like Yui's own inputs...her sensory organs," Sinon said.

It was Suguha, not me, who responded. "Yes. At school, Big Brother's in the mecha...mechaton..."

"Mechatronics," I corrected.

"*That*-nics elective course. He says he built them for class credit, but it's really just for Yui."

"*I keep ordering more features from him!*"

The three of us laughed. I took a sip of caustic ginger ale and argued, "Th-that's not all! If I can shrink the camera down and mount it on a shoulder or head, then we can take the machine anywhere..."

"Yeah, and that's for Yui, too, I'm saying!"

I had no rebuttal to that.

But the "AV Interactive Communications Probe," as we temporarily called it, was far from complete. For Yui to be able to sense the real world just like the virtual world, we needed total autonomous movement of cameras and mics, and we were way short on sensors. Ideally, this automatic terminal would be humanoid in shape. But that was impossible with a mere high school's resources, so I was hoping that some highly aggressive tech company built a beautiful girl robot soon...

While I was lost in my *purely* altruistic daydreams, Asuna, Klein, Liz, and Silica joined the group, and two tables were pushed together to hold all the food and drink. Last came an enormous plate of glistening spare ribs, to thunderous applause for the cook. Agil took off his apron to sit down, and we poured glasses of champagne both real and nonalcoholic.

"To earning Excalibur and Mjolnir! So long, 2025! Cheers!" I toasted briefly, and everyone joined in.

"...You know, I've been wondering," Sinon prompted, sitting in the seat to my right. It was an hour and a half later, and the feast had been totally picked clean. "Why is it Excalibur?"

"Huh? What do you mean?" I asked, not understanding her question. Sinon spun her fork in her fingers and explained.

"Normally in fantasy novels and manga and stuff, we Japanese usually pronounce it more like 'cali*ber*.' Excaliber. But in the game, it's pronounced Excali*bur*."

"Oh, that's what you're talking about."

"Oooh. You read those books, Sinon?" Suguha asked, perking up.

Sinon smiled shyly. "I practically owned the library in middle school. I read a couple books about the legend of King Arthur, but I'm pretty sure they all phoneticized it 'caliber.'"

"Hmm. Maybe the designer who put the item into *ALO* just called it that out of personal taste or a whim…" I offered without any real proof. At my left, Asuna smirked.

"I'm pretty sure that there were several more names in the original legend. Remember how in the quest, there was a fake version called Caliburn? Well, that was one of the real names in that list, I'm pretty sure."

The speaker on the table suddenly piped up with Yui's officious voice.

"The main variations seen most often are Caledfwlch, Caliburnus, Calesvol, Collbrande, Caliburn, and Escalibor, depending on the language."

"Sheesh, there are that many?" I marveled. In that case, the phonetic difference between "caliber" and "calibur" seemed like simple margin of error.

Sinon continued. "Well, it doesn't mean much…It just struck me as interesting, since 'caliber' has a very specific meaning to me."

"Huh? What's that?"

"Caliber is the English word for a bullet's size. My Hecate II is a 'fifty caliber' because its rounds are .50 inches wide. I think the English spelling is different from Excalibur, though."

She paused momentarily, then looked at me.

"…It can also refer to a person's quality of character. That's the source of the saying, 'a man of high caliber.'"

"Ooh, I need to remember that," Suguha noted. Sinon chuckled and said it probably wouldn't come up on any tests.

Meanwhile, on the other side of the table, Lisbeth spoke up at last with a smirk and said, "Then I guess they needed to make sure whoever owned Excalibur had the proper caliber. From what I've heard on the grapevine, a certain someone made quite a killing with a short-term job recently…"

"Urk…"

It was just yesterday that Kikuoka wired me the payment for assisting in the investigation of the Death Gun incident. But I'd already set aside most of it for better parts for Yui's desktop machine and a nanocarbon-fiber shinai for Suguha's kendo, so the remaining amount was already quite depressing.

But if I backed down now, that would only bring my *caliber* into question. I puffed out my chest and announced, "I-I intended to pay for today's party all along, of course."

Cheers erupted from all around, and Klein emitted an earsplitting whistle. As I raised my hand in response to the crowd, I considered something.

If there was one thing I'd learned about human potential throughout my experiences in the three worlds of *SAO*, *ALO*, and *GGO*, it was that "a single man cannot support anything on his own."

In each world, I'd been brought to my knees on many occasions and had only been able to continue walking thanks to the help of others. Today's spontaneous adventure was the perfect example of that.

So I was certain that my caliber—*our* caliber—was only as wide as when the entire group held hands in a circle and stretched as far as we could.

I would not use that golden sword for just my own gain.

With that oath in mind, I reached down for my glass on the table to lead another toast.

The Day of Beginnings

§ 1st Floor of Aincrad
November 2022

Game of death.

It was not a term with a clearly defined meaning. If it meant "a sport with physical risk," that could apply to ultimate fighting, rock climbing, or motorsports. There was probably just one criterion that separated those dangerous sports from a game of death.

In a game of death, fatality was listed in the rules as the penalty for failure.

Not as the result of unintended consequences. *Forced* death, as a punishment for player error, defeat, or breaking of the rules. Murder.

If that was your definition, then the world's first VRMMORPG, *Sword Art Online*, had just turned into a game of death. Not more than twenty minutes ago, the game's creator and ruler, Akihiko Kayaba, had stated as much in undeniable clarity.

If your hit points fell to zero—if you "lost"—he would kill you. If you tried to remove the NerveGear—if you "broke the rules"—he would kill you.

It didn't feel real. It couldn't. Countless questions swam through my mind.

Is that really possible? Is it possible for the NerveGear, a consumer game console for home use, to simply destroy a human being's brain?

And more importantly, why do such a thing at all? I can under-stand taking a player hostage for ransom. But Kayaba doesn't gain anything materially from forcing us to beat the game with our lives on the line. On the contrary, he's lost his standing as a game designer and quantum physicist and descended into being the worst criminal in history.

It made no sense. There was no logical sense.

But on an instinctual level, I did understand.

Everything Kayaba said was truth. The floating castle Aincrad, setting of *SAO*, had gone from a fantasy world full of excitement and wonder to a deadly cage with ten thousand souls trapped inside. What Kayaba said at the end of his tutorial—"this very situation *is* my ultimate goal"—was the truth. The deranged genius had built *SAO*, built the NerveGear itself...to make this game real.

It was my belief in that fact that had me, Level-1 swordsman Kirito, running at top speed.

All alone, through a vast grassland. Leaving my first and only friend here behind.

To ensure my own survival.

Aincrad was built of a hundred thin floors, stacked on top of one another in one mass.

The floors were larger on the bottom and smaller as you went up toward the top, so the entire structure was broadly conical in shape. The first floor was the biggest in the game, at over six miles across. The biggest city on the floor, known as the "main city," was called the Town of Beginnings, and it spread across the southern end in a half circle that was over half a mile wide.

Tall castle walls surrounded the town, preventing monsters from ever attacking. The interior of the town was protected by an "Anti-Criminal Code" that ensured no player could lose a single pixel of their HP, the measure of their true life remaining. Put another way, that meant you were safe if you stayed in the Town of Beginnings, and you could not die.

But the very instant that Akihiko Kayaba finished his welcoming tutorial, I made up my mind to leave the city.

There were several reasons why. I didn't know if the code would continue functioning forever. I wanted to avoid the infighting and distrust that were sure to develop among players. And the MMO gamer instincts that went down to my very core caused me to fixate on leveling up.

In a strange twist of fate, I loved games of death in fiction, and I'd lived vicariously through many in books, comics, and movies from all over the world. The actual subject of the games varied, but they all seemed to share a common theory:

In deadly games, there had to be a tradeoff between safety and liberation. There was no danger to your life if you stayed in the safe area at the very start. But unless you risked danger to proceed forward, you would never be free from there.

Of course, I wasn't possessed by some heroic desire to defeat a hundred floors of bosses and beat the game myself. But I was certain that out of the ten thousand players trapped in the game, at least a thousand were of that ilk. Whether alone or in groups, they would leave town, kill the weaker monsters around them, and begin earning experience points, leveling up, gaining better equipment, and becoming stronger.

That was where the second bit of theory came in.

In a game of death, the players' enemies weren't just the rules, traps, and monsters. Other players could be your enemy. I had never come across one that didn't turn out that way.

In *SAO*, the areas outside of town were PK-enabled. Surely no one would actually kill another player—but sadly, there was no guarantee that no one would succumb to the temptation of threatening that in order to take another's gear and money. Just the thought of a potential enemy with stats and gear completely overshadowing my own made my mouth turn bitter with actual fear and anxiety.

For that reason, I couldn't take the option to rely on the safety offered by town life and abandon the possibility of strengthening myself.

And if I were going to level up, there was no time to waste. I knew that the safest grasslands around the town would soon be jammed full of those players who chose action over safety. *SAO*'s monster pop rate was limited such that only a certain number would spawn over a certain period of time. When the first wave of prey was harvested, players would go bloodshot looking for the next one and be forced to compete with one another over the ones they found.

If I were going to avoid that state and level more efficiently, I would need to move past the "relatively safe" areas into "slightly dangerous" territory.

Of course, if this were a game I was playing for the first time, totally ignorant of what lay around me, that would be suicide. But for special reasons, I knew very well the terrain and monsters of the lower floors of Aincrad, despite this being the game's first official day.

If I left the northwest gate of the Town of Beginnings and cut straight across the open field, through a deep, mazelike forest, there would be a village called Horunka. Though small, it was indeed a safe haven just like the big city, with an inn, weapon store, and item shop; it was an excellent base of operations. There were no monsters in the surrounding forest with dangerous effects like paralysis or equipment destruction, so even playing solo, I was unlikely to meet an accidental death.

I would go from level 1 to level 5 in Horunka. The time was six fifteen in the evening. The fields around me were golden with the evening sun pouring through the outer aperture of Aincrad, and the forest in the distance was gloomy with dusk. Fortunately, even after night, there were no powerful monsters around Horunka. If I continued hunting until after midnight, I would have good enough stats and gear that I could move on to the next settlement by the time other players filled the village.

"…Talk about self-interest…I'm the very model of a solo player, I guess," I mumbled to myself as I sprinted out of the city.

I had to be light and joking about it, because if I didn't, there would be a different kind of bitterness than that of fear: the sour tang of self-loathing.

If only I had that friendly bandana-wearing guy with the cutlass along. At least helping him level up and aiding in his survival might overwrite my guilt somewhat.

But I left Klein, my only friend in Aincrad, back in the Town of Beginnings. Technically, I invited him to come with me to Horunka, but Klein said he couldn't leave behind his guildmates from a previous game.

I could have offered to bring them along. But I didn't. Unlike the boars and caterpillars that even Level-1 players could handle with ease outside the city, the forest ahead was full of more dangerous hornets and carnivorous plants. If you didn't know how to react to their special attacks, you could easily run out of HP... and actually die.

I was afraid of Klein's friends' dying—specifically, of the look he would give me if that happened. I didn't want something bad to happen. I didn't want to be hurt. That selfish desire caused me to abandon the first player to speak to me and invite me to play with him...

"...!!"

Even my self-deprecating line of thought couldn't cover up the true revulsion that swarmed up from my stomach. I clenched my teeth and reached back to grab the sword equipped over my back.

A blue boar popped in the grass just ahead. They were nonaggressive monsters, so I planned to just ignore them and race through the grassland, but a sudden impulse drove me to draw my simple starter sword and unleash the one-hit sword skill Slant on it.

Reacting to being targeted, the boar glared back at me and scratched the ground with its front right hoof: the animation for a charge attack. If I faltered now and stopped the skill, I'd suffer major damage. Both calm and irritated at myself, I stared down the foe and aimed the skill for the back of its neck, the monster's weak point.

My sword glowed a faint sky blue, and with a sharp sound effect, my avatar moved, half automatically. As it did for all sword skills, the system assistance largely helped me do the slashing motion on its own. Careful not to interfere with the timing of the movement, I intentionally sped up my launch foot and right hand to add power to the attack. I once spent nearly ten days in town firing off the skill against a combat dummy to practice that trick.

My Level-1 stats and starter gear were as weak as it got, of course, but with that little power boost and a critical hit on a weak point, the Slant would take the blue hog—officially called a Frenzied Boar—almost all the way down. My slash caught the charging boar fiercely on its mane, boldly knocking the four-foot-long beast backward.

"Greeeeh!"

The creature squealed, bounced on the ground, and stopped unnaturally in midair. *Spaash!* There was a burst of sound and light. The boar emitted a blue light and dispersed into countless tiny polygonal shards.

I didn't even bother to look at the readouts of experience points and dropped ingredient items as I charged right through the cloud of visual effects without slowing. There was no feeling of triumph. I thrust my sword back into the scabbard and ran toward the dark, approaching forest as fast as my agility stat would allow.

I made my way through the forest paths as quickly as I could, careful to avoid the reaction ranges of the monsters within, and made it to the village of Horunka just before the sun disappeared entirely.

Between the homes and shops there were only ten buildings in all, which I scanned quickly from the entrance. All the color cursors that popped into view had the NPC tag on them. I was the first to arrive—which made sense. I pretty much sprinted off without a single word to anyone the moment that Kayaba's "tutorial" speech ended.

First, I headed for the weapon shop facing the cramped center clearing. Before the tutorial, when *SAO* was still a normal game, I had beaten a few monsters with Klein, so I had a number of ingredient items in my inventory. I wasn't the crafting type, so I sold them all to the NPC storekeeper. I then used what little col I had to buy a brown leather half coat with pretty good defense.

I hit the instant-equip button without hesitation. The sturdy leather gear appeared with a brief glowing effect over my white linen starter-shirt and thick gray vest. Bolstered by a feeling of slight relief, I took a glance at the large full mirror on the wall of the shop.

"...It's...me..."

The old shopkeep behind the counter lifted an eyebrow curiously as he polished a dagger sheath, then went back to his work.

The avatar in the mirror, aside from height and gender, was completely different from the old Kirito I'd so painstakingly fashioned.

He was gaunt and thin, without a trace of manliness to his features. Black bangs hung low, and his eyes were black. In fact, they were *dark*. It was my own, real self, recreated in virtual form in startling detail.

The idea of *this* avatar wearing the same flashy metal armor the old Kirito had worn sent a pulse of horrifying rejection through my entire body. Fortunately, even light leather armor in *SAO* provided the necessary defense for a speed-minded swordsman. I couldn't play a tank that attracted all the enemies' attacks, but a tank build was pointless to a solo player anyway.

As long as circumstances permitted, I would continue wearing leather. As plain as possible.

With that in mind, I left the weapon shop. I only upgraded my leather coat, with no shield, and still held my starter sword. Next I raced into the item shop and bought all the healing and antidote potions I could, until my cash balance read zero.

There was a reason I didn't buy a new weapon. The Bronze Sword, the only one-handed sword sold at this village's shop, was more powerful than my starter Small Sword, but it ran out of durability faster and was weak to the corrosive effects of the plant enemies ahead. For hunting larger numbers, my Small Sword was better. But I couldn't rely on the weak blade for long. I left the item shop and sprinted for the house at the very back of the village.

An NPC stirring a pot in the kitchen, the very picture of a village wife, turned to me and said, "Good evening, traveling swordsman; you must be tired. I would offer you food, but I have none right now. All I can give you is a cup of water."

In a loud, clear voice—to make sure the system recognized my statement—I said, "That is fine."

I could have just said "sure" or "yes," but I preferred to play the role a bit more seriously. However, if I'd been more polite and said, "Don't mind me," she would take me at my word literally and not offer anything.

The NPC poured water from a pitcher into an old cup and set it down on the table before me. I sat down in the chair and downed it in one go.

The woman smiled briefly, then turned back to the pot. The fact that *something* was bubbling away in there, yet she claimed she had no food, was a hint. As I waited, eventually the sound of a child coughing came from the closed door to an adjacent room. The woman slumped sadly.

After several more seconds, a golden question mark appeared over her head at last. It was the sign of a quest. I promptly asked, "Is there a problem?"

That was one of the many acceptance phrases for NPC quests. The woman turned slowly toward me, the question mark flashing.

"Traveling swordsman, it is my daughter…"

Her daughter was very sick, so she tried herbs from the market (the contents of the stew) but that did not help, so her only choice was to try a medicine harvested from the ovule of the carnivorous plants in the western forest, but as the plants were dangerous and the flowering ones were rather rare, she couldn't harvest it herself and could you see your way to helping, traveling swordsman, because then she might just part ways with her ancestors' sword, which had been passed down for generations…

I sat and patiently waited out the very long speech, punctuated by various gestures. The quest wouldn't continue unless I listened to the whole thing, and with the way the daughter coughed in the background, it was hard to be rude.

She stopped talking at last, and a task updated on the quest log located on the left side of my vision. I stood and shouted, "Leave it to me!"—unnecessary but another part of the role—and darted out of the house.

Immediately, the little platform in the center clearing chimed the hourly melody that was common to every town in the game. It was seven o'clock.

What was it like in the real world by now? It had to be chaos. As my real body lay on my bed with the NerveGear attached, I was sure either my mother, or sister, or both, were sitting next to me.

What were they feeling now? Shock? Doubt? Fear? Or grief…?

But the fact that I was still alive in Aincrad meant that at the very least, neither of them had tried to rip the NerveGear off. That meant that, for now, they believed—in Akihiko Kayaba's warning and in my eventual return…

In order to leave this game of death alive, someone would need to reach the unfathomable hundredth floor of Aincrad, beat a final boss monster that was impossible to even imagine, and finish the game.

Of course, I didn't entertain the idea that I would do that—not at all. What I should do—what I *could* do—was simply struggle with all my might to survive.

First, I needed to be stronger. While I was on this floor, at the very least, I needed to be able to protect my own life, no matter how many monsters or antagonistic players attacked. I could think about what to do next after that.

"…I'm sorry for worrying you, Mom…I'm sorry, Sugu. I know you hate these VR games, and look what's happened now…"

Even I was surprised by the words that tumbled through my lips. I hadn't called my little sister by that nickname in three years or more.

If...if I got back alive, I'd look her in the face and called her "Sugu" once more.

With that decision made for no real reason, I headed through the village gate and into the eerie night forest.

There was no sky inside Aincrad, only the surface of the next floor up, looming three hundred feet above at all times, so the only way to see the sun directly was during a brief time in the morning and evening. The same rule applied for the moon.

But that didn't mean that it was dark during the day and pitch-black at night. The VR game took advantage of its virtual nature to provide proper sky-based lighting to allow for acceptable eyesight at all times. Even in the forest at night, there was just enough pale light around one's feet to allow you to run without falling.

But that was a separate issue from the psychological creepiness of it all. No matter how cautious you were, there was always that cyclical fear that something might be just behind you. Of course *now* I wished for the security of party members, but it was too late to go back. Both in terms of distance and the game system.

A Level-1 player started off with two skill slots.

I used the first on One-Handed Swords at the very start of the game right after one o'clock, and was planning to think hard about what to use on the other one. But after Kayaba's nightmare opening speech and leaving the Town of Beginnings, the fun of weighing my options was lost.

There were certain invaluable, necessary skills to playing solo. The most important were Search and Hiding. Both greatly increased one's survival, but the former aided in hunting effectiveness, while the latter was slightly less useful in this forest, for certain reasons. So I chose Search first and decided to add Hiding when my next slot opened up.

But both of those skills were not very useful in a party, where the added numbers and eyes provided the safety. So by choosing Search, I had basically locked myself into playing solo. Perhaps I would one day regret that choice, but for now, it was the right one...

As I ran along, I noticed a small color cursor pop into existence. The Search skill increased my detection range, so I couldn't see the owner of the cursor yet. The cursor was red, indicating a monster, but the shade was a bit darker, more of a magenta.

The depth of red was a rough indication of the relative strength of the enemy. Those monsters who were well beyond any reasonable attempt to fight would be a dark crimson, darker than blood. And the monsters so weak you'd hardly get any XP for killing them would be a pale pink that was practically white. An enemy about the same level would appear pure red.

The cursor in my view now was slightly darker than red. The monster's name was Little Nepenthes. For being "little," the ambulatory, carnivorous plant was nearly five feet tall. It was Level 3, which explained why the cursor looked purplish to a Level-1 player.

This was not a foe to be overlooked, but I wasn't going to be cowed, either. A thin yellow border—the sign of a quest target mob—bound the cursor.

I stopped short, made sure there were no other mobs around, then resumed running straight at the Little Nepenthes. Monsters without eyes like this one were basically impossible to hit with a back attack.

I stepped off the path and around an old tree, and it came into view.

As the name suggested, it had a torso like a pitcher plant, supported at the base by a multitude of wriggling, writhing roots. On either side were vines with sharp leaves, and the "mouth" at the top was opening and closing hungrily, dripping sour saliva.

"...No luck," I muttered. Every once in a while, one of these monsters would have a flower blooming on top. The "Little

Nepenthes Ovule" I needed for the quest in Horunka would only drop from those flowering Nepenthes. And the spawn rate for the flowering kind was less than 1 percent.

But if you kept beating the normal Nepenthes, the flower rate would rise. So fighting them wasn't a waste of time. There was just one thing to be wary of.

At the same rate as the flowering type was another rare Nepenthes spawn with a round fruit. That was a trap—if you attacked, it would explode with a tremendous blast and shoot out foul-smelling smoke. The smoke was not poisonous or corrosive, but it would draw distant Nepenthes down upon you. If the area was farmed out, that didn't mean much, but with the forest basically untouched right now, it would spell disaster.

I squinted and made sure the enemy had no fruit, then drew my sword. The Nepenthes noticed me, and the two vines rose up in a display of intimidation.

This mob would swipe with its daggerlike vines and expel a corrosive liquid from its mouth. That was more variety than the blue boars, who simply charged blindly, but compared to humanoid mobs like kobolds and goblins who used sword skills of their own, it was still pretty easy.

And most importantly, it was designed for attack and had weak defense. In the "old" Aincrad, I liked monsters like this. As long as you didn't get hit, you could wipe them out in short time.

"*Shuuuu!*" The carnivorous plant hissed and thrust its right vine forward. I detected its path instantly and leaped to the left, swinging around the side and striking at the connection between its thick stalk and the pitcher—its weak point.

It felt good. The Nepenthes's HP bar dropped nearly 20 percent.

The creature roared again and puffed up its pitcher, the warm-up motion for its corrosive spray. It could cover a good fifteen feet, so just backing up wasn't an option.

Not only would that take down my HP and armor durability quite a bit, the stickiness would impede my movement. But the angle of the spray was narrow, only thirty degrees facing forward. I waited for just the right moment, and when the pitcher stopped expanding, I jumped hard to my right this time.

Bshu! A pale green liquid sprayed out, hissing and steaming when it touched the ground. But not a single drop hit me. When my foot hit the ground, I held up my sword and whacked at the weak spot again. The Nepenthes arched backward with a scream, and yellow visual effects began to spin around it—I had inflicted a stun effect. The idea of a plant being stunned was weird, but I wasn't going to pass up this opportunity by thinking about it.

I drew back my sword, wide to the right. By holding it in place for a moment, a sword skill initiated, and the blade glowed pale blue.

"Raaah!"

With the first battle cry in this fight—since *SAO*'s release, in fact—I leaped forward. It was the single-strike flat slash Horizontal. The only difference between this and Slant was that the latter was diagonal, but this move made it easier to hit the Little Nepenthes's weak point.

The sword skill struck the exposed stalk of the stunned mob, which was just about halfway dead after the previous attacks. Naturally, I had thrown a little extra effort into my forward foot and swinging arm to boost the attack. The shining blade dug into the hard stalk, leaving me with a brief bit of feedback, and then—

Thwack! The pitcher was cut loose from the stalk and flew into the air. The rest of the HP gauge swung to the left, turning red. As it hit zero, the Little Nepenthes's body turned blue and froze. It exploded.

I came to a stop in the follow-up pose of the skill, sword held out in front of me. About twice as much XP flooded in as for beating the boar. The time of battle was about forty seconds. If I maintained that pace, I'd get quite an effective head start.

Naked blade still in hand, I looked around the area. A few more Little Nepenthes cursors popped up at the edge of my detection range. Still no players.

I had to hunt as much as I possibly could before others showed up here. I had to attempt to dry up the whole area's spawn rate myself. It was quite an egotistical idea, but there was no concept more paradoxical than a charitable solo player.

I settled on my target without emotion and resumed running through the deep forest.

In the next fifteen minutes, I dispatched over ten Little Nepenthes.

Sadly, no flowering mobs had appeared yet. In this type of quest, which gamers called "real luck dependent"—meaning they came down to whether you were personally lucky or not—I couldn't remember ever being showered with good fortune.

To my irritation, somewhere out there in the world, there were players who scored ultrarare drops with a success rate less than 0.01% percent, or succeeded in upgrading a weapon ten times in a row, or even managed to get close with a *girl* in the game. There was no way to compete with those lucky SOBs aside from sheer persistence and experimentation. In regards to scoring rare drops, of course—I had no intention of hitting on every girl I saw.

In fact, after Kayaba's godly act of turning all in-game avatars into their owners' actual appearance, I was certain that the number of girls in Aincrad had dropped dramatically. That saved me the trouble of wondering if every girl I saw was secretly a guy, but it had to be a real trial for those players who chose a starting name and gear because they wanted to role-play as a female. For their sake, I hoped that Kayaba had prepared a name-changing item or quest somewhere within the game.

This mental diversion was brought about by a bit of confidence as I finished off my eleventh Nepenthes. Just then, I heard a pleasant fanfare. A golden light shone all around my body. Including the experience I'd earned hunting boars with Klein before the game turned deadly, I had finally reached the threshold for a level-up.

If I were playing in a party, I'd hear a rousing round of "gratz" for the feat. Instead, all I heard was the rustling of the breeze among the leaves as I put the sword back into my sheath. I swiped downward with my right index and middle fingers to bring up the menu window. Over in my status tab, I put one of the three stat points I earned into strength, and the other two into agility. Without magic spells in *SAO*, these were the only two stats I could see, so there wasn't much point contemplating my options. In exchange, there was a great number of battle and crafting skills to choose from, so when I started earning more skill slots, that's where the really big choices would come in.

But for right now, I had to focus on surviving the next hour. I needed to level up until I had built up a good "safety margin" before I could stop and consider the future.

Done with my level-up, I closed the window—and heard two abrupt, dry pops.

"…!!"

I leaped backward and put my hand on my hilt. I'd been so absorbed in my menu that I failed to pay attention to my surroundings—a terrible newbie mistake.

Cursing my own lack of discipline, I assumed battle stance and saw a humanoid monster, one that shouldn't actually spawn in this forest. No…it *was* a human.

And not even an NPC. A player.

It was a man, slightly taller than me. He wore the light leather armor and buckler sold in Horunka. Like mine, his weapon was the Small Sword. But he wasn't holding it. His empty hands were held together in front of him, and his mouth hung open.

Meaning the pops were actually from this man—no, boy— clapping to congratulate me on the level-up.

I let out a little breath and lowered my hand. The boy smiled awkwardly and bowed.

"…S-sorry for startling you. I should have said something first."

"…No, it's my bad…I overreacted. Sorry," I mumbled and put my hands into my pockets for lack of anything else to do with them. The boy's smile widened in relief, his features giving him a first impression of being earnest and serious. He put his right hand up to his right eye for some reason, then realized what he was doing and self-consciously dropped his hand. I guessed he wore glasses in the real world.

"C-congrats on leveling up. That was quick," he said, and I automatically shrugged. I felt awkward, like he'd somehow sensed I was just thinking about *if* I had been in a party at this moment. I shook my head.

"No, it wasn't that fast…If anything, you're pretty quick here, too. I thought I had another two or three hours before anyone arrived at this forest."

"Ha-ha-ha, I thought I was first, too. The road here's pretty tricky to remember."

And with that, I finally came to a belated realization.

He was *just like me.*

Not in terms of weapons or gender. Not in the fact that we were both *SAO* players and prisoners of this game of death.

This boy knew the game like I did. The location of Horunka. The reason not to buy a Bronze Sword. And where the most Little Nepenthes spawned. Meaning…

He was a former beta tester. Just like I was.

Today was November 6th, 2022, the first official day of *Sword Art Online*, the world's first VRMMO. But three months earlier, they'd run an experimental beta test with a thousand players, chosen by lottery.

With a tremendous amount of real luck (or as I thought of it now, bad luck), I was chosen out of the hundreds of thousands of applicants. The test ran all through August. Thanks to my summer vacation, I was able to dive in from morning until night—or in my case, midday to early morning. I ran all over Aincrad when it wasn't a horrible prison, swinging my sword and dying. A lot. Over and over.

Through an unlimited process of trial and error, I gained a massive amount of knowledge and experience.

Little paths and shortcuts not listed on the map. The locations of towns and villages, and the wares on sale there. The prices of weapons and their stats. Where quests were offered and how to beat them. Monster spawn locations, their strengths, their weaknesses.

All of this knowledge was what brought me here alive—to this forest far from the Town of Beginnings. If I were a total newbie who hadn't played the beta, I probably wouldn't even think of leaving the city alone.

And the same could be said of the boy standing a few yards away.

This swordsman, with slightly longer hair than mine, was undoubtedly another beta tester. I could tell that he was totally comfortable in the *SAO* VR engine just from the way he was standing, not to mention his presence here, on the other end of a maze of forest trails.

With all of this deduced over a few seconds, the boy confirmed it all by asking, "You're doing the Forest Elixir quest, too, huh?"

That was the very quest I'd accepted in the woman's home just minutes ago. There was no way to deny it now. I nodded, and he put his hand up to his nonexistent glasses, grinning.

"Anybody using one-handed swords has got to do that quest. Once you get that Anneal Blade as a reward, it'll take you all the way to the third-floor labyrinth."

"…Even if it doesn't look that impressive," I added, and he laughed. When he was done, he paused for a moment, then spoke. It wasn't what I was expecting to hear.

"Since we're both here, want to work on the quest together?"

"Uh…but I thought it was a solo-only quest," I responded automatically. Quests were divided into those that could be finished with a party and those that couldn't, and the Forest Elixir was the latter. Since only a single Little Nepenthes Ovule would drop from a single mob, a party would need to hunt down multiple items to finish as a group.

But the boy seemed to expect that answer. He grinned.

"Yeah, but the flowering kind gets more likely, the more normal ones you kill. It'll be more effective than the two of us working separately."

In theory, he was right. As a solo player, you could only go after solitary monsters, but as a duo, we could handle two at a time. It would shorten the amount of time needed to pick out a proper target, allow us to kill them faster, and increase the probability of coming across a flowered mob as we went.

I was just about to agree with his plan when I stopped my avatar short.

Just over an hour ago, I'd left friendly Klein behind…Did I really have the right to go forming a new party, just after I'd abandoned my first friend here?

But the boy interpreted my hesitation in a different way and quickly added, "I mean, we don't have to form a party. You were here first, so you can get the first key item. If we keep going with the probability boost, I'm sure the second will show up in short order, so you can just go along with me until then…"

"Oh…uh, right…well, if you don't mind…" I said awkwardly. If we formed a party to fight, any key items we earned would go not into our individual inventories but to a temporary shared storage, which would make it possible for him to claim the item and run off. He probably thought I was concerned about that. I hadn't been thinking that far ahead, but it wasn't worth correcting him.

The boy smiled again, walked closer, and held out his hand.

"That's great. Well, here's to working with you. I'm Kopel."

As a fellow beta tester, I might have actually known him back then, but the name wasn't familiar to me.

He could certainly be using a different name now, and the color cursor didn't display his official character name, so it might not even be his real name. I could have used an alias as well. But I wasn't very good at coming up with names; in every online game I played, I always used the same handle, clumsily adapted from my real name. So I wasn't clever enough to come up with another one on the spot.

"…Hiya. I'm Kirito."

Kopel reacted oddly to my introduction.

"Kirito…Wait, have I heard that…?"

It seemed that he knew *of* me in the beta test, if not directly. I sensed incoming danger and immediately interrupted.

"You're thinking of someone else. C'mon, let's hunt. We've got to earn two ovules before the other players catch up."

"Y-yeah…That's right. Let's do this."

And with that, Kopel and I raced off toward a pair of Little Nepenthes clumped together.

Kopel's battle instincts were impressive, just as I'd expected from another tester.

He understood the right range for a sword, the monsters' various tells, and how to use a sword skill. From my perspective, he was a bit too passive and defensive in his style, but given the circumstances, I couldn't blame him. We naturally assumed a pattern of teamwork in which Kopel drew aggro first, and I led an all-out assault on the enemy's weak point. This worked well, and we tore our targets to polygonal shreds one after the other.

The hunt was going smoothly, but the more I thought about it, the odder the situation became.

Kopel and I hadn't shared a single word about the state of *SAO* yet. Was Kayaba's proclamation true? If we died in the game, would we die for real? What would happen to this world we were trapped in…? He had to be thinking about the same questions as I was, yet we never spoke a word about anything other than items and the quest. Yet despite that, our conversation was totally natural, not forced.

Perhaps that was just a sign of what MMO addicts we were. Even in a realm of death without a log-out button, as long as we were in a game, we were going to quest and earn levels. It was pathetic in a way, but considering that Kopel had applied to beta test *SAO*, it should be obvious that like me, he was an online gamer to the bone. We were just able to put our impulse to power up our characters in front of our fear of dying…

No.

That wasn't right.

Both Kopel and I...we just weren't able to face reality yet.

Our brains were busy calculating experience gains, spawn rates, and other numbers, but they weren't considering the big picture. We were avoiding the reality that if our HP reached zero, the NerveGears we were wearing would fry our brains with high-powered microwaves, and the only way for us to escape that was to blindly face forward. You might even say that all the players still hanging out in the Town of Beginnings were reacting to the situation with more clarity than we were.

But if that was the case, then the reason I could face these fearsome monsters with absolute composure was only because I wasn't facing reality. I was only able to avoid the sharp vines and dangerous acids, which were perfectly capable of killing me, because I wasn't feeling the true danger that was present.

The moment I came to this realization, an insight hit my brain.

I was surely going to die...and very soon.

If I didn't understand the first rule of this game, that true death lurked everywhere, then I wasn't seeing the line that I should not cross. I might as well be walking alongside a deadly cliff in pure darkness, trusting luck to keep me alive. In that sense, leaving the town alone and heading into a dark forest with poor visibility was already an extremely reckless move...

A shiver of cold burst through my spine into all of my extremities, hampering my movement.

At that moment, I'd lifted my sword to strike the umpteenth Nepenthes in a row on its weak point. If I held that spot for half a second more, it would hit me with a very painful counterattack.

I came back to my senses and restarted my Horizontal skill, which just barely severed the plant's stalk in the nick of time. The creature exploded and the intangible bits of glass passed through me as they expanded outward.

Fortunately, Kopel was dealing with another Nepenthes with his back to me, so he didn't notice my momentary lapse. Five seconds later, he finished off the monster with a normal attack, exhaled, and turned back to me.

"...They're not popping..."

There was fatigue in his voice now. Over an hour had passed since we started hunting together. Together, we'd killed about a hundred and fifty Nepenthes, but there were still no flowering types.

I worked my shoulders hard, trying to dislodge the chill that still rested between my shoulder blades.

"Maybe they changed the pop rate since the beta...I've heard about other MMOs tweaking drop rates on loot between beta and full release before..."

"It's possible...What should we do? We've gained a couple levels, and our weapons are pretty worn down. Maybe we should go back to—" Kopel started to say, when a faint red light appeared at the foot of a tree not forty feet away.

A number of rough, blocky models were being drawn in midair, combining together and taking shape. It was a familiar sight to me—the process of a monster popping.

As Kopel said, I'd gained a ton of XP from our run of slaughter, and we were both Level 3 now. From what I remembered of the beta, the expected level for beating the first floor was 10, so it was still too early to push onward, but there wasn't much point waiting for a single Nepenthes. The enemy's color cursor was now regular red, not magenta.

"..."

Kopel and I stood in the grass, watching the monster spawn. Within a few seconds, the hundred-and-somethingth Nepenthes of the night took shape and began to walk, vines wriggling. It had a vivid, gleaming green stalk, a carnivorous pitcher with its own individual markings, and on top—shining red in the gloom—an enormous tuliplike flower.

"..."

After several seconds of blank stares, our faces snapped toward each other.

"—!!"

I made a silent scream. We brandished our swords and prepared to leap onto the long-awaited flowering mob like cats stalking a mouse.

But I stopped suddenly, reaching out with my free hand to hold back Kopel as well.

He looked at me in bewilderment, so I held up my index finger, then pointed beyond the flowering Nepenthes as it walked away from us.

It was hard to see among the trees, but farther in that direction was the shadow of another Nepenthes. I'd only noticed it because of the increased level of my Search skill. Kopel didn't have that skill yet; he squinted into the darkness, but after several seconds, noticed it at last.

If it were just a normal Nepenthes hiding behind the flowering one, there would be no reason to hesitate. But of all the odds, the second one also had a large mass bobbing over its large pitcher head.

If that was a flower, too, I was ready to lower my "real bad luck" sign forever. But dangling from the second creature's thin stalk was a round ball about eight inches across—a fruit. It was bulging as if ready to burst at any moment, and if we harmed it in any way, it would instantly rupture and release foul-smelling smoke. That smoke would draw an army of crazed Nepenthes, plunging us into a trap we couldn't escape from, even after leveling up.

What to do?

I wasn't sure. In terms of skill, it was certainly possible that we could defeat the fruit-bearing one without touching the fruit. But it wasn't an absolute guarantee. If there was any risk of death whatsoever, perhaps we should wait for the two Nepenthes to separate a bit before moving in.

But then a rumor I recalled from the beta made me hesitate further. I thought I remembered hearing that if you waited for too long after a flowering Nepenthes popped, it would eventually turn into the exceedingly dangerous fruit model.

It wasn't out of the question. In fact, it sounded quite likely. If we stood here and watched, the petals on the flowering Nepenthes fifty feet away might begin to fall, eventually leaving us with two fruit-bearing monsters on our hands.

"What to do..." I murmured without thinking. The fact that I didn't have an immediate answer was proof that I didn't have that clear line between danger and safety established yet. If I wasn't sure, the reasonable decision was to pull back, but I couldn't even trust my sense of reason at this point.

As I stood there, practically locked in a stun effect, I heard Kopel whisper, "Let's go. I'll grab the fruit one's attention while you take out the flowering one as quick as you can."

Without waiting, he strode off, his starter boots crunching the grass.

"...All right," I answered, following him.

I hadn't gotten over my ambivalence. I just kicked it down the line. But once things went into motion, I had to focus on controlling my sword and avatar. If I couldn't do even that, I really would die.

The flowering plant noticed Kopel's approach first, and it turned around. The edges of the pitcher, grotesquely similar to human lips, opened and hissed, *"Shaaaa!"*

Kopel moved to the right, heading for the fruit-bearing Nepenthes in the back, but the flower stayed on him. I approached it from behind and raised my sword, my mind empty.

Despite being a rare variant that appeared less than 1 percent of the time, the flowering Nepenthes had basically the same stats as the normal kind. Its defense and attack were slightly higher, but now that I was Level 3, that difference was negligible.

While my brain raced with questions, the physical instincts I'd built since the beta test moved my avatar automatically, dodging and parrying the Nepenthes's vine attacks, then countering. In ten seconds, its HP bar was yellow. I jumped back and prepared the finishing sword skill.

All that battle had raised my One-Handed Sword skill, and I could feel the initiation speed and range of the attacks increasing. Before the Nepenthes could even half inflate its pitcher to spit acid, my Horizontal skill cut across with a blue line of light, severing the stalk.

It let out a scream that was a bit different from the usual kind. The severed pitcher rolled to the ground and burst into little polygons—but not before the flower on its head fell off.

A faintly glowing orb about the size of a fist rolled out and toward my feet, coming to stop against my boot toe just as the monster's torso and mouth shattered.

I crouched down and scooped up the glowing Little Nepenthes Ovule. I'd killed about a hundred and fifty of the monsters just to gain this item, grappling with many questions along the way.

It was enough to make me want to fall to my butt in the grass, but I couldn't relax yet. A short distance away, Kopel was doing me the favor of distracting the dangerous fruit-bearing Nepenthes, and I needed to help him.

"Sorry for the wait!" I shouted, looking up. I dropped the ovule into my belt pouch—I'd feel better having it stored safely in my inventory, but I didn't have time to perform all those actions now. I held up my sword and ran several steps—

But my feet stopped for some reason.

Even I didn't know why. Up ahead, my temporary partner Kopel was avoiding attack nimbly with sword and buckler. He was good at defense, because he was able to glance over at me now and then, even in the midst of battle. Those earnest, narrow eyes, staring at me. That stare.

Something in that stare stopped my feet.

What was it? Why would Kopel look at me like that? Doubting, perhaps pitying.

He deflected a vine attack with his buckler and broke away from the fight, glanced quickly at me, and said, "Sorry, Kirito."

Then he turned to the monster and held his sword high over his head. The blade started glowing blue. He was starting a sword skill—the motion for the overhead slice attack, Vertical.

"Wait…that's not going to work…" I said automatically, while my mind still puzzled over what he'd just said to me.

The weak stalk of the Little Nepenthes was hidden beneath its prey-trapping pitcher, so vertical attacks were minimally effective. And Kopel had a very clear reason not to use a vertical slice now. He must know that.

But once a sword skill started, it wouldn't stop. With the system behind the wheel, his avatar leaped forward on autopilot and drove the glowing sword downward upon the Nepenthes's pitcher—and the bobbing fruit hanging above it.

Powww!

The forest shook with a tremendous blast.

It was the second time I'd heard that sound. The first was in the beta test, of course. One of the temporary party members at the time had accidentally struck it with a spear, and a swarm of Nepenthes descended on us. The *four* of us, all levels 2 or 3, died before we could escape.

After smashing the fruit with a Vertical, Kopel quickly sliced the Nepenthes's pitcher loose, killing it. The monster promptly blew up, but the green gas hanging in the air and the stench in my nostrils did not go away.

As Kopel leaped away from the smoke, I mumbled, dumbfounded, "Wh...why...?"

It wasn't an accident. It was intentional. Kopel hit the fruit of his own volition to make it explode.

The beta tester who had worked with me for the last hour did not look me in the face.

"...Sorry."

I saw a number of color cursors appear on the other side of him.

To the right. To the left. Behind us. They were all Little Nepenthes, summoned by the smoke. It had to be every single individual currently present in the area. There were at least twenty of them... no, thirty. The moment I recognized that it was pointless to fight, my legs started to run, but that in itself was pointless. Even if I broke free of the net, the Nepenthes' max speed was much higher than you'd imagine from their appearance, and another monster would just target me before I could break free. Escape was impossible...

Was it suicide?

Was he planning to die here and take me down with him? Had the threat of true death driven this man to try resigning from the game altogether?

It was all I could think about as I stood stock-still.

But my guess was incorrect.

Kopel put his sword back into the scabbard on his left side, not looking at me anymore, and started running into the nearby brush. His stride was steady, full of intent. He hadn't given up on life. But...

"It's pointless..." I said, all air and no voice.

The swarm of Little Nepenthes was coming in from every direction. It would be difficult to slip through them or fight your way out, and even if you succeeded, another foe would just hold you back. In fact, if he was going to run, why would Kopel use Vertical on it at all? Was he planning to die, then got frightened by the swarm and decided to make one last struggle?

As my half-numb brain tried to grapple with all this, I watched Kopel leap into a small overgrowth of brush. His avatar was covered by the thick leaves, but his color cursor...

Disappeared. He wasn't more than seventy feet away, but his cursor vanished from view. For a moment, I wondered if he'd used a teleport crystal, but that was impossible. They were incredibly expensive, unaffordable at this stage, and they weren't sold on the first floor or dropped by any monsters here.

Which left just one answer. It was the effect of the Hiding skill. His cursor disappeared from the view of players, and he no longer attracted the attention of monsters. Kopel's second skill slot wasn't open; he used it on the Hiding skill. That was how he snuck up on me before our first meeting without me detecting him...

As the mass of monsters thundered closer and closer, I finally—and very belatedly—realized the truth.

Kopel wasn't attempting suicide or fleeing in fear.

He was trying to kill me.

That was why he struck the fruit and drew all those Nepenthes here: He could use his Hiding skill to escape the danger. All thirty-plus monsters would be left to concentrate solely on me. It was an orthodox trick, an MPK—monster player kill.

Knowing that made his motive much clearer: to steal my gear and the Little Nepenthes Ovule I put in my pouch. If I died, all items I had equipped or in my pouch dropped on the spot. Once the swarm of Nepenthes left, he could scoop up the ovule, return to the village, and complete the quest.

"…I see…" I mumbled. Meanwhile, the beasts themselves were finally coming into view.

Kopel, you weren't hiding from the reality of the situation. Just the opposite. You recognized this game of death and took your place as a player. You decided to lie, cheat, and steal your way to survival.

Strangely, I felt no anger or enmity toward him.

My mind was strangely calm, despite being put in a deadly trap. Perhaps that was partially because I'd already recognized a hole in Kopel's plan.

"Kopel…I'm guessing you didn't know," I said to the brush, though I had no way to tell if he could hear me or not. "It's your first time taking Hiding, right? It's a useful skill, but it's not all-powerful. The thing is, it doesn't work very well on monsters who rely on *senses other than sight.* Such as the Little Nepenthes."

Part of the hissing horde coming down on us like an avalanche was clearly heading for Kopel's hiding spot. By now, he had to be realizing that his Hiding attempt wasn't working. This was the exact reason that I chose Search first.

Still calm, I spun around and stared down the charging line of plants. The ones behind me would attack Kopel, so I didn't need to concern myself with them for now. If I could wipe out the enemies ahead before the battle behind me finished, I might have a chance at escape. Even if that chance was a hundredth of 1 percent.

I gripped my Small Sword, still not recognizing the full reality of the situation, despite death bearing down on me. After over a hundred battles, the sword was considerably worn, the blade chipped here and there. If I was too rough, it might even break in this fight.

I would keep the number of attacks to a minimum. I would only use Horizontal, boosted by my movements, so that I hit each enemy on its weak point and killed it in one hit. If I couldn't manage that, I was sure to end up dying due to a broken weapon, a truly miserable end.

Behind me, I heard monster roars, the clashing of attacks, and Kopel screaming something.

But I didn't pay attention. Every one of my nerves was fixed on the enemies ahead.

What happened over the next few minutes—it couldn't have been more than ten—I couldn't fully remember afterward.

I lost all higher thinking. All that existed was the enemy before me, my sword, and the body swinging it—the movement signals my brain was emitting.

I tracked the monsters' trajectories, evaded with minimal movement, and countered with my sword skill. It was the same thing I'd done in every other battle, only executed with perfect precision.

There were no auto-homing magic attacks in *SAO*. So theoretically, if a player had good-enough decision-making and response time, he could evade every single attack. But I wasn't that skilled of a player, and there were too many enemies, so I couldn't dodge everything. The vines coming from all directions nicked my limbs, and the deluges of corrosive spit put holes in my new leather coat. Each hit took down my HP bar, bringing virtual and real death one step closer.

But I dodged all the direct hits just in time and kept swinging my sword.

If I got knocked into a delay of even half a second by a direct hit, I would be battered about continuously until I died. Either they would eventually whittle my HP down to zero first or they'd knock me still and wipe me out in an instant.

I'd been in this kind of desperate situation countless times in the beta test, and in all the other MMOs I'd played before this. Each time, after a brief struggle, I'd let my HP drain away, grumbling about the experience penalty or hoping I didn't lose my weapon.

If I really wanted a taste of reality here, I should try that now. At least then I'd find out if Kayaba was telling the truth or just playing a very nasty, tasteless prank.

I thought I heard a little voice whispering that suggestion into my ear. But I ignored it, continuing to use Slant and Horizontal on the endless stream of Nepenthes.

Because I didn't want to die? Of course I didn't.

But there was another motive that drove me to fight, something different. Something that twisted my mouth into a fierce grimace—or even a smile.

This is it.

This was *SAO.* I spent at least two hundred hours diving into the beta test, but I never saw the true nature of the game. I wasn't fighting in the true sense.

My sword wasn't an item of the weapon classification, and my body wasn't simply a movable object. There was a place you could reach only when those things were combined with the mind when in a situation of extremes. I had only glimpsed the entrance to that world from a distance. I wanted to know what came next. I wanted to go further.

"Ruaaaahhhh!!"

I howled, leaped.

The Horizontal even outstripped the light, blasting two consecutive Nepenthes' pitchers skyward.

Then, from far behind me, I heard a sharp, nasty crash, a brief blasting apart of a body.

It was not anything like the sound of a monster exploding. It was the death sound of a player.

Beset upon by at least a dozen of the monsters, Kopel had finally perished.

"...!!"

I just barely stopped myself from turning to look, and made sure to quickly finish the last two in my vicinity.

Only then did I turn around.

Having finished off their first target, the Nepenthes were looking at me with bloodthirsty interest. There were seven of them. Kopel must have killed at least five of them. I was certain that the lack of a scream from him was a sign of his beta-tester pride.

"...GG," I said, the standard compliment for a player of a game well played, and I held my sword out. Perhaps escape *was* an option by then, but the thought didn't even enter into my head.

Among the seven Nepenthes bearing down on me, of all the irony, one of them had a bright red flower blooming atop its carnivorous pitcher.

If Kopel had kept working hard, rather than trying to MPK me, he could have soon earned his own ovule. But that lesson was lost on him. Choice and result: that was all there was.

My HP bar was under 40 percent and would soon fall into the red, but I no longer felt sure I was going to die. Sensing that the two on the right were about to enter the spitting animation, I raced toward them and dispatched them both at once while they were charging their attacks.

Over the next twenty-five seconds, I finished off the other five, bringing the battle to an end.

In the spot where Kopel vanished, I saw his Small Sword and buckler. They were both about as ragged as my gear.

He fought for several hours in the floating castle Aincrad, then died. Technically, his HP dropped to zero, and his avatar disintegrated. But there was no way for me to know if, somewhere in Japan, lying down on his bed, the player controlling that avatar was truly dead or not. All I could do was see off the warrior named Kopel.

I thought for a moment, then picked up the sword and stuck it into the base of the biggest tree around. Then I picked up the

ovule from the second flowering plant and laid it next to the weapon.

"It's yours, Kopel."

I got to my feet. The durability of the abandoned items would slowly tick away and they would disappear, but for at least a few hours they would serve as a grave marker here. I turned on my heel and started toward the path to the east that would take me back to the village.

I'd been tricked, nearly died, witnessed the end of the one who tricked me, and somehow just barely survived, but my sense of the "reality" of the game of death was still hazy. At the very least, my desire to be stronger had grown somewhat since before. Not to leave the game alive, but the secret, shameful desire to know the ultimate pinnacle of sword battle in *SAO*.

Our long hunting trip must have really dried up the spawn rate, as I made it back to Horunka without encountering a single monster along the way.

It was nine o'clock. Three hours had passed since Kayaba's tutorial.

By this time, there were a few players in the clearing of the village. They were probably former testers, too. At this rate, if all the testers kept moving forward, it would lead to a major rift between them and the vast majority of inexperienced players… but it wasn't really my place to worry about that.

I didn't feel like talking to anyone, so before any players could notice me, I headed down the back path to the end of the village. Fortunately, the NPC hadn't yet entered her late-night activity pattern—there was still orange light in the window of the house.

I gave the nonfunctional knocker a little rap, then opened the door. There was the mother, still boiling something at the window. There was a golden exclamation point over her head that indicated an in-progress quest.

I walked over and took the Little Nepenthes Ovule out of my waistpouch, the center of the orb still glowing a faint green.

She broke out into a smile that immediately took twenty years off of her age, and she accepted the ovule. As she fired off thanks after thanks, my quest log updated on the left side of my view.

The now-young mother dropped the ovule into the pot, then walked to a large chest on the south end of the room and opened the lid. From inside she pulled out a faded, but clearly more impressive longsword in a red scabbard. She returned to me, and with another bow of thanks, presented the sword with both hands.

"...Thank you," I said simply, taking the weapon. I felt its weight press down against my right hand. It felt about half as heavy as the Small Sword. I'd used this Anneal Blade quite a lot in the beta test, and it would take some time to get comfortable with it again.

A message floated up informing me I'd completed the quest, and the bonus XP from that feat pushed me into level 4.

The old me would have leaped up and out of the village to challenge the Large Nepenthes found farther into the western woods to test out my new blade.

But I no longer had the motivation for that. I stored the new weapon in my inventory and slumped into a nearby chair. The quest was over, so the young mother would no longer bother to offer me water. She turned her back on me, stirring away at the pot.

A fresh wave of exhaustion flooded through me, and I gazed at her as she busied herself. How many minutes passed with us doing just that? But as I watched, she took a wooden cup off the shelf and scooped a ladleful of the pot's contents into it.

Carrying the steaming cup even more carefully than the sword earlier, she walked toward the door in the back. Without much reason, I stood up and followed her. The NPC opened the door and proceeded into a dimly lit room. I was pretty sure I remembered trying to open the door myself in the beta, and it had been locked by the system. Hesitantly, I crossed the threshold.

It was a small bedroom. The only furniture was a set of drawers against the wall, a bed near the window, and a small chair.

Lying on the bed was a little girl, about seven or eight years old.

Even in the light of the moon, I could tell she was sickly. Her neck was scrawny, and the shoulders poking out above the bedsheet were bony.

The girl's eyelids fluttered open when she sensed her mother's presence, and then she looked at me. I stopped still, surprised, and then her pale lips rose in a tiny smile.

The mother reached out and helped her sit up, holding a hand to her back. Suddenly, the girl tensed and coughed. Her brown braid ran limp down the back of her white negligee.

I checked the color cursor for the girl again. Sure enough, it had the NPC tag right on it. Her name was Agatha.

Agatha's mother rubbed her back gently and sat down in the bedside chair.

"Look, Agatha. The traveling swordsman brought this medicine from the forest. If you drink this, I'm sure you'll feel better."

She held up the cup with her other hand and gave it to the girl.

"...Okay," Agatha said in a cute, high-pitched voice. She held up the cup with both hands and drank it, gulp by gulp.

No, there was no golden light that shone down from the heavens, color didn't immediately return to her face, and she didn't leap to her feet and run around the room. But if it wasn't my imagination, I thought Agatha's cheeks were a bit rosier than before when she lowered the cup.

She gave the empty cup back to her mother, then looked at me again and grinned. Her lips moved, and she lisped a few words, like tiny little jewels.

"Thank you, Big Bwudda."

"...Ah..."

I gasped, unable to come up with a different response, my eyes wide.

In the past—*long, long* in the past, I remembered a similar experience.

My sister, Suguha, was bedridden with a cold. Our father was overseas for work, as usual, and our mother had to go to work for a little bit, so I was in charge of watching over her for two hours. At the time, I was…some grade in elementary school. Honestly, I'd been annoyed by the whole thing, but I couldn't just leave her behind and play, so I wiped away Suguha's sweat and changed out the cooling pack for her forehead.

To my surprise, she suddenly asked for ginger tea.

I had to call Mom to ask how to make that. All I needed to do was put ginger juice and honey into hot water—it was even easier than cooking in Aincrad. But for a kid with no cooking experience, it was a challenge. Despite nearly slicing up my fingers on the grater, I managed to put together a cup of ginger tea and bring it to her. Instead of her usual insults, she looked at me with a blissful expression, and—

"…Ung…kh…"

I couldn't keep the sound from escaping my throat.

I wanted to see them.

I wanted to see Suguha, Mom, and Dad.

The overwhelming impulse rocked my avatar, and I faltered, putting my hands on Agatha's bed. I lowered my knees to the floor, squeezed my white shirt, and sobbed again.

I wanted to see them. But that wasn't allowed. The electric field from the NerveGear cut off my conscious mind from the real world and trapped me in this place.

Using every ounce of willpower to hold in the sobs threatening to rip free of my throat, I felt like I finally understood the "truth" of this world.

It wasn't about dying or living. There was no way for me to "earn" a real understanding of death here to begin with. Because in the real world, a place where death was just as permanent as here, I'd never been close enough to death to know.

No, it was the fact that this was an alternate world. That I couldn't see the people I wanted to see. That was the one truth. The reality of this world.

I buried my face in the sheets, gritted my teeth, and trembled violently. There were no tears. Perhaps there were tears falling on my real cheeks, as I lay on my bed back home in the real world. Perhaps they were in view of Suguha, watching over me in person.

"...Wut's wong, Big Bwudda?"

A soft hand touched my head.

Eventually, it started to clumsily caress my hair. Over and over.

Until the moment my crying ended, the little hand never stopped moving.

(The End)

AFTERWORD

Hello, this is Reki Kawahara. Thank you for reading *Sword Art Online 8: Early and Late*.

This is my first short story collection since Volume 2. As the title suggests, it covers from the latest story of *SAO* (technically, the story in *Mother's Rosario* happens a week later) all the way back to the earliest (again, technically the first chapter of Volume 1 begins an hour earlier, ha-ha).

As those of you reading ever since the first volume (or before that, from my web version), the story of *SAO* jumps ahead after the very start and covers only the three weeks before *Sword Art Online* was beaten, a full two years after it began. After that, I wrote the four short stories in Volume 2 to fill in some of the gaps of the past. But as a matter of fact, when Dengeki Bunko offered to publish them in book form, I was faced with a real dilemma. I wondered if it would be better not to simply publish my web version in book form but to take all the material of the first two volumes and rearrange it into a full story, filling in more blanks as I went, to thoroughly explore the game of death from start to finish.

Obviously, I only considered that idea and never went with it (mostly because I was terrified of how much fresh writing I'd need to do to fill it all out), but in truth, the image of Kirito immediately after leaving Klein behind in the Town of Beginnings always stuck in the back of my mind. When the beater chose the quickest route to personal strength, what was he thinking and feeling? My desire to explore that moment never really went away.

When I learned that Volume 8 would contain two stories I already published on the web ("The Safe Haven Incident" and "Calibur"), I decided, "Why not write a new story about what happened after Kirito ran out into the wilderness on the first day?" And what I produced was the "Day of Beginnings." Given that nearly ten years have passed since I wrote the very start of *SAO*, there might be a bit of inconsistency in Kirito's depiction, but I'd be very lucky if you considered that part of the fun.

If I get the chance in the future, I'd like to write another story about Kirito taking on the first floor with his new trusty blade. Just be patient with me!

And now, for the standard apology section...With the "Safe Haven Incident," as is the danger with all retroactive sequels, it does introduce a few inconsistencies with what I wrote in the first volume. (For example, in Volume 1, Kirito claims that he has never entered an NPC restaurant with Asuna, but he does exactly that in this story...) I briefly thought about cheating around the issue by changing the owner of the restaurant to a player, but that didn't really solve the fundamental issue, so I didn't bother. I'm sure there are other spots here and there that caused you to raise an eyebrow, but I hope that you can understand the very strange circumstances of this long story's development and overlook the small things!

While I'm on a roll with apologies, let me address the reveal of the trick and the resolution to the mystery story contained in "Safe Haven Incident." I'm sure that the big mystery-novel fans among you are outraged at its un-believability. I do enjoy reading mysteries, so I thought I would tackle the genre as a writer, and I apologize for not knowing what I was doing! I'd like to keep working at it and try again someday.

This is not an apology, but a bit of advertisement. The "Calibur" story you read in this book is what happened if the quest was successful. I also wrote a "what if they failed" version that appears in the June 2011 issue of *Dengeki Bunko Magazine*. If you get the chance to read that after this one, you might just enjoy the story 1.2 times more!

To my editor, Mr. Miki, whom I put through hell for forgetting to submit this afterword when he was super busy with the editorial office moving, and to my illustrator, abec, for doing yeoman's duty with a cramped June–August two-month turnover, thank you so much! And to everyone else, I hope you return for the fourth story arc, beginning in Volume 9!

Reki Kawahara—May 2011